Other Ballroom Dance Mysteries

Quickstep to Murder
Dead Man Waltzing

MORE PRAISE FOR
THE BALLROOM DANCE MYSTERY SERIES

Quickstep to Murder

"Perfect for all your dance-show fans. Barrick brings a light step and an upbeat tempo to her debut. Readers will like the adjacency to the greater D.C. area (plot potential there) and the interplay between generations. Who wouldn't want to spice up their lives with a little ballroom?"
— *Library Journal*

"This snazzy, jazzy, and brilliantly choreographed mystery provides a clever twist and unexpected turn on every page."
— Agatha, Anthony, and Macavity award–winning author Hank Phillippi Ryan

"Ella Barrick dances through a complex plot without a false step in this fast-paced series debut."
— Sheila Connolly, national bestselling author of *Sour Apples*

"A new series that looks like fun."   — CA Reviews

"Barrick keeps them hopping with a classy little mystery set in the world of professional dancing."
— *Romantic Times*

"[A]n engaging debonair amateur sleuth ... will have readers dancing the Lindy."— Genre Go Round Reviews

continued . . .

"[A] great mystery." —Fresh Fiction

"Absolutely delicious. . . .The mystery is substantial, the murder is piquant, and the characters are fun-loving, quirky, and provocative. . . . 10s across the board."
—*Seattle Post-Intelligencer*

Dead Man Waltzing

"Ella Barrick waltzes right into your heart with this lively murder mystery. . . .Barrick's writing is charming and impressive. The author of *Quickstep to Murder* is quickly dancing her way to the top of the mystery genre. This is a waltz you'll definitely not want to sit out."
—Fresh Fiction

"Looking for something hip and fun to help fill the time until Bruno, Len, and Carrie Ann return to your screen? Check out *Dead Man Waltzing*; it's definitely worth your time." —The Season for Romance

"*Dead Man Waltzing* is a quick look into the sometimes glamorous world of international ballroom dancing, with the fancy costumes and smoldering looks, but also with the reality as physical in activity as it is, many still view it as a pleasant pastime rather than a competitive activity that makes some of its participants very emotional about their work." —The Mystery Reader

The Homicide Hustle

A BALLROOM DANCE MYSTERY

ELLA BARRICK

AN OBSIDIAN MYSTERY

OBSIDIAN
Published by the Penguin Group
Penguin Group (USA) Inc., 375 Hudson Street,
New York, New York 10014, USA

USA / Canada / UK / Ireland / Australia / New Zealand / India / South Africa / China

Penguin Books Ltd., Registered Offices: 80 Strand, London WC2R 0RL, England
For more information about the Penguin Group visit penguin.com.

First published by Obsidian, an imprint of New American Library,
a division of Penguin Group (USA) Inc.

First Printing, April 2013

Copyright © Laura DiSilverio, 2013

ISBN 978-0-451-23974-7

Printed in the United States of America
10 9 8 7 6 5 4 3 2 1

PUBLISHER'S NOTE
This is a work of fiction. Names, characters, places, and incidents either are the
product of the author's imagination or are used fictitiously, and any resemblance
to actual persons, living or dead, business establishments, events, or locales is
entirely coincidental.

   The publisher does not have any control over and does not assume any
responsibility for author or third-party Web sites or their content.

ALWAYS LEARNING   PEARSON

For Thomas, husband, best friend, and soul mate

ACKNOWLEDGMENTS

The lovely and talented ballroom dancer Tatiana Keegan shared her expertise and anecdotes with me and I owe her a big debt of gratitude. All errors are mine.

I find myself thanking the same group of folks again and again, and I do so one more time. Thanks to the women in my critique group—Lin, Amy, and Marie—who take the time to read my awkward and incoherent early drafts and make them better. Thanks to my agent, Paige Wheeler, who takes the time to check in with me and see how I'm doing, even if there's no deal or problem in the works. Thanks to my husband, mother, girls, and friends, who support me with cheerleading, brainstorming, and the occasional pint of ice cream in the face of rejection, less than glowing reviews, or self-doubt. Thanks especially to my editor, Sandy Harding, for caring enough about my novels to champion them and work with me to make them better.

Chapter 1

If Nigel told me one more time to manufacture a wardrobe malfunction for the show's first night of live competition, I was going to slap him.

"Stacy-luv," he said, Cockney origins evident in his accent, "we can make this strap a breakaway so sometime during the dance it will separate and—pop!" He ran a stubby forefinger with manicured nail down the pink spaghetti strap of my costume, stopping with his finger indenting my left breast through the satin. "Pop goes your boob and pop go the ratings!" He beamed.

I slapped him.

Three weeks ago, when Nigel Whiteman, coproducer of the hit series *Ballroom with the B-Listers*, phoned to announce the show was going to film its next season in the Washington, D.C., area, and said he wanted Graysin Motion to be one of the featured studios, I leaped at the opportunity. The chance to teach a Hollywood has-been or never-quite-was to dance on national TV was not one I was likely to pass up. The television exposure would be great for business, and if there was one thing I wanted more than a Blackpool Dance Festival title, it was for Graysin Motion to be the premier ballroom dance studio in the country. I immediately said "yes," not stopping to consider that my new business partner, Octavio "Tav" Acosta, might object.

Sitting on the edge of my desk, facing Tav where he sat on the loveseat under the window that looked out on Old Town Alexandria, I gauged his initial reaction to the news. His silence gave me time to admire the way the sun slanting through the window highlighted his cheekbones and the straight line of his nose. I squelched the thoughts. Tav Acosta was my business partner and I'd learned the hard way that mixing business with romance was a bad idea when I caught my former fiancé, Tav's half brother Rafe, in bed with a Latin specialist. Rafe's murder—no, I hadn't shot him—had brought Tav to Virginia. In his late thirties, he looked far too much like Rafe—lean face, long legs, dark hair and eyes—for my peace of mind. He'd inherited Rafe's share of my beginning-to-be-successful ballroom studio and had decided to open a branch of his import-export business in the area and stay for a while to help run the studio. He was a whiz with money, payroll accounts, expenses, and taxes—all the things that made me want to drive a skewer into my temple. I handled the teaching and our instructors and the competing. Our partnership had been working well. Until now.

When he didn't react immediately, I hurried to give him more details. "It's not like that other ballroom dancing show, where it all happens in Hollywood," I said.

"*Ballroom with the B-Listers* goes to a different city each time and pits local ballroom dance studios against each other by giving them each two celebrities, a man and a woman, to train. The broadcasts are done from different local venues, so it's sort of a dance show, reality show, and travel show in one." Swinging one leg with excitement, I kicked so hard my flip-flop flew off, landing in Tav's lap. "Sorry."

He gave a half smile and handed me the orange rubber shoe. Then his handsome face got serious. "But, Stacy, how does a studio have time to work with the celebrities and do everything the show requires, and still run classes and train its private students? I came by this morning to tell you we got a tax bill saying that an error in the city's record keeping has resulted in us owing more than one hundred thousand dollars in back taxes on this place." He gestured to the building that was both my studio and my home that my great-aunt Laurinda had willed to me. "We cannot afford a drop-off in business right now. I am meeting with officials today to try and work out a payment plan since there is no way we can come up with a sum like that." His faint Argentinean accent was more pronounced than usual.

The news hit me hard and distracted me momentarily from my excitement about the TV show. Graysin Motion didn't have a tenth of that in the bank. "Please tell me you're kidding."

His expression said he wasn't.

"What happened?"

"I will find out more at the meeting, but apparently your great-aunt was not conscientious about paying the property taxes in her final years."

More likely, she'd refused to pay taxes because the

city hadn't filled potholes in the streets or repaired cracked sidewalks. Aunt Laurinda had insisted on value for her money. She had gumption. She'd died two years ago, at ninety-seven, in the midst of writing a scathing letter to the mayor about the city's unsynchronized traffic lights. I missed her.

"That makes it trickier," I said. "We'll have to cut back on some of our classes, and rearrange private lesson times, but our students will be as excited about the show as we are, hopefully."

Tav looked decidedly unexcited, so I added hastily, "There's prize money—enough to make a dent in the taxes. And think of the amazing free advertising we'll get when twelve million people watch the show every Saturday night!"

"There is that," Tav admitted. "Still, we cannot afford to discourage any of our regular students. Long after this *Ballroom with the—* What did you call them?"

"B-Listers. It means sort of second-tier celebrities." Or third or fourth tier, I added to myself, recalling previous seasons' competitors. "Everyone calls it *Blisters*." The nickname, although unflattering, sort of fit, and I wondered if the show's producers had foreseen it when they titled the show.

"Thank you. Long after the show is over, Graysin Motion will depend on the competitive students to pay our bills and keep us in business." A shock of black hair fell onto his forehead and he brushed it aside impatiently.

"They'll still be here," I said. "The show only runs eight weeks, after all. Don't forget we'll have tons of new students brought in by *Blisters*, too." Levering myself off the desk, I approached Tav and bent so our faces were on the same level. My blond ponytail dangled over my shoulder and I breathed in his cedary scent. "Don't you want to be on TV?"

"*Por Díos*, no!" He looked so horrified at the thought that I laughed.

"Well, I do." I'd been on television before, of course, as a participant in international-level ballroom competitions, but this was different.

Tav threw up a hand. "Okay, Stacy. You win. Tell them Graysin Motion will be happy to compete."

Since I'd already committed the studio, I was relieved I'd gotten Tav to agree. I pushed the tax bill out of my mind, figuring we'd find some way to pay it before the city repo-ed my house or threw me in jail for tax delinquency. Optimism was my middle name. "It'll be fun," I said. "You'll see."

"Oh, my graciousness, this will being fun!" Vitaly Voloshin exclaimed later that day, clapping his hands together. With lank, straw-colored hair, a willowy build, and a face that was all sharp nose and angles, Vitaly came across as totally ordinary, maybe even a bit loserish. But when he stepped on a dance floor . . . Pow! Originally from Russia, Vitaly now lived in Baltimore with his life partner. We'd become ballroom partners after Rafe's death.

We were warming up in the ballroom, the long room that ran the length of my historic Federal-era town house, which housed Graysin Motion on the top floor and my living quarters on the ground floor. Harsh July sunlight poured through the front windows, making my eyes water, and I moved to draw the draperies.

"'My graciousness'?" The phrase didn't sound like Vitaly. I *shush*ed the drapes closed.

"John's mother, she is visiting," he explained, "and

this she is saying all the times." He smiled at himself in the mirrors that lined our ballroom studio, admiring his teeth, I knew. His partner John had paid for extensive cosmetic dentistry not long ago and Vitaly was still fascinated with the toothpaste ad smile that had replaced his formerly crooked and tannish teeth.

"Where's she from?"

"The Alabamas. She is nice, but I am not liking the grist for breakfast."

"Grits."

"*Da.*"

I joined Vitaly in lunging the length of the ballroom, adding a high kick every time I straightened. "We've got a lot to do to get ready. We'll have to let all our students know, see what changes we need to make in the class schedule . . . maybe Maurice can pick up some of the classes I teach and work with your private students, since he won't be competing." *Blisters* assigned only two celebrities to each studio and they'd specifically said they wanted me and Vitaly to partner this season's competitors.

"Our studio will winning," Vitaly pronounced.

I certainly hoped he was right since the prize money for the winning studio would put Graysin Motion on firmer financial ground.

One week later, on Tuesday, once again in our ballroom, Vitaly stared at his *Blisters* partner in disbelief. "You is taller than Vitaly."

"You are a runt." Phoebe Jackson looked down her nose at him. Perhaps half an inch taller than his six feet, with medium dark skin and a half-inch-long Afro that hugged her skull, she exuded strength in a tank top that showed defined biceps and triceps. Strong, slightly arched brows drew in toward a broad nose as she extended a hand for Vitaly to shake.

Vitaly appraised her, running his gaze from her shoulders to the muscled thighs and calves displayed by a short denim skirt. "You seem reasonably athletics," he said approvingly. "Why are you being famous?"

"You've never heard of me?" Her tone hovered between affront and amusement. "I'm a kick-butt action star, baby. I whupped up on Jackie Chan in *Shanghai Serenade* and beat the crap out of Sly Stallone in *Rambo Meets Bimbo*. He was even shorter than you," she added, "but, baby, was he in good shape, even though he's got to be in his sixties. Mm-mm." She smacked her full lips appreciatively.

I guessed Phoebe was in her early forties, but she looked fit for her age. "Nice to meet you, Ms. Jackson," I said. "I'm Stacy Graysin." We shook hands and eyed each other. The microphone pack was uncomfortable at the small of my back and I wiggled.

"Call me Phoebe. Miz Jackson is my granny." She smiled. "You'll get used to the mike pack."

"Okay, okay," Nigel Whiteman broke in from where he stood, arms crossed, behind the cameraman. He had a compact body, a spray tan, and eyebrows that winged up from the bridge of his nose like Nike swooshes. His light brown hair was receding at the corners of his forehead, creating a widow's peak effect I didn't think he'd had in his youth. He wore blue jeans and a gray T-shirt, which would have made him look like just one of the guys, if he weren't also wearing a platinum Rolex and Italian loafers. I'd learned in the three days since I'd met him that his smile rarely made it to his eyes, and even when he laughed at people's jokes, it was more to avoid looking surly than because he found anything funny.

"Stace, Phoeb. Let's not make nice, hm? Viewers like conflict and tension, not nicey-nicey. Try it again. Think two lionesses meeting up on the savannah, fighting over a mate." He gestured at Vitaly.

Vitaly looked offended and I folded my lips to keep in a giggle. We were getting a quick lesson in how much was real about reality shows. "Sure, Nige," I said.

"Grrrrr." I growled at Phoebe.

She burst into laughter, showing enough white teeth and gum to intimidate a real lioness, then high-fived me while Nigel frowned. "I like your style, girl."

Vitaly and Phoebe and I filmed our "first meeting" three more times until Nigel was satisfied that we'd snarled enough.

"Where's my partner?" I asked. I'd been on pins and needles for days, wondering who I'd be paired with.

"He couldn't make it today," Nigel said. "You'll meet him tomorrow."

"But you can tell me who it is now, right?"

"Uh-uh." Nigel smiled, closemouthed. "We want to record the real surprise when you two meet for the first time. Makes for better television."

I stifled my frustration and my urge to point out that we'd just filmed Vitaly and Phoebe's "real" reaction to each other four times. "I can't wait," I said brightly, conscious that the camera was running and that I'd signed a contract saying the show could use whatever footage they obtained. I didn't want to come across as surly or uncooperative; that would scare away potential clients. I began to get an inkling that being part of *Blisters* for two months might not be all fun and dancing.

I said as much to Maurice Goldberg in my office moments later. Nigel had shooed me out of the ballroom so they could film Vitaly's first efforts to teach Phoebe the basics of ballroom dancing.

"Surely you didn't think reality shows were completely unscripted, Anastasia?" Maurice said, blowing on his coffee and then taking a sip. He looked up at me through graying eyebrows. Maurice Goldberg was our other instructor, a former cruise ship dance host who admitted to being "sixtyish" but whom I suspected was more like seventy. He was a big hit with our more mature, well-off female clients, the bread and butter of any ballroom studio.

I eyed him where he sat in the chair in front of my desk, one gray flannel–clad leg crossed over the other, navy blazer neatly buttoned. "I never thought about it," I confessed. "Maybe I should have before I signed us up, but you know how I am."

"Impulsive." He gave a small smile. "Do you know which other studios are competing?"

I shook my head, blond hair swishing across my shoulders. "That's another thing they're keeping secret. We won't know until the night of the press conference. Nigel and Tessa are big on secrets and surprises and we can't tell anyone anything. With all the confidentiality agreements they had us sign, I won't be able to tell myself when I need to go to the bathroom."

"Who's Tessa?"

"Tessa King. The coproducer. I haven't met her yet,

but she's Nigel's partner. She's probably got all the empathy of a starving crocodile, just like he does."

"That's very funny," a voice said from the doorway. Maurice and I turned our heads to see a tall, lanky woman in a designer pantsuit standing in the doorway. Large gray eyes tilted down a bit at the outside corners and medium brown hair was bobbed at chin length, looking more like the work of a Super Cuts stylist than the kind of hairdresser someone wearing Armani could afford.

I got a sinking feeling in the pit of my stomach. "You're—"

"Tessa King."

I winced, stood, and offered my hand. "I'm sorry. That was rude. I—"

She shook my hand strongly and waved away my apology. "No, no. You need to say it again when the cameras are rolling. It's good TV. You're spot on: Nigel's testy in the morning until he's snagged a baby wildebeest." Her hair fell from a deep side part, and she swept it aside. "You are?" She extended her hand to Maurice.

Rising, he said, "Maurice Goldberg. *Enchanté*, mademoiselle." He kissed the tips of her fingers, rather than shaking her hand.

I stared at him. I'd never seen this version of Maurice before. Sure, he was smooth and charming with all his students, but this. . . . I wondered if this was his cruise ship persona and, if so, why he'd resurrected it.

"I like you," she said, running her eyes from his smoothed-back white hair, down his fit and immaculately clad body, to his soft black practice shoes. "You'd go over big with our older demographic. You remind me of someone . . ." She snapped her fingers. "George Hamilton!"

"It's the tan," Maurice said.

Tessa laughed, a warm, throaty sound. I already liked her better than Nigel, although I got the feeling she could bring down a wildebeest or two herself, if the occasion demanded. Something in the way she squared her shoulders, and the directness of her gaze, told me her success in the male-dominated world of reality show production was no accident.

"We'll make sure you get some screen time," Tessa promised Maurice.

I couldn't tell if he was pleased by the prospect or appalled. I had a feeling it didn't matter: if Tessa King wanted it to happen, it was going to happen.

Chapter 2

Nigel and Tessa had insisted on filming my "meet cute" with my celebrity partner in my home, rather than at the studio. "People want to get to know you," Tessa explained, poking her head into the kitchen, raising her brows, and then proceeding toward what Aunt Laurinda had called the "parlor" at the front of the house, trailed by the cameraman. She surveyed it for a moment, then said, "This is taking minimalism to extremes, isn't it?"

I didn't feel compelled to tell her I'd recently sold most of the fusty, 1930s-era furniture that had been Great-aunt Laurinda's. I'd made some decent money from it, but hadn't yet gotten around to picking out new furnishings that said "me." All I'd bought so far was a comfy chair-and-a-half plus matching ottoman in a goldy-apricot shade that lit up the empty front room. I'd placed it near the window, where I could sit and enjoy both the fireplace—which wouldn't work until I'd gotten a chimney sweep to do his thing—and the window facing the street. Great-aunt Laurinda looked down at me—approvingly, I hoped—from the portrait above the fireplace. I couldn't bring myself to sell the painting of my aunt as an early twentieth century debutante.

The doorbell donged. "Never mind," Tessa said. "He's here. Larry." She motioned the cameraman into position.

Rubbing my fingers against my palms, surprisingly nervous, hoping my partner would be reasonably cooperative and appealing, not obnoxious like the soccer star who'd been on the previous season, I swung the door inward.

"You must be Stacy. I'm so excited about dancing with you." The Adonis on the doorstep leaned forward to kiss my cheek and proffered a handful of tulips, my favorites. Tessa had wanted me to squeal when meeting my partner, and I'd told her I wasn't the squealing type. However, a small squeal escaped before I could stop it.

Zane Savage had kissed me. My hand went involuntarily to the spot his lips had touched. Zane Savage, teen star of *Hollywood High*, the love of my life when I was thirteen or so. How many hours had my sister Danielle and I spent giggling over Zane, fantasizing about meeting him accidentally on a plane or at the mall, saving him or being saved by him from some unspecified and highly unlikely peril, marrying him in a lace dress with a twelve-foot train and six bridesmaids? Okay, the dress fantasy was Dani's; I favored something simpler. I wondered what had happened to the Zane Savage poster that had hung over my bed for a year or two. Maybe even until I was sixteen and *Hollywood High* went off the air.

"You're Zane Savage." God, could I sound any stupider? I remembered this was being filmed for the entertainment of millions and winced.

He laughed. "Yes, I am. These are for you." He thrust the tulips at me again, and I took them this time.

"Thanks. Uh, come in."

Zane Savage had pretty much disappeared after *Hollywood High* got canceled. Another child actor who never converted his success to adult stardom. I seemed to recall that he'd gone to college somewhere prestigious, maybe even played a sport for his university—lacrosse?—but I might be thinking of someone else. I eyed him covertly as he moved into the drawing room. He must be in his mid-thirties, but he still had the wholesome, boy-next-door cuteness that had captivated millions of tweenage girls: longish, sun-streaked hair; hazel eyes fringed by outrageous lashes; a smile that quirked up on one side. In addition, he now sported a haze of mustache and goatee that I found incredibly attractive. He wore aging khakis and a white shirt, open at the collar, working hard at looking casual, approachable, and hot. He was succeeding wildly at the latter, as far as I was concerned.

"So, where've you been for the last fifteen years or so?" I asked.

His eyes widened, as if he was surprised by my bluntness, but then he laughed. "Around. But not in front of the camera, so it's the equivalent of being deader than Busby Berkeley musicals. Is there some place to sit?" He gestured at the nearly empty parlor.

"Kitchen." I led the way, too aware of Tessa and the camera guy listening in. I looked for a vase and finally filled Great-aunt Laurinda's parrot-shaped ceramic cookie jar with water and plopped in the tulips. I liked the whimsical effect. "Thanks for these," I told Zane, placing the makeshift vase on the table and sitting across from him. "This is your comeback, then?"

"You could say that." Zane turned to Tessa where she

hovered near the refrigerator, out of the shot. "Have you got enough, Tess?" Reaching around, he detached the mike pack from the waistline of his khakis and laid it on the table.

"Perfect," Tessa said after a tight-lipped moment.

I got the feeling she wanted more footage, but she was giving in to Zane. I wrinkled my brow, not sure how the power dynamics played out between the two. Not my problem, I decided.

Tessa nodded at Larry who lowered his camera. "We'll go away and let you two get acquainted. Be upstairs in twenty so we can film your first lesson with Stacy."

Zane nodded his acknowledgment and waited until Tessa and Larry had left, using my interior staircase to return to the upstairs studio. Then, he leaned toward me, close enough that I could smell his subtle cologne.

"Now I can tell you how much I've been looking forward to this. Since seeing Tessa's footage of you dancing at Blackpool, I've been impatient to meet you. I made dancing with you part of my contract with *Blisters*. You've got a certain something the viewers will love, and I've got a feeling that we can go all the way. Win this, I mean," he added with a smile, making sure I caught the double meaning. "I probably shouldn't show you my ambitious side at a first meeting, but being on *Blisters*, winning, will show casting directors that I'm not cute Hayden Hansen of *Hollywood High* anymore; it'll make me competitive for new roles, dramatic roles, romantic leads, let me take my career to the next level." His hazel eyes searched my green ones. "You want to win, right?"

"I always want to win." My dad frequently said I'd been a competitive little cuss from the moment I emerged from the womb, and that I'd walked at nine months only because our neighbor went on and on about how her son took his first step at just over ten months.

I gave Zane an assessing look. "Ballroom dancing isn't all sequins and spray tans. It's damn hard work. You need to be flexible, aerobically fit, and strong. On top of that, you need a great sense of rhythm and showmanship— pizzazz. If you really want to win, I'll have to work you like you've never worked in your life."

He didn't hesitate. "Bring it on."

Upstairs in the ballroom, we redonned the mike packs and I took Zane through some warm-ups, and tested his flexibility. With knees locked, he could stretch his fingertips only to his ankles. "We need to work on your flexibility," I said as I demonstrated a simple waltz box step for him, feeling a bit self-conscious with the two producers and the cameraman paying close attention.

"Step forward with your left foot on one. Step to the right with your right foot on two, and bring your left foot to your right foot on three. That's the basic step. Easy, right?" I moved through the steps five more times while he watched.

"I think I've got it." Zane stepped forward and completed the sequence correctly, counting under his breath.

"Excellent. Now let's talk about frame."

We worked for three solid hours and he made quick progress, listening intently, his gaze fixed on my face, whenever I explained something. He had a naturally elegant frame and sense of rhythm; once he got over wanting to watch his feet, he was going to be a good dancer. I told him so.

He pulled me close in a way that had more to do with

middle school slow dancing than ballroom, letting his hands drift to my waist. He smiled down at me, such warmth and mischief in his gaze that I had to remind myself he was an actor and the cameras were rolling.

"What a relief. I was afraid you'd be disappointed to end up with me."

"Disappointed? Zane Savage—Zane Savage!—actually suggested you might be disappointed at getting to spend several weeks with him, dancing with him, in his arms?" From atop a step stool, my sister Danielle stared down at me incredulously that evening. "Get out!" A strip of wallpaper slid from the wall, leaving a trail of glue slime. "Oh, damn."

Her apartment complex had recently converted to a condo and she'd bought the unit she'd lived in for almost six years. Now, she was intent on redecorating every inch of it and I'd promised to help after pointing out that I had zero expertise with any aspect of home improvement. She'd appointed me chief wallpaper cutter and soaker.

"That's what he said."

"You told him that you were thrilled, over the moon, ecstatic to be partnered with him, right?"

"Not in so many words." I hoped my expression hadn't said all that for me. "We're not thirteen anymore, after all. I told him I thought we'd do well in the competition. He's about the right height for me, which helps, and he's in great shape." Ridged abs had shown through the thin mesh of his practice shirt, and I figured that would go over well with every female demographic, and some of the male.

Danielle sighed and reached above her head to

smooth the limp strip onto the wall. "I could be so jealous of you, if I let myself."

I looked up, catching something in her voice, but her back was to me. "What about Coop?"

"Oh, Coop." Danielle dismissed her longtime boyfriend with another sigh. "We're ... I don't know ... getting stale, you know?" Turning her head, she looked down at me over her shoulder. "What about Tav?"

"What about Tav?"

She waggled her brows at me.

I fought to keep from blushing. I bent to cut another length of wallpaper, breathing in the new vinyl odor. "He's my business partner. Period. After the way things turned out between me and Rafe—I'm not going to make the same mistake twice." Truth was, I'd almost given in to my attraction to Tav and gone on a date with him. I'd actually said, "Yes," when he asked me out, but then backed out the morning of the day we were supposed to have dinner. I'd felt bad about it—awful, actually—when I'd seen the look in his eyes, but I thought I was doing the smart thing by hinting Tav away. I just wasn't ready for a serious relationship, especially not with someone who was a virtual clone of my dead fiancé.

"Chicken."

I stared at Dani. "I'm not afraid. I'm being ... sensible. Everyone's always telling me not to be so impulsive, but the moment I try cautious on for size, you call me 'chicken'?"

"Bawk, bawk!" Dani flapped her arms, elbows out. "Rafe cheated on you and he died. I get it. You don't want to get hurt again. But Tav's not Rafe. When do I get to meet him?"

She lost me for a moment, but then I realized she was

back to Zane Savage. Fine. I'd rather talk about him than Tav. "Meet Zane? I'm teaching him to dance, not serving as his social secretary. I don't expect to see him outside the studio."

Danielle jumped off the stepladder, landing with a thump, and stood facing me with her pasty hands on her hips. "You're planning to keep him to yourself, aren't you? Even though I was the one who was most in love with him."

She must have been joking, even though she sounded semiserious. "'Most in love with him'? You're kidding, right? We had crushes on him when we were thirteen. That was more than fifteen years ago. We grew out of it, grew up, threw away our posters."

Danielle mumbled something.

"What?"

"I said I still have mine." She eyed me, half-defiant, half-embarrassed. "At least, I think I do. In a box with my other high school stuff."

I laughed. "Oh, that's great! Maybe he'd autograph it for you. You could probably get big bucks for it now, as a collector's item. Oops." I pulled an extremely soggy roll of wallpaper from the water tray, and held it up by thumb and forefinger, letting it drip paste and water into the tray.

"Don't you dare tell him," Danielle said, sounding like a teen ordering her best friend not to reveal her crush on the basketball team captain.

"Cross my heart and hope to die." I marked a cross on my chest with my forefinger, smudging glue on my orange T-shirt, and wondered if I'd stepped into a time machine that had transported me back to my teenage years. Pretty soon we'd start squabbling about whose turn it was to do the dishes or take out the trash, and she'd accuse me of stealing her favorite green shirt (which I was pretty sure I still had in the back of my closet).

"You're making fun of me!"

I tried to pacify her. "Look, if I can figure out a way to introduce you, I will."

"Hmph." She went at the wallpaper with a brush, apparently planning to beat the air pockets into submission rather than smooth them away.

I stared at Danielle for a moment, puzzled by her unusual snappiness and having trouble believing this was really about Zane Savage. Before I could ask if there was anything wrong, she snatched the drippy wallpaper from me and ascended the step stool.

Muttering under her breath about how wet the strip was, she tried to plaster it to the wall. It tore. The bottom third sagged down, landing on my head where I bent over the water tray. Glue oozed down my temple. Ick. I sprang back, knocking against the stepladder. It rocked.

"Are you trying to kill me?" Danielle steadied herself with a hand on the wall and glared at me.

"Maybe you'd do better without me." I was on the verge of losing my temper, too, as I dragged the wallpaper off my head; I'd need half a bottle of shampoo to get the paste out of my hair.

"Maybe I would."

"Fine." I dropped the scissors with a clang and walked out.

Chapter 3

Walking into the studio the next morning, Thursday, the first thing I saw was Tav chatting with—flirting with?—a pretty young woman with copper-colored curls framing a heart-shaped face. She was leaning toward him over his desk, displaying a bosom that stretched the white T-shirt tucked into faded jeans. "I've never been to Argentina," she said as I came through the door.

"You should definitely visit some day." Tav's smile was an invitation and for a moment I saw Rafe. Rafe had flirted nonstop . . . with students, judges, store clerks. Tav wasn't Rafe, I reminded myself; he was just being friendly. His smile broadened when he spotted me. "Stacy. Have you met Ariel?"

Of course she was named Ariel. She looked like a sprite or a mermaid: petite, slim, curvaceous, and no more than twenty-five. "Hi."

"She does makeup for the show."

That explained why she was studying my face so closely.

"With those cheekbones and those brows, you must

be extremely photogenic," Ariel said. "And I love your coloring. Is that blond hair natural?"

I warmed up to her, and smiled. "Mostly." What are a few highlights among friends?

She started to say something else, but a thumping noise from the ballroom cut her off.

"Can you not remembering for two minutes? Step back with *left* foot."

"Well, if you were a better teacher, maybe I'd pick it up quicker," Phoebe answered Vitaly.

Sharing a worried look with Tav, I hurried to the ballroom door and peeped in. Tav followed and looked over my shoulder; I could feel his breath stirring the hairs on the top of my head. Vitaly and Phoebe stood two feet apart, glaring at each other. The action star looked buff and energetic in a yellow workout bra and spandex bike shorts. Vitaly looked frustrated, his dirty blond hair sticking out in all directions like he'd run his hand through it. I'd never seen him get irate with a student before.

"You must be fuller of graces. The arms is not windmills." He flailed his arms wildly over his head.

Phoebe settled into a boxer's stance, fists raised. "These arms are enough to put you on the floor, homeboy. No one messed with me in prison."

Curiosity replaced frustration on Vitaly's face. "You were in the jail?"

I wasn't as astonished as Vitaly because I'd read in *People*, pretty much my only reading material, about Phoebe Jackson's journey from middle-class Atlanta runaway, to drugs and life on the streets, to prison, and then to movie stardom. Well, if not megastardom like Julia Roberts or Ethan Jarrett, then at least steady movie employment. She was the black female Robert Downey Jr., some reporter said, who had conquered her demons and reinvented herself. She was a role model for young girls in trouble, the reporter added, and spent a lot of time and money helping girls like her get ahead.

"I was," Phoebe said, almost proudly, "and every woman on my cell block was tougher than you, so don't let your mouth write any checks your body can't cash."

"Great." Tessa's voice cut in and I leaned farther into the ballroom, spotting her and Larry the camera dude in the far corner. I breathed out a sigh of relief, realizing that Vitaly's spat with Phoebe had been at least partially scripted. I'd been worried for a second that their partnership was doomed from the get-go.

"My money is on Phoebe," Tav whispered. He cocked his head as if assessing the odds.

"I don't know . . . I'll bet Vitaly has a few tricks up his sleeve." I giggled at the thought of Vitaly and Phoebe in a wrestling match and Tav drew me away from the door, his hand warm on my bare arm. We almost tripped over Ariel who had come up behind us. "Is it always like this?" I asked.

She rolled her eyes. "This is nothing. Wait until the third or fourth week of competition. Nigel and Tessa will have people at each other's throats . . . or in each other's beds. It's all about the ratings, baby. Tessa and Nigel live and die by the ratings. Either one of them would give their firstborn to a tribe of Gypsies if it would boost ratings a point or two."

She said it matter-of-factly, not bitterly. Tav arched his brows. "Tessa seems nice enough," I ventured. I already suspected Nigel was a toad.

She snorted. "When nice will get the results she wants, Tessa's nice."

Sauntering off, she left us to draw our own conclusions about how Tessa did business when nice didn't cut it.

Chapter 4

Luckily, the cameras weren't rolling two weeks later when Nigel suggested we engineer a wardrobe malfunction and I slapped his hand away. They wouldn't be, of course, since he was trying to talk me into a display that would make the FCC sensors froth at the mouth.

"Do not ever poke me again," I said in a low voice so the costume designer and seamstress didn't hear me. They stood near the doorway of the room we called the "studio" to distinguish it from the "ballroom." We used it for individual lessons and small groups.

Anger flared in Nigel's pale blue eyes, but then he forced a smile, showing all of his strangely even teeth. "Feisty," he said. "That will play well with the younger audience members. They like a bit of brangling when they turn on the telly."

I was weary of being told what would "play well" or "go over big" with various demographic groups, but I said, "Happy to hear it."

Nigel turned away from me, saying, "Anyone seen Tessa? She should've been here two hours ago." He paused to chat with the costumers near the door and one of them nodded, sliding me a sideways glance. Suspicion tickled me and I moved as quickly as the pinned-on gown would allow, catching Nigel in the hall.

Stopping him with a hand on his arm, I said sweetly, "You know, Nige, if my bodice should happen to *accidentally* come apart while I'm dancing, your life won't be worth living." Okay, so the phrase sounded like it'd come from the sort of straight-to-DVD movie most of this show's celebs "starred" in, but I couldn't think of a more realistic threat on the spur of the moment.

"Accidents happen, Stace, don't they?" Without bothering to see how I responded, he continued down the hall, bellowing, "Where the *hell* is Tessa?"

I was debating chasing after him, when Zane stepped out of the powder room wearing a classic black tux with a pink bow tie and cummerbund to match my dress. He would have passed muster at any Standard ballroom competition, except for the tousled hair and goatee; judges prefer a clean-shaven look. He spread his arms wide, and said, "Ta-da! I look like Fred Astaire, only more ruggedly handsome, right?"

Studying Zane's costume, I assured him that he not only looked like a ballroom dancer, he was one. He'd improved tremendously in the two weeks we'd spent practicing. I'd been relieved to discover that the production crew and cameras spent only a small portion of each day filming us since they had to spend equal time at the other studios participating on *Blisters*. Zane and I got a lot more real practicing done when Tessa and Nigel weren't standing in a corner, offering suggestions. It was evident from our second practice that the producers were urging Zane and me to become romantic, to contrast with the arguments they sparked between Phoebe and Vitaly, I suspected. I was glad I'd gotten the scoop from Ariel.

"Let me take this off"—I gestured to the pinned-on pink gown—"and we can get in another hour of practice. Your footwork is still atrocious."

"I can help you get out of that," Zane said, not bothered by my criticism. He started forward with a smile.

"Down, boy." I held him off with stiff arms. "The cameras aren't rolling."

"All the better." Grabbing a wrist in each hand, he pushed my arms apart and brought us chest to chest, arms out. Slowly, he lowered our arms until they rested at our sides. "We could play hooky this afternoon," he said in a low voice, the look in his eyes leaving me in no doubt about what he'd prefer to practice.

His woodsy scent, combined with the heat left over from our vigorous dancing, was playing havoc with my hormones. He leaned in closer, ostensibly to whisper in my ear, and his cheek brushed mine, the stubble rasping gently across my skin. Warmth flooded me.

"There you are."

Zane and I whipped our heads toward the sound and he released me. I knew I was blushing, and it made me mad.

"Danielle," I said. "I wasn't expecting you." I hadn't seen her since wallpaper night.

"You must be Zane." She ignored me, coming toward Zane with her hand out and a sparkle in her eye. "I'm Danielle Graysin, Stacy's sister. Call me Dani."

Shooting me a quizzical look, he shook hands with her. "Nice to meet you. Stacy didn't tell me she had a sister."

"Of course not." Danielle's laugh sounded forced. "I just stopped by to see if she'd like to lunch. Maybe you could join us?"

"I can't—" I started.

"Oh, too bad," she said with fake disappointment. "I guess it's just you and me, then." She smiled up at Zane in a way I had to admit was charming and engaging, even though I wanted to strangle her.

Zane didn't hesitate. "Delightful, Dani. Or should I say Delightful Dani? Let me change." He closed the door to the powder room, leaving Danielle and me facing each other.

"How's it going?" I asked. A pin stabbed my rib cage and I winced.

"Fine." She didn't meet my eyes, pretending to inspect a hangnail.

"Good." A long pause ensued. I shifted from foot to foot, not knowing what to say. I was mad at her for showing up like this and hijacking Zane, but I didn't want to fight, either. "Danielle—"

Before I could suggest we get together later, Zane reappeared in jeans. "Ready?" He looked from me to Danielle.

"Always!" Linking her arm in his she drew him toward the door that led to the exterior staircase.

Zane looked over his shoulder at me as she opened the door. "Sure you can't join us, Stacy? We'll be back in time for the press conference."

"She's busy," Danielle said and yanked him onto the small landing before I could respond.

I'd never wanted a sister.

"Too bad the cameras weren't here to film that," Phoebe observed with a laugh in her voice. With sweat beaded on her forehead, she crossed the hall to get a bottle of sports drink from the small fridge in the powder room. I could hear Vitaly changing out the CD in the ballroom.

"I don't know what you're talking about," I said loftily.

That only made her laugh harder. She paused beside me and twisted off the bottle's cap to glug down three-quarters of the water. "Remind me that tequila shooters and dance practice don't mix," she said with a comic eye roll.

I laughed. "Tequila shooters?"

"We all went clubbing in D.C. last night and things got a little wild."

She gave a strained smile that said "major hangover" to me, and I offered, "I've got some ibuprofen."

"You're a goddess."

I ducked into my office, retrieved the bottle, and brought it back to Phoebe, who was slumped against the wall. She took several pills with the rest of the water and straightened. "Don't tell that Russian slave driver in there, but I can't remember the last time a workout made me so sore."

"Phoebe. No more the lollygaggings," Vitaly called out, right on cue.

Laughing, I returned to where the seamstress was waiting to unpin me from my gown, while Phoebe reluctantly reentered the ballroom. Back in my practice clothes of cropped top and capri-length warm-up pants, I traipsed barefoot to my office, admiring the new teal polish on my toenails as I went. With Vitaly and Phoebe practicing in the ballroom, Nigel and his crew haunting dancers at another studio, and Tav engaged in downtown

D.C. with his import-export business, I hoped I could get some scheduling done and call some students to rearrange their practice times yet again. So far, everyone had been cooperative, excited about Graysin Motion appearing on *Blisters*, but I knew the constant schedule shuffling would get irritating before long.

Done with the final call, I tuned my computer to a radio station, hoping for a weather report. Instead, I got news about a gang killing in D.C., a hit-and-run that left a homeless man near death, and a domestic murder-suicide that left two small children and their parents dead. Nothing but cheeriness, I thought, waiting it out to get the forecast: a high of ninety with matching humidity and a chance of showers in the late afternoon. Not unusual for early July in this area.

My door flew open without a knock and I looked up, startled.

"Tessa here?" Nigel stood in a half crouch, as if hoping to spot her under my desk. His British accent was more noticeable when he was stressed.

"I thought you were gone."

"I was. If you see her, tell her to give me a bell. We've got a problem over at Take the Lead." He left, not bothering to close the door, and not seeming to notice he'd supplied me with the name of one of the competing studios. It probably wasn't a big deal since the press conference this evening was designed to reveal all the competitors.

Take the Lead with Ingelido was a studio I knew well. It was the flagship for a ballroom dancing franchise owned by Marco Ingelido, a dancer I'd had run-ins with while trying to figure out who killed the grande dame of ballroom dancing, Corinne Blakely. Even worse, Take the Lead was where Solange Dubonnet taught. I wrinkled my nose in distaste at the prospect of competing head-to-head with the woman I'd caught in bed with Rafe back when he was still my fiancé. I wondered if it was possible that Nigel Whiteman knew about that and had deliberately pitted us against each other hoping we'd start a cat fight that would bump the ratings up. Nah, I decided. There was no way he could know. I was being paranoid. Still, I hoped Solange had an old, overweight, obnoxious "b-lister" as a partner. I wasted some time trying to think of who would make the most revolting and least capable partner, but finally returned to my scheduling.

Nigel and Tessa had scheduled a press conference for the evening to announce all the competing studios and their b-listers. The judges would be present to talk about each star's potential, and the show's host, Kristen Lee, who had zero dance experience but looked great in slinky evening wear, would also be on hand. I was excited about the opportunity to see who we were up against, celebrity-wise and pro-wise, and it was hard to sit still as Ariel drew on heavy navy eyeliner.

"I could do that myself," I said. "I've been doing makeup for competitions since I was ten." Wearing the pink dress that was my waltz costume for the first live show Saturday night, I leaned forward to inspect her collection of bottles, tubes, brushes, and wands.

"Ssh." She batted my hand away when I tried to pick up a lipstick. "Are you trying to do me out of a job?"

I grinned and relaxed back into the chair that sat in a long trailer parked near the Alexandria City Hall in Market Square where the producers had decided to hold the press conference. Zane sat in the next chair, a smock protecting his costume, and Vitaly and Phoebe were having their faces applied on the other side of a partition. I'd exchanged greetings with the head judge, Carmelo, a dancer I knew slightly, before he disappeared into a private room at the back. The trailer smelled gloriously of hair and makeup products, and I breathed in deeply.

"Have fun with my sister?" I asked Zane, obediently looking up as Ariel flicked mascara on my lower lashes.

"She's a sweetheart."

I heard the smile in his voice, even though I couldn't look at him. "That's one word for her." The hum of the trailer's air-conditioning partially drowned out his answer and before I could ask him to repeat, the door swung open, letting the humidity rush in, along with a bright, brittle voice. "I hate this freaking humidity. Look what it's done to my hair. I told Nigel we should've gone to Phoenix."

A petite blonde I recognized as the show's host, Kristen Lee, swept down the aisle and plunked herself into a stylist's chair. "You have to fix it again, Giorgio."

She reminded me of a cat. Not one of those big fluffy ones with the pushed-in noses, but a small, sleek, compact one. All toned arms and pronounced collarbones, she had hair a couple shades lighter than my blond, a pointy chin, and feline eyes that tipped up at the corners.

"You're Anastasia Graysin," she announced after a narrow-eyed moment of studying me.

"Stacy."

"I told Nigel we shouldn't use you," she said matter-of-factly. "Ow, not so hard, Giorgio. Your coloring is too similar to mine. We'll look . . ."—she waved one hand, unable to find the word—"too . . . *something* standing side by side for the post-dance reactions. Wardrobe is going to have to make sure we're always dressed in contrasting colors. Viewers will think we're twins."

You wish, I thought but didn't say. Kristen Lee was forty if she was a day, compared to my not-quite-thirty, and she was a good four inches shorter than I, and two cup sizes smaller, at least. "I'm sure that will work," I said.

Giorgio fizzed half a can of hairspray over her hair, slicked stick-straight to below her shoulders, and I coughed.

Surveying her reflection in the mirror, Kristen proclaimed, "Better. I wish to hell Tessa would show up. I need to talk to her, and Nigel is chewing nails. You know how he gets."

There was a generalized "mm-hm" from the crew of makeup and hair artists and Kristen swept out in a rustle of black taffeta.

Ariel moved down the counter to find something, and I leaned closer to Zane. "No one's seen Tessa all day. Is that usual?"

"No," he said, brows drawing together. "I'm worried. I told Nigel we should tell the police she's missing, but he almost snapped my head off. Said *that* was not the kind of publicity we wanted this early in the show."

That led me to wonder if police-related publicity would be good farther into the show's run, but I didn't bring it up. "Has anyone checked her hotel room? Maybe she's ill."

"I don't know." His square jaw jutted forward in a determined way. "If she doesn't turn up for the press conference, I'll go over there myself."

Chapter 5

The press conference started only ten minutes late. As I'd expected, Marco Ingelido and Solange Dubonnet were there, as were a husband and wife dance team who ran a ballroom studio in Fairfax County, on the other side of the Beltway. The other celebs were a pet psychic who had a call-in radio talk show, a Disney channel phenom, a disgraced evangelist, and a reality show personality known for his big mouth and his "guns," which he flashed at every opportunity. I was pleased to see that Solange was stuck with the evangelist who was muscle-bound in a bulky way that suggested he wouldn't be too agile. Reporters and onlookers gathered in front of a dais where the b-listers sat at a long table studded with microphones, while their professionals stood behind them.

The reporters fawned over the Disney singer-actress, a seventeen-year-old beauty named Calista Marques who reminded me of a young Eva Longoria. With a breathy voice, a throaty laugh, and the trick of looking up from under her lashes, she was the odds-on favorite to win the Crystal Slipper, the dance shoe–shaped trophy *Blisters* awarded to the winner. Rumor had it she'd studied tap dancing and ballet, hoping to break into musical theater, before Disney signed her for the *Hannah Montana*-ish show that launched her career when she was only thirteen. If so, her dancing background would certainly give her an edge. I kept a smile pinned to my face as a reporter asked her if she liked being a teen role model.

"I am absolutely honored," she said, leaning into the table mike. "My fans are *so* wonderful and *so* loyal. I'd never do anything to disappoint them. I am *so* grateful to Disney for taking a chance on me and for giving me the opportunity to be Lisa on *It's a Double Life*. I know some young actors who are in a hurry to move to more adult roles, but I'm happy to be a teenager and to play a teenager for as long as I can, because teens are my fans and they are just *so* awesome."

I couldn't tell if she was sincere, or needling Zane. He responded with something that made the reporters laugh again and Nigel, as the moderator, managed to direct attention to Mickey Hazzard, the evangelist.

"Doesn't your religion forbid dancing?" a female journalist asked.

Hazzard's forehead sloped steeply so his deep-set eyes seemed shaded by an outcropping of thick brows. His voice was deep and sonorous, the kind that made even everyday phrases like "Pass the ketchup" sound like a benediction. He'd been a hugely popular minister with a flock of thousands until the scandal broke. "God gave us bodies to celebrate life," he said. "Dancing is a form of celebration."

I wondered if anyone else had noticed he hadn't really answered the question. "Is bonking underage girls a celebration, too?" someone called from the middle of the audience.

Hazzard's cheeks turned a mottled red and Nigel hastened to ask the professional dancers to sum up their partners' strengths and weaknesses. We'd been coached on this beforehand, and when my turn came I gave my canned answer with a roguish smile and an inward wince. "Zane's strengths are his passion and how hard he works," I said. "His weakness . . . well, he's just so sexy it's hard to concentrate on dancing. This *Hollywood High* alum is *all* grown up." Whistles and catcalls from the female members of the audience greeted my remarks and grew to deafening proportions when Zane rose and swept me into a seemingly passionate embrace, arching me back like we'd rehearsed.

"We could make this real," he said, his lips a whisper from mine.

I was not remotely tempted to make out with him on national television. I pushed him away with an eye roll and he took his seat again, grinning.

After the interviews, and the posing, and a bare minimum of mingling, Zane grabbed my hand, all trace of the devil-may-care persona he'd put on for the cameras gone. "Come to the hotel with me, Stacy. I've got a bad feeling about Tessa."

Startled by his request, I asked, "Why me?"

"You're a woman. You might spot something 'off' in her room that I'd miss. Come on."

I let him pull me away from the press conference and changed hurriedly in the wardrobe trailer, infected by his anxiety.

*　　　*　　　*

The production company was housing the b-listers and crew at one of those executive suites places that were like a cross between a hotel and an apartment complex, intended for people who needed temporary lodging for two or three months. EAKINS EXTENDED STAY—YOUR HOME AWAY FROM HOME proclaimed the neon sign atop the porte cochere. The complex had two wings, five stories each, on either side of a central lobby with a breakfast area. Four men and two women sat around the big-screen TV opposite the registration desk, munching popcorn and watching a baseball game. I felt a shiver of apprehension as I trailed Zane into the elevator and up to Tessa's fifth-floor room. Thick carpet hushed our footsteps and we passed no one before Zane, with his longer stride, stopped in front of a closed door. He felt along the top of the doorjamb. "The advantage of knowing a woman's habits," he said, holding up a key.

"Tessa?" Zane knocked lightly and paused. When Tessa didn't appear, he slid the key into the lock, pushing the door inward.

The apartment was dark, the draperies closed, and smelled like nothing more sinister than stale air-conditioning. Zane pressed the light switch. I let my breath out in a whoosh of relief at the sight of the neat, unransacked, empty room. Tessa wasn't here. It was an efficiency apartment, with a kitchenette in an alcove, and a sitting area with a desk in addition to the king-sized bed, but we could see from the foyer that the place was empty. The TV was off, files and papers were stacked neatly on the desk, and the only sound was a faint hum from the refrigerator. The place couldn't have felt emptier if it'd been unoccupied for weeks.

"She's not here." Zane stated the obvious.

Without answering, I crossed to a half-closed door I thought must be the bathroom. Taking a deep breath, I used one finger to push the door wider. I peered inside. Folded towels, cosmetics and lotions on the countertop, toilet paper edge fashioned into a point . . . no body. If the toilet paper was anything to go by, Tessa hadn't been here all day, at least not since the housekeeper went through.

"See anything, Stacy?" Zane asked. He stood close enough that I could feel his breath on my neck.

Backing away from the bathroom, I walked into the sleeping area. "She wore those clothes yesterday," I said, pointing to the brown slacks and caramel-colored silk shell draped over the desk chair. "She must've come back here after work yesterday."

"We know that," Zane said impatiently. "We all saw her at Club Nitro. She wasn't missing then. She's just been missing today."

I tried not to take offense at his tone, realizing he was worried about Tessa. What was their relationship, I wondered. Friends? Something more? What had he meant about "knowing a woman's habits"? "Well, I don't see any nightclubbing clothes, so it looks to me like she didn't come back last night."

Zane yanked on the closet door and peered into it. "You're right. She was wearing black pants with a stripe—"

"Tuxedo pants." Very chic.

"—and a silvery . . ." He brushed his hand up and down near his chest.

"Cami? Tank top?"

"Yeah. They're not here."

"Mystery solved."

Zane looked at me with a confused expression. I rolled my eyes. "Do I have to spell it out?" Apparently so. "She met someone at the club. A guy. She went home with him."

Zane was shaking his head before I finished speaking. "No way. I mean, it's possible she met someone and let him pick her up, but it's not possible that she blew off work today to hang with some guy, no matter how hot the sex. Never happen."

I didn't know Tessa well, but she gave off the kind of ambitious, competent vibes that made me think Zane was right. "Well, if she's not playing footsie with a new boyfriend, where is she?"

"I don't know." Zane looked around with frustration.

"Why don't you leave her a note," I suggested, "in case she comes back."

"I already left six voice mails." Still, he stalked to the desk, ripped a piece of paper from a small notepad and wrote "CALL ME. Z" in block letters. He left it on top of the laptop. "I'll walk you home."

Without waiting for an answer, Zane ushered me out of the room, locked the door and returned the key to its spot, and escorted me onto the elevator. We rode down in silence. On the ground floor, the door whooshed open and a couple of photographers surged forward, cameras clicking and whirring. I would have stopped in astonishment if Zane's hand at my waist hadn't kept me moving forward.

"Zane!" one called. "Are you a couple off the dance floor as well as on it?"

"No comment." Head slightly lowered, Zane bulled past the paparazzi, grabbing my hand to pull me along.

The baseball watchers stared curiously and I felt like I'd done something wrong, even though I hadn't. If this was fame, the Hollywood crowd was welcome to it. We emerged into the muggy July night and walked briskly for half a block before I tugged on Zane's hand to slow him down. "My shoes." I pointed to the kitten-heeled sandals that showed off my pedicure, but weren't meant for racewalking down Old Town's brick sidewalks.

"I am going to kill Nigel," he ground out, skin tightening around his eyes.

"You think he sicced the photographers on you?"

"Not a doubt about it. He's from the school that thinks any publicity is good publicity, so I'm sure he's let every photog in town know where all the celebs from *Blisters* are staying. He's hoping they'll stake out the hotel and get a good shot or two, preferably something scandalous that can go viral on the Internet." He looked down at me, forehead puckered, streaky blond hair feathering over his eyebrows. "I'm sorry you got caught up in it, Stacy."

"No biggie," I said, shrugging. I started walking toward my house again, at a slower pace, a little disconcerted by the concern in Zane's eyes. He was a nice guy. His niceness, combined with his hotness, made him hard to resist . . . not that he'd actually made a move or anything. If he did, what would I do? Danielle's face popped into my head. I chased it away. Then, Tav's face, so like Rafe's, seemed to float in front of me. Any relationship with Tav was doomed, I thought sadly, reliving the moment I'd walked in on Rafe and Solange. I didn't necessarily think Tav would cheat, but his life was in Argentina, mine was here, and we both had memories of Rafe getting in the way at inopportune moments. If I let myself start something with him, our business partnership would suffer when things went south, as they inevitably would. We reached the town house. "Well, here we are," I said brightly.

A blue glow came from my neighbor's window, along with the faint sounds of crashes and gunshots that suggested she was watching a cop show or thriller. The gray cat that lived behind me skittered along the base of the staircase beside my house and a young couple strolled by, arms twined around each other. The sticky humidity clung to my arms. There was a moment of hesitation when my gaze met Zane's. Was he going to kiss me? Was I going to let him? I caught my breath.

"I'll see you in the morning," Zane said with a smile. "I *am* going to master that turn series tomorrow." He leaned forward and kissed my cheek, watched until I let myself in, and then walked back toward the hotel.

Idiot, I told myself, kicking off my shoes and heading for my bedroom. Stripping, I let my clothes fall to the floor, and pulled my sleep cami over my head. I brushed my teeth with more fierceness than my poor gums deserved, still beating myself for that moment of almost-hope on the front sidewalk. I did not need the complications that a relationship, no matter how shallow and temporary, with Zane Savage would bring. So I was glad he hadn't tried to kiss me. Really, really glad. Immensely glad.

Chapter 6

Tav greeted me when I climbed the interior stairs to the studio Thursday morning. I was makeupless and draggy, and my hair needed washing. I'd intended to do some cleaning before the film crew arrived—we'd cut costs by letting the janitorial service go—and I wasn't expecting to see anyone. When I entered the office and saw him at his desk, I jumped. "Tav!"

"Good morning, Stacy." He wore a suit that told me he was headed into the city on business, and a frown. He looked unusually forbidding and formal.

Something must be wrong. He never stopped by this early. My stomach knotted. "Is everything okay?" I asked hesitantly. "Your family?"

"My family is fine," he said, his accent more noticeable than usual. His expression didn't lighten. He passed a folded newspaper across to me. "You can imagine how I felt when I saw this this morning."

I gazed at the photo of me and Zane getting out of the elevator. My head was tucked down in a way that made me look like I had a double chin. Ugh. "What?"

"That is you and Zane Savage at his hotel." He took the paper back and read: " 'Former child star and *Ballroom with the B-Listers* contender Zane Savage leaves the Eakins Extended Stay apartments with his dance partner, Anastasia Graysin, leading to speculation that they are partners off the dance floor as well as on it.' " He dropped the paper on his desk.

I felt a confused jumble of emotion. First, I was pissed off with the newspaper for the unflattering photo and innuendo. Second, I was annoyed that Tav was annoyed—he had no right to be. Third, I was a little bit pleased that Tav was annoyed. The combination of feelings irritated me. "Zane and I went to the hotel to check on Tessa King, who is missing. We didn't find her. We left. He walked me home."

Tav looked taken aback, either by my explanation or my tone. He leaned forward, palms on his desk. "Look, Stacy, I know I have no right—"

"No, you don't."

His brows soared.

"You have no right to assume I'm sleeping with Zane or anyone else, merely because a newspaper prints a photo of us in a hotel lobby."

"I did not think—"

Now it was my turn to cock a brow.

"All right. I did think." He smiled ruefully. "I am sorry."

The genuine contrition in his eyes melted my anger. "It's okay. Forget it. What are you up to today?"

He filled me in on his schedule, saying he hoped to return from a downtown meeting in time to watch some of the filming, and then left, stuffing the newspaper into the trash can. A glance at the clock told me I no longer had time to scrub the bathroom before my student arrived for a private lesson, so I contented myself with sweeping the ballroom quickly and darted downstairs to shower.

An hour and a half later, sweaty from practicing jive flicks and kicks with the government worker who'd taken up ballroom dance to get a little exercise and meet women, but now competed successfully at the Silver level, I needed another shower. I rinsed off quickly and was reapplying deodorant when the phone rang. I answered it, simultaneously trying to pull up the stretchy shorts I was wearing for today's *Blisters* practice session. It was Danielle.

"I can't believe you'd do this to me," she yelled.

Holding the phone away from my ear, I said, "Take a chill pill, Dani. What are you talking about?" I knew what she was talking about, of course—the photo—but I wanted to hear her accuse me of sleeping with Zane Savage.

"You knew I was interested in him, but you still had to have him."

I rolled my eyes and set the phone on the dresser so I could tug up the shorts. I could still hear Danielle's aggrieved voice.

Admiring my tight abs in the mirror as I pulled a cropped top over my head, I picked up the phone again. "I haven't 'had' him," I said, and explained about the photo. "But if I wanted to have him, I could. There's no 'Property of Danielle Graysin' sign tattooed on his forehead." I couldn't help but poke at her, even knowing it would make her furious. It was a sister reflex.

"We'll see about that," she said, and hung up. I felt sorry for any of the union employees who wanted her to arbitrate a grievance today.

Upstairs, the filming chaos matched my mood. Nigel Whiteman, the camera guy, and both our celebrities had arrived while I was changing and they were all gathered in the ballroom, along with Vitaly.

"Nigel, you've got to go to the police," Zane was saying as I slipped into the room and began stretching at the barre. "Phoebe, tell him."

Phoebe shrugged muscular shoulders. "Tessa's a big girl."

Zane almost growled with frustration. "It's not like her to disappear like this."

"You would know," Phoebe shot at him.

I pursed my lips. What did that mean? I was getting the distinct impression that there was something between Zane and Tessa besides star and producer.

Nigel made a calming motion. "Zane. You're concerned. I get it. Me, too. But the coppers aren't going to give a rat's ass about an adult woman who's been missing—what?—about thirty-six hours. If she hasn't shown up by—"

"If you won't go to the police, I will." Zane's mouth was set in a grim line.

"Excuse me." The voice came from the threshold.

I recognized it and whipped around, snagging my heel on the barre and almost falling on my face. Catching myself with my palms on the floor, I stared up with dismay at the man entering the ballroom. At first glance, he didn't look like much, in his mid-fifties with thinning dishwater-colored hair, too-red lips, and freckles spattering his face and even his ear lobes. Black, Clark Kent–type glasses made him look like an escapee from the 1960s. His suit said Penney's or Men's Wearhouse rather than Hugo Boss or Calvin Klein, but his shoes were polished to a mirrorlike shine. It was the badge hooked over his belt, though, that brought conversation to a halt.

"Detective Lissy," I blurted, getting a bad feeling. I straightened, face red, and unhooked my foot from the barre. "What are you—?"

His gray gaze swept me, moved from Zane to the camera guy, and finally settled on Nigel. "I'm looking for a Nigel Whiteman."

"I'm Whiteman." Nigel stepped forward, shorter than Lissy, but overshadowing the detective with his smile and personality. "How can I help you, constable?"

"It's detective. Detective Lissy of the Alexandria Police Department." He seemed completely unfazed by Nigel's attitude. "I understand you work with Tessa King."

"Oh, my God," Zane breathed. He took a hasty step forward, coming to a halt between Nigel and Lissy. "What about Tessa? Have you found her?"

Detective Lissy gave him a considering look. "And you are?"

"Zane Savage," he said impatiently. "Where's Tessa? Is she hurt, in the hospital?"

Lissy pursed his lips and I think we all knew what he was going to say before the words left his mouth. "She's dead."

"Impossible," Nigel huffed.

"Is badly," Vitaly said.

"Oh, my God," Zane said again.

"Tessa. Poor Tessa," Phoebe said. "I can't believe it. Was it a car accident?"

I strode forward, hands on my hips. I knew a homicide detective wouldn't be standing in my ballroom if Tessa had died in a garden-variety car accident. "What happened?"

Lissy's eyes cut toward me. "Ah, Ms. Graysin. I saw your photo in the paper this morning." His gaze flicked from me to Zane. "Not very flattering." He didn't answer my question, merely announcing, "I will need to interview each of you individually. The officer" — he gestured toward the hall where I could see a uniformed sleeve — "will take your details. Your office will work best, Ms. Graysin." Taking my agreement for granted, he crossed the hall to my office door and stopped in the opening. "I'll start with you, Mr. Whiteman."

Nigel sputtered, but then joined Detective Lissy, leaving the rest of us looking at each other with varying degrees of confusion, grief, and anxiety.

"I guess we are not dancing today," Vitaly said, plucking his grapefruit juice bottle off the stereo cabinet and taking a long swallow.

"Excuse me." Phoebe hurried from the room, one hand pressed to her lips.

"Turn that damn thing off, Larry," Zane snapped.

Larry, tall and gawky with a fringe of curly hair around a bald pate, shrugged and complied, lowering the camera from his shoulder.

I realized the camera had been running the whole time and wondered if any of the footage would make it onto the air. Another thought hit me. Maybe they'd cancel the show. I asked Zane about it and he gave a bark of unamused laughter.

"Cancel? Nigel? He's in there right now, talking to that detective, trying to figure out which media contact to call first to get the biggest ratings bump out of this. Nigel wouldn't even slip the schedule — forget canceling — unless *he'd* been killed. Come to think of it, he's probably got a clause in his will that would keep the cameras rolling even in the event of his death." Zane rubbed his palms along his stubbly jaw.

"I'm sorry about Tessa," I said, putting a hand on Zane's arm. "It seems like you two were . . . close."

"We dated for a few months. Even though it's been over for two years, I still care about her." His face was a stony mask, as if he was willing himself to show no emotion for fear that letting a hint of sadness show might loose more emotions than he could handle.

I'd sensed that there was more between them than actor and producer. Still, his admission took me by surprise; I wasn't sure how I felt about it. It certainly explained his concern when Tessa went missing.

We stood silently for perhaps five minutes until Nigel came through the door. "You're up," he told Zane. "Nosy bugger."

I assumed he meant Detective Lissy and not Zane. As Zane crossed the hall, Nigel texted from his iPhone, and directed Larry to pack up. "Did you get all that?" he asked, and the camera guy nodded. "Bloody hell," Nigel muttered savagely, slinging his briefcase across the room. It smacked against the wall. The room went dead quiet. "Bloody damn hell." Nigel retrieved the case and walked out, not looking at any of us. Zane and Phoebe left immediately following their interviews with Detective Lissy, so I didn't get a chance to find out what he asked about. Vitaly was in and out of the office in less than two minutes and left to meet his John with a somber, "I will seeing you tomorrow."

With a little trepidation, I walked into my office. Lissy had made himself at home behind my desk, aligning the file folders I'd had out with their spines along the edge of the desk, and sizing my framed photos from shortest to tallest. I sank into the love seat, glancing out the window. The usual noonday traffic clogged the street, stopped by the traffic light at the end of the block, and pedestrians hurried down the sidewalk, meeting friends for lunch or getting in a quick workout before returning to their offices for the afternoon. Sunburns, cameras, and shopping bags made the tourists easy to spot. Reluctant to talk about sudden death on this bright summer day—or any day, for that matter—I dragged my gaze away when Detective Lissy cleared his throat.

"Ms. Graysin, I'm interested in your observations on this case."

"You are?"

His nonconfrontational tone surprised me. We'd first met when he investigated Rafe's murder and he thought for a long time that I'd killed my fiancé. We met again when Corinne Blakely was killed because Maurice was lunching with her when she keeled over and that made him a suspect. I got the feeling toward the end of that case that maybe Detective Lissy was thawing toward me a little bit. I sat up straighter, ridiculously pleased that he didn't seem to consider me a suspect this time. It was a nice change of pace.

"You've known Ms. King how long?"

I thought back. "About two weeks."

"How did you meet?"

I explained about the call from Nigel, about agreeing to participate on *Blisters*. "She was one of the show's producers, as you probably know."

He nodded. "Did you get along well with her?"

"Pretty much. I didn't see her all that often. It was mostly Nigel here when we were filming practices. I think Tessa spent more time at the other studios. They were—"

"I've got the names, thank you. How would you describe her mood lately? Did she act any differently the last couple of days? Scared, worried, depressed?"

Biting my lip, I thought. "I don't think so. She was always professional, not like . . ." Not like Nigel Whiteman, who wore his mood—usually testy—on his sleeve and could go off like a rocket when he was angry.

"Did you ever see her socially, outside the studio?"

Shaking my head so my ponytail swished across my shoulders, I said, "Nope. Not once."

"But you saw Zane Savage socially."

Something new had crept into Lissy's pedantic voice and I eyed him narrowly. "No, I didn't."

The detective gave me a disbelieving look. "That photograph in the newspaper this morning suggests otherwise. Are you lying about your relationship with Savage because he was still involved with Tessa King?"

"He wasn't— We weren't—" I glared at him. "You're not interested in my observations. You're trying to trick me."

Giving a small, satisfied smile, he leaned forward. "Tricks don't work with someone who's got nothing to hide."

I jumped up. "I'm telling the truth. Zane and I went to the Eakins to check out Tessa's room. We are not dating. I didn't know until today that he used to date Tessa. They ended it a couple years ago and were just friends. Not that it mattered to me," I added hastily.

"According to . . . ?"

"To Zane."

Making a notation in his notebook, Lissy laid down his pen. He fussed with his cuffs momentarily, and then pinned me with his gaze. "Where were you Tuesday night?"

I thought back, trying to remember. "I took a ballet class at five and left the studio about seven, after I showered." I gave him the name of the ballet studio and the teacher, and he wrote them down. Great. Now everyone I knew would wonder why the police were asking questions about me again. "I walked home and made myself dinner. Then I watched a couple of *NCIS* episodes—they were doing another marathon—until bedtime. I went to bed around ten. Alone."

Lissy's expression said he wasn't surprised I had no real alibi. "Thank you, Ms. Graysin, I think that's all . . . for now."

"How did she die?"

Adjusting his tie tack so it sat straight, Lissy gave me a considering look. "We don't have the autopsy results yet, but she was fished out of the Potomac by a kayaker early this morning." Apparently satisfied with my horrified expression, he tucked his notebook into his inner pocket, said good-bye, and left.

Chapter 7

I barely had time to wrap my mind around what Detective Lissy had told me when the door to the exterior stairs, the ones students and staff used so they didn't have to come through my living area to get to the studio, creaked open. The clicking of toenails on the wooden floors told me who had arrived. Sure enough, a moment later, Hoover trotted into the office, tail wagging, and laid his large head on my desk. The doleful expression in his brown eyes told me he hadn't had a morsel to eat in forever and that he'd appreciate a nibble of the peanut butter crackers he could smell in my desk drawer. I was happy to split a packet of crackers with him. The size of a calf, Hoover was the harlequin Great Dane who belonged to Mildred Kensington, one of our more elderly students who danced with more enthusiasm than technique. He came to classes with her, usually lying in a sunny spot on the floor, and had become an unofficial studio mascot.

I waited half expectantly for Mildred's cheery voice, but it was Maurice Goldberg who walked into the office.

"Dog sitting again?" I asked, crumpling up the cracker wrapper and slipping it into the trash can. Hoover swiped a long tongue over his muzzle, disposing of crumb evidence, and we both turned innocent gazes on Maurice.

"Mildred's gone to visit her daughter in Oshkosh and you know she hates to kennel Hoover. I'm house-sitting for her."

"What about Cyd and Gene?"

"The cats are with me, of course. They keep Hoover in line."

Hoover woofed his outrage at the idea that he answered to any member of the feline species, and we laughed.

"Where is everyone?" Maurice asked. "I thought they were filming today."

"They were. We were. Right up until Detective Lissy walked in and told us Tessa King was dead." Maurice looked aghast and I added, "They're treating it as a homicide." Saying the words aloud gave me pause. "You know, he didn't actually say they thought someone killed her. He said they fished her out of the Potomac this morning. It could have been an accident."

"Or suicide. What a tragedy."

"Oh, I can't see Tessa—" I bit off the rest of what I was going to say. How well did I know Tessa King, anyway? Not well at all. She might have an incurable illness, for all I knew, or boyfriend troubles, or a history of depression. Lissy *had* asked about Tessa's moods. Maybe the police had a reason to suspect suicide. The thought both relieved and saddened me. I told Maurice about Lissy's interrogation.

Maurice listened thoughtfully from where he sat on the love seat with one ankle resting on the opposite knee, absently picking white Hoover hairs off his gray flannel trousers. "It's a tragedy," he said, "no matter how it happened. She was so young." He straightened. "However, we must be practical, Anastasia. Another death associated with Graysin Motion is not going to look good."

"Corinne wasn't associated with the studio," I said weakly.

"But Rafe was. And now Tessa."

"She's from Hollywood," I said. "She didn't live here. So no one can say—"

"You know the newspapers will mention Graysin Motion when they report her death. If it turns out to be murder, and the killer is someone associated with the show . . ."

He trailed off to let me assimilate the bad publicity consequences for my studio. I slammed shut my half-open middle desk drawer with unnecessary force. "Being on *Blisters* was supposed to be good publicity for us!"

"You need to get out in front of this, find out the truth about what happened before it turns into a media circus and the studio loses clients." Maurice eyed me seriously. Hoover lifted his head, disturbed, perhaps, by Maurice's tone.

"Me?"

"You have a knack for investigation, Anastasia."

"I'm a ballroom dancer, not Jethro Gibbs."

"Be that as it may." Maurice smiled the smile that must have beguiled many a lonely widow or divorcée on one of his cruise ships.

I *did* have the afternoon free since clearly filming was disrupted for the day. "Fine. Where do we start?"

Maurice and I agreed we needed more information about how and when Tessa had died. "If it was an accident, or a suicide, and Detective Lissy was just covering his bases with his questions this morning, it won't get much play in the media," I pointed out. Thus, we scanned Internet reports of her death. They didn't tell us anything we didn't already know, but they reinforced our fears for the studio's reputation since several of the articles mentioned that Tessa was in town to oversee production of *Blisters* and named the competing studios and celebrities.

Tapping a peach-polished fingernail on my tooth, I pondered my options after Maurice went into the ballroom to teach a Standard class. Tango music thrummed through the studio. Detective Lissy was not going to tell me anything about how Tessa died. Who else—? The answer came to me: Kevin McDill. A longtime reporter for the *Washington Post* I'd met investigating Rafe's death, he had to have contacts in the coroner's office, someone who could tell him what the autopsy report said. And he owed me. I had the phone in my hand, preparing to dial, when someone knocked on the outside door. I got up to answer it, Hoover padding curiously at my heels.

An attractive woman I didn't recognize stood on the landing. Her suit, hair, and makeup said "high maintenance."

"Can I help you?"

"This *is* Graysin Motion, where *Blisters* is filming, right?" Her voice suggested she didn't really think she might be wrong.

"Yes, but—"

"Good. I need to see Zane right away." Her designer-shod foot tapped and she slid her large sunglasses onto her head, revealing hard eyes and unlined skin.

I eyed her, wondering if she really knew Zane or if she was some kind of stalker. "Zane's not here."

"Oh, please. I heard about what happened to Tessa. I've got to assure myself he's all right." She made as if to push past me, but I blocked her. She was about my height—five foot six—and her sleeveless sheath revealed toned arms, but I figured I could take her.

She gave me a frosty look. "If you don't let me in to see Zane right this minute, I'll get your ass fired from this show. Zane will say he'd rather dance with a rabid baboon than you, and your tight little dancer's fanny will be out the door."

Who was this witch? Zane's agent, maybe. I didn't care who she was: no one talked to me like that. "You're trespassing," I said flatly. Hoover stuck his head past my thigh and growled deep in his throat. I patted him. *Good dog.*

The woman gave Hoover a wary look. "I'm allergic to dogs."

I didn't respond. I was tempted to let Hoover chase her down the stairs, but I wasn't sure if the studio's insurance would pay up if she took a tumble, so I kept a hand on his collar.

"Look," she said in a more conciliatory voice, "we got off on the wrong foot. I was just worried. You can't blame a mother for getting a little uptight when her son might be in peril." She tried a thin, closed-lip smile.

It took me a split second to process what she'd said. "You're Zane's *mother*?" I mentally upped her age a good ten years. I didn't see much resemblance to Zane. She had dark hair where his was blond, and brown eyes to his hazel. Her nose was too straight, lacking the slight bump that gave his character.

"Kim Savage." She extended a slim hand and I reluctantly shook hands with her.

"Come on in, I guess." I pulled the door wider. "Zane's really not here, though. After the police questioned him, he left. I don't know where he went."

"The police interrogated him? That's just great! After all I've been doing to rejuvenate his career, he gets tangled up in a murder." She huffed a sigh and strode past me into the studio, looking around curiously. "I've been lobbying for eighteen months to get him on *Ballroom with the B-Listers*, calling in favors and—" She shot me a look. "Well, never mind. His career's been in the doldrums ever since *Hollywood High* got canceled, and this is his best shot at a comeback. I've been in talks with James Cameron about his new movie, and I can't believe it might all fall apart because of that—" She folded her lips together. "One shouldn't speak ill of the dead. But she was never good for Zane, never."

Without a knock or a by-your-leave, she opened the ballroom door and peered in at the class. Music swirled into the hall. They'd moved on to a foxtrot and Kim Savage watched the dancers for a moment. Maurice caught sight of us and lifted his brows, but I shook my head.

"He's not here," she said.

I resisted the "duh" that sprang to my tongue. "Did you try the hotel?"

"He's not there, either. Where could he be?" A line appeared between her brows.

She was acting more like Zane was a fifteen-year-old who'd missed his curfew instead of a man in his mid-thirties. I guessed Kim Savage might be the poster child for "stage mothers."

"Look, I'm sorry I barged in like this. If Zane comes by, or if you hear from him, would you let me know?"

She handed me a card with her name and a phone number on it. Perhaps inferring from my expression that I was unlikely to tattle on Zane, she said, "Tell him to call me, okay?"

Turning on her stiletto heels and making a big circle around Hoover, she headed for the door. She turned, hand on the doorknob. "Oh, and Stacy—I can call you Stacy, right?" Without waiting for an answer, she went on, "When things settle down a bit, you and I should have a chat. I've got some ideas for dance routines that will help Zane—and you—get viewer votes." Sliding the sunglasses over her eyes, she was gone.

"An attractive woman," Maurice observed from behind me. I hadn't heard him come out of the ballroom. His students trickled into the hall, taking a water break. I heard the toilet flush.

"Zane's mommy dearest."

"Really?" Maurice crossed to the window at the end of the hall that looked onto the street fronting the house. I joined him. We watched Kim Savage slide, with a display of shapely calf, into an illegally parked Jaguar convertible. "Well preserved."

"If you like your women Monroe-esque and stuffed into Spanx." I knew I wasn't being quite fair; Kim Savage had the kind of hourglass figure many men found irresistible, even if she needed a little undergarment help to make that knit sheath fit so smoothly.

"I do." Maurice grinned at me. "I remember her now. She made a couple of movies in the seventies, pretty campy stuff. She gave Raquel Welch and Ann-Margret a run for their money when it came to the sex kitten roles. Va-va-voom." He waggled his brows.

I was mildly interested that Kim Savage had been an

actress, but that didn't make me like her any better. "She has choreography ideas she wants to 'share' with me."

"Ah-hah. That's why you're being snippy. Presumptuous of her, I grant you." Rounding up his students, Maurice herded them back into the ballroom for the second half of the lesson. Hoover followed them in.

I traipsed to the door at the far end of the hall marked PRIVATE and descended the interior stairs to my living quarters. I'd decided a little privacy was in order for my conversation with Kevin McDill. I made myself a cup of coffee and settled in at the scarred kitchen table, wishing for the thousandth time I could afford to have the garish turquoise tile counter replaced with granite or one of those new recycled glass countertops. However, given that I cooked only about twice a month, I had to use my limited funds on higher priorities—like keeping my dance studio afloat.

McDill seemed pleased but wary to hear from me. When I told him why I was calling, silence came over the line, broken only by sounds I finally identified as the reporter working his mouth around his omnipresent toothpick. I visualized his seamed, walnut-colored face, and the reading glasses that would be halfway down his nose. "I've got someone I can talk to," he finally said. "If they only found the body this morning, though, the autopsy might not be complete. I'll give you a call when I know something. You owe me." He hung up.

I set the phone down, satisfied. A few minutes' thought told me it made no sense to sit here and wait for McDill to call back; it might be hours before he knew anything. If I was going to find out what happened to Tessa King, I needed to know more about her. Zane obviously knew plenty, but he was out and about somewhere, if his mother was to be believed. I could talk to Nigel . . . I wrinkled my nose at the thought of seeking out the caustic producer, but he probably knew Tessa best, of all the cast and crew. He was the logical person to start with if I wanted to learn more about her. Reluctantly, I picked up the phone again and dialed.

Chapter 8

Nigel's assistant said the producer was too busy to meet with me, but let fall the information that he was currently coping with "talent issues" at Take the Lead with Ingelido, one of the other studios competing on *Blisters*. I thanked the assistant sweetly, grabbed a yogurt to eat on the way, and headed out the back door to my yellow Volkswagen Beetle where it sat under the carport. Take the Lead with Ingelido was in the Tysons Corner area and I zipped around the beltway to get there, hoping I'd be home again before rush hour traffic clogged I-495.

Marco Ingelido's ballroom studio occupied a former roller skating rink. A neon top hat logo signaled potential dancers from atop a sign that towered over the private parking lot. As always, I eyed the lot enviously. In crowded Old Town Alexandria, parking was at a premium and my town house didn't have any off-street parking to offer students. I knew a fair number of our female clients didn't feel comfortable attending our evening events because they didn't like the parking situation. I'd long lusted after the property that abutted my lot, a sixties-era building that had been a home, a dental office, a bodega, and now sat empty. I'd love to buy the property and raze the building to turn it into a parking lot, but the cost was way out of my reach.

I sighed and walked into Take the Lead. The color scheme inside the building was black and gold like the logo, with flocked wallpaper and gilt mirrors in the entryway. Tacky, I sniffed, preferring the gracious elegance of my historic townhome that had once been owned by James Madison's cousin. Old linoleum covered the floors, still showing black streaks where skaters had skidded. The fact that Marco Ingelido hadn't replaced the lino made me wonder if the studio was doing as well as he always claimed it was. An unmanned reception counter originally used to pass out roller skates now held class schedules, brochures, and a selection of dance shoes.

From the half-open door leading to the dance floor came the sounds of an argument. I crept closer to listen, putting my eyes to the crack. The dance floor was huge, the former rink covered with wood flooring. The waist-high wall that encircled it had gaps for dancers to enter or leave the floor. Nanette Fleaston, the pet psychic, stood ten feet inside the door, her back to me, gesturing at Nigel Whiteman.

"Tessa's death is a bad omen for the show," Nanette said, her voice high-pitched and fragile. She was delicately built, with sharp features and caramel-colored hair. If she'd been a dog, she'd have been a Pomeranian. "Jezebel is most unhappy about it."

"Who the f— hell is Jezebel?" Nigel bit out, his gaze landing on the camera in time to censor his language. "You haven't changed agents, have you?"

"My pig," Nanette said reproachfully, gesturing toward the floor.

I leaned farther in, curious. A small, vaguely pink pig with a black spot on her back sat near Nanette, snout pointed upward as if she was following the conversation. She was cute in a piggy sort of way.

Nanette continued, "She's a pedigreed, potbellied Viet—"

"Forgive me, luv, but I don't give a flip what Miss Bacon-on-the-hoof thinks about anything."

An indignant oink came from Jezebel and she sprang to her feet. I suppressed a giggle.

"Well, I do," Nanette said, drawing herself up with dignity. "In fact, I don't know if I can continue on with this show, not under the circumstances. Jezebel says—"

"Let me remind you that you signed a contract," Nigel said, his jaw tightening. "I've got a raft of lawyers ready to sue you for any breach, so lace up your dance shoes and make like Little Miss Twinkletoes, hm?" He smiled broadly, but his swooping eyebrows gave him a menacing aspect.

I couldn't see Nanette's reaction, but I heard her gasp. Before she could say more, however, Marco Ingelido glided over to them. Six feet of tall, dark, and handsome, even if a bit long in the tooth at near sixty, Marco put an arm around Nanette's shoulders. "Let's try the promenade again, Nanette. You really have a feel for the waltz and, with a little more practice, we could be the high-scoring couple Saturday."

Some of the rigidity left her shoulders and she let Marco lead her onto the dance floor, Jezebel trotting behind. Nigel gave a satisfied nod and I was about to approach him when his iPhone buzzed. He answered it and I hesitated.

"Absolutely, luv," he said after a moment of listening. "Everything's under control. What do you have on—"

"Spying on the competition, Stacy?"

The hateful voice made me straighten and turn, furious at being caught in such an ignominious position. I might as well have had my ear against a glass pressed to the wall. "Just waiting for Nigel to get off the phone, Solange," I said as airily as I could.

The svelte redhead snorted delicately. Her hair was more a strawberry blond now than the flame it had been when she filled in at Graysin Motion, but she looked as fit and revoltingly sexy as ever in a mint-colored top that flaunted her six-pack and leggings that showed a mile of slim leg. "I hope your ankle's not going to hold you and your partner back," I said with spurious sympathy.

"All better." She rotated it in both directions to demonstrate. "Thanks for asking." She pretended like she thought I was truly concerned. "Mickey's got a real aptitude for ballroom dance," she went on, "especially for someone who used to think all dancing was sinful. Luckily, he's seen the error of his ways. I'm doing what I can to convert him." She smiled. "How's it going with the boy wonder? Zane Something, right? I can't have been more than two or three when his show got canceled, so I don't think I'd ever heard of him until the press conference."

She was probably three or four years younger than me, but no way had she been a toddler when *Hollywood High* went off the air. "Most of the *Blisters* voting demographic were wild for Zane and *Hollywood High*," I said, "and they're going to be amazed by his dancing. He's got the grace and charm of Gene Kelly, and the athleticism of Derek Hough."

"Really?" Solange's thin eyebrows soared. "Well, Mickey's very strong and he can convey the emotion of each dance so well it'll make the women cry. You know tears mean votes on this show."

"I heard his congregation was in tears when he got caught with that underage prostitute. Think they'll vote for him?"

Solange lifted her chin to come back with another "my celeb's better than your celeb" zinger when I noticed Nigel had hung up and was coming toward us. "Sorry, Solange," I said. "Gotta go. Nigel!" I intercepted him as he came through the door.

White teeth glinting, he looked from me to Solange and back again. "Do I smell female testosterone in the air? A catfight brewing? Splendid idea! Let's get it on film. Larry!"

"No, no," I said, laying a hand on his arm. "Solange and I were just chatting while I waited for you."

I could see Solange weighing the potential benefits of an on-air spat with me, and my eyes urged her to turn Nigel down. "Think how hard it would be for Ariel to cover scratch marks on our faces," I said to Nigel, hoping it would give Solange pause.

After half a beat of hesitation, Solange smiled with fake sweetness and said, "Stacy and I go way back, Nige. We're like . . . sisters."

I sent Danielle a silent apology for every argument we'd ever had, and especially for the time I told her she was the worst sister ever.

"That's not what I heard," Nigel said, studying us

from under his brows, "but it can wait. It might be better after a round or two of competition."

Solange melted away, joining her evangelist partner, Mickey Hazzard, on the dance floor. I wanted to watch them dance, scope out Hazzard's potential, but talking to Nigel was more important. "I'm horrified by what's happened to Tessa," I said.

"You're horrified, luv? They made me identify her body," Nigel said, looking like he'd appreciate a shot of liquor. He seemed a bit green, but maybe it was the lousy lighting in the foyer. Marco should invest in higher wattage bulbs.

I didn't want to think about what Tessa must have looked like after more than twenty-four hours, possibly, in the Potomac at the height of summer. "Don't think about her like that. Try to remember her as she was the last time you saw her alive," I urged Nigel. "Which was when?" Sometimes, my subtlety amazes me.

"Late Tuesday afternoon," he said absently, scrolling through a couple of texts. "We were at the studio in Fairfax and she left to go back to the hotel. I met a friend for dinner."

"So you didn't go to the nightclub that night with everybody else?"

"Not my scene, Stace," he said, flashing a sharky smile. "Can't do business with a deafening techno-pop sound track."

"You and Tessa were all about business, I guess." I trailed after him as he headed for the door and the parking lot. "How did you two become partners?"

Nigel halted and a reminiscent smile played around his lips. "On a blind date. A mutual friend hooked us up. After we got the sex out of the way, we realized we had more in common as business partners than lovers and we made it legal: we formed a limited partnership, White King Productions."

"How romantic," I murmured.

He caught my tone. "After what happened with Rafe Acosta boning the sultry Solange, I'd think you of all people would appreciate the benefits of a business partnership untainted by sex."

I drew back slightly and fumbled for a response. "You must have some research team," I finally said.

"That's the least of what they uncovered researching all of the *Blisters* possibles. You don't think the chemistry on this show just happens, do you? No. It's the end result of months of hard work by a large team, the least of which is the talent." He gave me a dismissive look. "Replacing Tessa will be hard, maybe impossible, but even without her this is going to be the show's best season ever. Explosive!"

I didn't like his secretive smile. He pushed through the door and the harsh afternoon sunlight made me blink.

"Got a meeting," Nigel said, striding toward a Mercedes roadster. "Filming tomorrow. Your place. Eight. Ta, luv."

"Can you think of anyone who was mad at Tessa?" I called after him. "Someone who might have wanted to hurt her?"

He spun around, sunlight glinting off his platinum watch, and took two steps toward me. He studied my face. "You're investigating Tessa's death, aren't you, like you did your partner's?"

I couldn't read his expression. I thought he'd be angry, but he seemed more thoughtful.

He didn't wait for me to reply, but said slowly, "This could be big. Huge. Hot ballroom dancer tracks down murderer." Bouncing his fist lightly off his mouth, he said, "We could have the camera follow you while you do interviews. If you come up with anything, we can be there for the confrontation . . . on live TV. Brilliant!"

I stared at him, openmouthed, aghast. "No! I mean—" How did I get myself out of this one? Footage of me trying to ID a murderer was a) going to royally piss off Detective Lissy and b) totally link Graysin Motion and murder in the minds of the viewing public, exactly what Maurice and I had been trying to avoid.

"We don't even know that she was murdered," I said desperately. "It was probably an accident or . . ." I couldn't bring myself to say the S-word. "I was just curious about Tessa. She seemed so competent and ambitious. Forget I said anything. It's none of my business." I backed up as I spoke, trying to reach my Beetle and escape. Sweat poured down my sides and I didn't know if it was all due to the heat rising off the asphalt or from anxiety about the way my plan was backfiring.

Nigel furrowed his forehead, thinking. "She was murdered. That police detective called and told me so not five minutes before you walked in. We'll offer a reward," he said slowly, "maybe fifty thou for information leading to the arrest of Tessa's killer. We'll make a big announcement, lots of hoopla, get more publicity for the show. It's a brilliant idea, Stace—brilliant." Sliding into the low-slung Mercedes two-seater, he gunned the motor and was gone with his last "brilliant" still hanging in the air.

I climbed into the Beetle feeling anything but brilliant. Moronic, doltish, idiotic, stupid . . . those words better summed me up.

Chapter 9

A message from Kevin McDill waited on my answering machine when I got home and I returned his call. His voice, with its former smoker's rasp, held an undertone of excitement.

"You've got a nose for news, I'll give you that," he greeted me.

I winced, sure I knew what was coming since Nigel had already told me.

"She drowned," McDill said, and I let out a sigh of relief. "Her BAC was 1.3, well over the legal limit."

"It was an accident," I breathed. Nigel misunderstood! "She got drunk, fell into the river somehow, and drowned."

"Not so fast," McDill said with an edge of "gotcha" in his voice. "Both her legs were broken. Miscellaneous abrasions and contusions."

"What?"

"The coroner thinks she might have been struck by a car and either knocked into the water by the impact, or someone tossed her into the drink after hitting her. With two broken legs—hell, she never had a chance."

I gasped. "That's horrible." Poor Tessa. "What was she doing near the river, anyway? From what I've heard, she was last seen at Club Nitro. That's on Pennsylvania, nowhere near the river."

"Not in the autopsy report." McDill chuckled.

Trying to push the grimness of Tessa's death aside, I asked, "Do they know where she went into the water?"

"Not yet," McDill said. "But that's the right question to ask. I'll make a reporter of you yet."

"I don't think so." I told him I owed him one, thanked him, and hung up.

Although I didn't want it to, my mind insisted on flashing pictures of a hurt, drunk Tessa flailing in the river, trying to keep her head above water. I only hoped she'd been unconscious when she went in. In an attempt to get the images of her last moments out of my mind, I backed the reel up a bit, trying to focus on Tessa in the nightclub. I imagined her dancing, silvery tank top glittering under the strobe lights, laughing and flirting with some man. J. Lo's "On the Floor" reverberated in my head as the scene played out.

Tessa and the mystery man have a couple more drinks, maybe kiss, and he invites her home with him. They stagger from the club, tipsy and laughing. They get in his car—something upscale, I'm sure, because Tessa wasn't the type to go home with someone driving a Corolla— and they drive off. Somewhere along the way, he says or does something that makes Tessa mad . . . or scares her. She demands that he let her out. He laughs and goes faster. Really scared now, she waits for him to slow for a turn, then opens the door and jumps out, breaking her legs. Maybe they're on one of the area's many river roads and she rolls down the bank and into the water. Heartless and/or scared, the man drives away. Or, maybe they're crossing a bridge when she jumps out. The man skids to a stop and comes back to where she's lying helpless in the roadway. He's scared she'll have him arrested for attempted rape or abduction—he's drunk, too, and not thinking straight—so he hoists her up and over the guardrail. Plop—into the water. A grimmer scenario came to mind . . . he was some kind of Mr. Goodbar and he planned to kill her all along, seduced her away from the club with that intent.

I shivered, disturbed by my imaginings. So real was the scene, I was almost convinced I'd witnessed it. I hoped Detective Lissy was interviewing everyone who'd been at Club Nitro Tuesday night, asking questions about who Tessa had been dancing with and what time she left. I called him to suggest it.

Detective Lissy was silent for a long, heavy moment after I fed him my theory. Then he said, "If this were the Old West, I could give you a star and deputize you. Since it's not, I'll merely remind you—again—that I've been doing this job for twenty-seven years. My superiors seem to think I know what I'm doing, as do the many, many perps I've sent to prison. Why, then, Ms. Graysin, can I not convince you of that?"

Before I could formulate a response, he hung up. Fine. He was always testy when I offered suggestions or volunteered my theories. I knew he'd been a detective for three decades, but that didn't mean he wouldn't overlook something. I sniffed. It was after five by now and I was tired and hungry. Normally, I'd have called Dani to see if she wanted to get a bite, but she was mad at me for "stealing" Zane. I could be the big one, and apologize first, but I didn't have the energy to do it this evening. I could drive out to see Mom and the horses, but that, too, would take energy, especially at rush hour. I pulled a bowl from the cupboard and was dumping cereal in it when the phone rang.

"Stacy?" It was Zane.

"How are you doing?" I asked in a concerned voice.

"I've been better. Look, I'm going to drop by Club Nitro later on, see if I can spot some folks who were there Tuesday night, who might remember seeing Tessa. Would you come with me?"

I was flattered. My weariness disappeared. Nightclubbing with Zane Savage! I hastily damped down my inappropriate enthusiasm. This wasn't a date ... it was a fishing expedition. Apparently, Zane lacked faith in the Alexandria Police Department, too. "Sure," I said.

"Pick you up at nine."

Club Nitro had a line of people snaking around the block when Zane and I arrived at nine thirty. It was located in a stand-alone building on Pennsylvania Avenue, near where 395 terminated—not remotely close to the famous house at 1600 Pennsylvania. Geography and direction are not my strong suit, but I thought we were closer to the Anacostia River than the Potomac. What looked like a small park across the street seemed to have a lot of foot traffic for this hour of the night and I figured there were drug deals going down. I stuck close to Zane when the valet gave me a hand out of the car. I appreciated his assistance since the shortness of my skirt and the height of my heels made exiting a car something of a challenge. Despite the line, we had no trouble gaining entry. As the valet drove off in Zane's rented Audi TT, a man in black jeans—I missed his name—greeted us and escorted us inside, past the waiting partiers who were variously disgruntled and awed. I heard Zane's name whispered several times.

"My people called ahead," Zane said in answer to my questioning look. I wondered how it felt to have "people." His hand at my waist felt good and I let myself revel in the reflected glow of celebrity, just a teeny bit, as we entered the club. I knew I looked my best in a midnight-blue miniskirt shot through with silver threads, and a silver cami that draped my curves in a sensual but non-trashy way. High-heeled silver sandals, blond hair in a messy knot, and smoky eyes completed the look: casual glamour with a sexy edge. Hey, when your living depends on your looks almost as much as your talent, you get into the nuances.

The music thrummed through me and I found myself moving with the beat as we followed our escort—one of the owners?—to a semicircular booth beside the dance floor. It was easily large enough for eight people. Lots of young professionals were getting an early start to the weekend on a Thursday night and the dance floor was packed. It was a crowd of mixed ethnicity—black, white, Asian, Hispanic—but if the clothes were anything to go by, the economic level was yuppie to the core.

Zane slid onto the banquette and I wiggled in beside him. His lips practically touching my ear so I could hear him over the music, he said, "We sat in these three booths Tuesday night, all of us. Tessa wore a shirt just like that." He nodded to my silver cami and a frisson ran up my spine. I wished I'd worn something else.

A server appeared, holding a small tray aloft with practiced expertise. She was young, brunette, cute, and had eyes only for Zane. "Mr. Savage," she said, leaning over the table to display impressive cleavage and a name tag that said MAYA. "It's good to see you again. G&T with a twist?"

Zane nodded and looked at me. I'd allow myself one drink before switching to club soda, I decided. It wasn't that I was afraid of getting drunk. Alcohol is chock-full of calories and I couldn't afford to gain an ounce before the *Blisters* debut. The camera added ten pounds to start with, and my opening-night costume fit closely enough that an extra olive or single pistachio was going to show. "The same," I said.

"Maya," Zane said, stopping the server before she could leave. "Tuesday night . . . I was here with some friends. One of them was wearing a silver shirt like that"—he pointed to my cami—"only she had dark hair, cut to about here." He chopped a hand at his jawline. "Do you remember her?"

Maya nodded. "Sure. The one who died."

That opened my eyes, and I could tell it surprised Zane, too. Before I could ask how she'd made the connection between news reports about Tessa King, who wasn't exactly a household name, and one of thousands of patrons who must cycle through Nitro weekly, she added, "The police were asking about her. They had a photo."

"What did you tell them?" Zane asked.

Maya shrugged. "She danced, she drank, she left. I told them I didn't notice her particularly. Now, if they'd asked about *you* . . ." She trailed off flirtatiously, winked, and left to get our drinks.

Zane slumped against the leather back of the booth, staring broodingly out at the dancers. Several of the women had clearly sussed out who he was and were dancing provocatively within his line of sight, all but ignoring their poor partners.

"Who all was here with you Tuesday night?" I asked, almost shouting. My voice was going to be hoarse in the morning.

He slid closer, so we could talk more easily, and his hard thigh pressed along the length of mine. Tendrils of warmth curled in my belly, but I ignored them. Mostly.

"Everyone," he said.

"Define 'everyone.' Nigel said he wasn't here."

"Me, Phoebe, Kristen, Tessa, Ariel—she was one of Tessa's best friends—Larry, Nanette, Calista, Mickey . . ." He went on to name another eight or ten crew members. "I think that's it," he said, "but I might have missed someone. Oh, and Carmelo." Carmelo was *Blisters'* head judge. "People were coming and going . . . dancing, getting drinks at the bar, taking a leak. You see how it is." He gestured to the writhing mass of people around us, the crowd so thick now that navigating from one end of the club to the other was a test of agility, determination, and diplomatic skills.

Maya came back, placing our drinks carefully on the table. Zane slid her a bill and she smiled brilliantly. "You know," she said. "The cops spent a long time talking to Gabriel about your friend, but I don't know what he told them." She gestured to a narrow-faced, dark-haired man behind the bar. He was moving with the smooth efficiency of a man who'd been bartending for many years.

"Think he'd talk to us?" Zane held up a hundred-dollar bill between his forefinger and middle finger.

"I'll ask." She nipped the bill away.

We watched as she forced her way through the throng and beckoned to Gabriel. They conversed for thirty seconds, with him glancing at us across the crowd's bobbing heads when Maya slipped him the bribe. Maya made it back five minutes later, delivering some drinks on the way. "He goes on break in forty minutes. He'll meet you across the street in the park." She brought two fingers to her mouth as if puffing on a cigarette. "That door"—she nodded toward a hall to the right of the bar where an exit sign glowed—"is the closest one."

"I feel like Jason Bourne," I admitted a bit sheepishly when she left. "Meeting sources in dark corners of the nation's capital." I sipped my G&T, savoring the gin's zing on my tongue.

A smile crept onto Zane's face, but before he could respond, a gorgeous blonde slithered up to the table. "Would you like to dance?" she cooed at Zane, acting as if I wasn't there.

"Sorry, babe, but I'm taken." Zane put his arm around my shoulders and smiled down into my eyes in a way that made the blonde merge back into the crowd without another word.

I caught my breath and had to remind myself that the man was an actor. "Is that why I'm here?" I asked a little breathlessly. "To keep away the hordes of love-crazed fans?"

"Partly," Zane admitted, "and partly because you're so hot I can hardly keep my hands off of you. Let's dance." Downing most of his G&T in a single swallow, he grabbed my hand and led me onto the floor.

The song was a fast one with a driving beat, but body contact was unavoidable since other dancers pressed in on us from all sides. Zane rested his hands lightly on my hips and we moved together, freestyle, going with the music. I let my hips do their own thing and raised my arms above my head. I could feel my hair tumbling from the loose topknot and sweat dampening my forehead. Zane was likewise flushed and I watched a bead of sweat streak from his neck into the open V of his gray silk shirt, disappearing into a moderate thicket of chest hair. The DJ kept the tunes coming and we stayed on the floor until Zane glanced at his watch.

"It's time." He sounded reluctant, and his gaze lingered on my lips for a long moment. I could lean forward a breath and let him kiss me. Being with Zane would be fun, easy, and temporary . . . no complications at the inevitable parting. It might even be good for the studio for me to be seen with a celebrity. I imagined Tav's frown of disapproval at my train of thought and bit my lip.

I pulled away and said, "Let's go."

Chapter 10

We danced our way off the floor and serpentined our way to the hall Maya had pointed out. It was dark and a bit quieter than the dance floor. A man wheeled a dolly with a metal keg on it from a storage room on our right and I peered in, spotting cases of liquor and wine stacked several boxes high, and a walk-in cooler with sliding doors clouded with condensation. The man paid us no attention as we headed for the door at the hall's far end. We emerged into what looked like the valet parking lot on the building's east side and I caught the glow of a cigarette over by an attendant's hut and heard the murmur of voices. I'd thought the night air would cool my flushed face and arms, but the day's heat still lingered, even though it was coming up on midnight, and humidity kept the sweat from evaporating. My heels tapped on the sidewalk as Zane drew me toward the street. Hopeful partiers still waited in line to get into Club Nitro but I knew we were nothing more than people-shaped shadows to them as we crossed the street. The only illumination was the bluish light spilling from the nightclub's

door since the streetlights seemed to be uniformly non-
functional. Glancing at one as we passed by, I saw why:
thieves had opened the lamp's base and removed the
copper wiring. Bits of insulated wire dangled from the
opening.

The sweetish smell of marijuana drifted from the park
and two teens eyed us narrowly, stuffing something into
their pockets as we passed them. Zane pulled me closer
to him and whispered, "I hope the police don't raid this
park tonight—that's all we'd need, to get hauled downtown as part of a drug user roundup. Think Nigel would
be thrilled or enraged?"

I giggled. "I don't know, but your mom would go bal-
listic."

He almost stopped in surprise. "How do you know my
mom?"

"I forgot to tell you that she stopped by the studio
earlier. She wants you to call her." For some reason,
maybe the G&T or the tension, this felt much funnier to
me than it had earlier. I bit back another giggle. "There."
I pointed to a bench where the thin bartender sat in a
relaxed posture, drawing on a cigarette.

Gabriel looked up at us but didn't stand as we approached. Something rustled in the bushes behind him
and I jumped. "Cats." He lit a new cigarette off the stub
of the first and said, "Maya tells me you want to know
about the dead chick."

"We worked together," Zane said, as if Gabriel had
asked a question. "We were friends."

A thin woman with fried blond hair, out-of-proportion
boobs bouncing in a tube top, a skirt about the size and
tightness of a tourniquet, and six-inch heels, swayed past
us, an older man in her wake. They disappeared into the

shrubbery twenty feet past us and Gabriel snorted at my expression. "Capitalism at its finest. The law of supply and demand at work." He gestured with the cigarette. Its glow showed the aquiline cast of his nose and deep-set eyes. He looked a weary forty, but was probably only my age. "I could tell you what I told the police about your friend, Terry."

"Tessa."

Gabriel stayed silent, looking up at Zane with his brows slightly raised. It took Zane a moment to get what the bartender wanted. With an impatient sigh, he pulled a money clip from his pocket, shielding it from the view of the park's nocturnal denizens. Withdrawing another hundred, he offered it to Gabriel. "Tell us what you saw in the club."

The bill disappeared into Gabriel's pocket. "Thanks." He didn't look one whit embarrassed or self-conscious. Drawing on the cigarette so hard his cheeks went concave, he blew out a long stream of smoke. "I didn't see her in the club," he said. "It was out here, while I was taking my break."

"Go on," Zane said grimly.

I shifted from foot to foot, the silver sandals pinching my toes. I couldn't imagine why Tessa would come to this fetid little park. If she wanted a breath of fresh air, she'd have been better off lingering just outside the club. "What was she doing out here?" I asked.

Gabriel tapped ash from the end of his cigarette. "What everyone else is doing here: looking to score."

"Bullshit," Zane burst out, bunching his hands into fists.

Gabriel shrugged. "All one to me, man, whether you believe me or not." He made as if to get up.

Putting a calming hand on Zane's arm, I said, "No, please, tell us exactly what you saw. What time was it?"

"It was coming up on one o'clock," Gabriel said. "I remember because I'd had to take my break way late. Sharita, the other bartender, cut her finger on a broken glass and had to go to the ER for stitches. It was hopping in there for a Tuesday night and I couldn't get away for my cancer stick"—he waved the smoldering stub—"until quarter to one. I had barely lit up when I saw her coming across the street."

"Alone?"

Gabriel nodded. "She was wearing a top kinda like yours, and she seemed a bit uncertain. One of the local entrepreneurs"—he put the word in air quotes—"approached her. She seemed cool with it. They talked for a couple minutes and then she went off with him."

"Tessa did not do drugs," Zane said. "She used to say her brain was her greatest asset in an industry that worshipped physical beauty, and there was no way she was risking losing one brain cell to a temporary high. End quote. I've never seen her do so much as a line of coke at a party."

I gave Zane a troubled look.

Gabriel held up his hands. "Hey, I didn't say the chick was scoring drugs. There're other things for sale in this park, you know?"

As if on cue, the blond hooker emerged from the shrubbery and sashayed toward the street. Her customer followed a moment later, still tugging at his zipper. He ducked his head as he hurried past us. Zane frowned. "I don't know what you're smoking there, but Tessa did not come out here for *that*, either."

Gabriel stood and ground out his cigarette with his

shoe. "I can only tell you what I saw. Hey, I gotta get back to work."

"Did you know the guy, the one Tessa talked to?" I asked, detaining him with a hand on his arm.

He flinched away from me. "Not to say *know*. I mean, folks mind their own business out here, right?" His eyes cut toward a shadowy area farther down the street from where we'd entered the park. A large black man, at least six foot seven and coming up on three hundred pounds, loomed over a man wearing a hoodie. They were too far away for me to hear their conversation, but the shorter man scuttled away after a few seconds, tucking something into the kangaroo pocket of his jacket.

"Him?" I breathed.

"I gotta go," Gabriel reiterated, striding down the path.

"Let's see what he has to say," I said, starting off toward the supersized drug dealer.

Zane grabbed my hand to halt me. "Are you insane? I can't be seen talking to a drug dealer. My fan base is tweenage girls—that kind of publicity would sink my already foundering career."

I thought he was overreacting. I made a show of looking around. "I don't see any paparazzi hiding under the park benches."

"It's not funny, Stacy. Everyone's got a camera on their cell phone these days, and a YouTube account. Besides, he's gone." Zane lifted his chin toward where the big man had been; the sidewalk was empty.

Telling myself that Gabriel had told the police the same thing he told us, and the police would take care of asking the "entrepreneur" about his interactions with

Tessa, I let Zane lead me away, conscious of the feel of his hard palm against mine. "Did you see Tessa in the club after one o'clock that night?"

Running a hand through his tousled hair, Zane said, "I don't remember! We'd all had a few drinks, we were all up dancing with each other and with total strangers, like you do. I don't remember seeing her specifically, but I don't remember *not* seeing her. I mean, it didn't hit me that she wasn't there anymore, if you know what I mean. I didn't look around and wonder, 'Where's Tessa?'"

I knew what he meant. We waited for a car to pass, and crossed the street to where Club Nitro glowed like a beacon of safety after the unsettled furtiveness of the park, although I suspected there were just as many drugs being sold in the club's restrooms or other out-of-the-way corners as there were in the park. "So, when you all got ready to leave, did you miss Tessa then?"

"We didn't leave at the same time," Zane said. "Some people left way early, before midnight, and others closed the place down and then went out for breakfast, from what I hear. I knew you were going to kick my butt on the dance floor that morning, so I went back to the hotel to catch some z's." He gave me a half smile, the first lightening of his expression since we entered the park. "Look, I don't want to go back in the club, okay?"

"Sure," I agreed, my mood also quenched by our conversation with Gabriel. We crossed the valet lot to the attendant's hut and a kid reading a graphic novel jumped up to retrieve the rental Audi. As I buckled myself in, I had a thought. "Who did Tessa come with that night, or did she drive herself?"

Zane gave me an interested look, then put the car in gear and zoomed out of the lot. "Good question. I'm pretty sure she drove herself. I think I heard Ariel say something about catching a ride with her."

"Then where's her car?"

We pondered that question in silence for a couple of beats before Zane said, "Maybe the cops know."

"If they do, they won't tell us," I said, yawning. "Detective Lissy never learned about sharing in kindergarten."

"Is the bridge we came across the only way back to Virginia from here?"

I laughed sleepily. "Oh, no. If you went that way"—I pointed over my shoulder down Pennsylvania—"you'd cross a bridge that leads to 295."

I held on to the edge of my leather seat as Zane flipped an abrupt U-ey. I raised my brows, but didn't say anything. We sped down Pennsylvania Avenue, past Club Nitro and the park, and onto the bridge spanning the dark waters of the Anacostia River.

"Where to now?"

"South on 295. That'll take us to the Woodrow Wilson Bridge, which will spit us out by Route 1, which is just a hop, skip, and a jump from Old Town. Or, there's another bridge by Nationals Park that would put us in the same place, I think."

"I'm thinking that this doesn't look like a very nice neighborhood," Zane said. "If Tessa got turned around leaving the club, or her car broke down—"

I shivered and Zane turned down the air-conditioning, even though it wasn't the A/C making me cold. "A woman alone in this area would be pretty vulnerable," I admitted. The southeast side of D.C. was one of the city's less desirable areas. Slums, drugs, and gangs abounded. We saw nothing unusual or unsettling as we traveled south to the Woodrow Wilson Bridge, crossed it, and headed up Route 1. Within twenty minutes, Zane was pulling up outside my town house. I opened the door and slid out before he could come around. Still, he insisted on walking me to my front door, which I appreciated.

"Thanks for coming with me tonight, Stacy," Zane said, as we stood on my stoop and I fumbled the key out of my tiny purse. "Next time, we'll have an evening that doesn't include interrogating witnesses."

I felt myself flush with pleasure at his implicit promise there would be a "next time" and was about to say I'd look forward to it when he bent his head and kissed me. There was none of the first-date awkwardness I remembered from my dating life pre-Rafe. His lips found mine unerringly and he kissed with an assurance and competence that left me breathless. He was breathing hard when he lifted his head long moments later, and his eyes glittered. "Perhaps we should continue this inside?" he suggested.

I pulled away slightly, knowing his closeness was affecting my judgment. His hands slid down my back, molding me to him, and my whole body buzzed with lust. "Too fast," I murmured, unable to keep my eyes off his full lips.

They grazed mine again, teasingly. "You're sure?"

"No, but you've got to go anyway."

Laughing, he released me. With a foot of air between us, I could feel sanity returning and I unlocked the door.

"See you tomorrow at practice," Zane said, as I slipped inside. "Eight o'clock, Nigel said." The hall light

I'd left on struck gold from his tawny hair and high-lighted the planes of his face.

"Don't think I'll take it easy on you just because you were up late," I warned, and closed the door on his laugh. I leaned back against it to prevent myself from opening it and hauling him inside.

Chapter 11

I gave a private, forty-five-minute lesson at seven Friday morning to one of my reshuffled students who had generously agreed to come in before work for his lesson, so I was glowing with the joy of dancing (and perhaps a bit of perspiration) when the film crew arrived. Vitaly bounced in moments after the camera guy and Ariel arrived, and Phoebe and Zane arrived together, both clutching large coffees and looking like they would have preferred an extra two or three hours' sleep.

Ariel whisked me into makeup in the small powder room before I had a chance to do more than exchange "Good mornings" with Zane. Wearing her usual tight white T-shirt and faded jeans, she complained that makeup would slip off my sweaty face.

"I thought this was a 'reality' show and we were supposed to look natural," I countered as she swept damp toner pads over my skin.

She grinned and her red hair spilled over her shoulders as she dabbed foundation on my cheeks and forehead. "Trust me—you'll look natural, only better," she said. "There are varying degrees of 'reality,' don't you think?"

"That's way too profound for this early in the morning."

She laughed and made me close my lids so she could dust them with a pale taupe powder and lightly line them with a brown pencil. She added just enough mascara to darken my lashes and stepped back, surveying the effect. "There. Natural, but better. Not so . . ."

"Washed out? Death warmed over? You can say it, Ariel; I know what I look like in the morning."

Laughing again, she began getting out the shades that would look good on Phoebe. "Can you tell Phoebe I'm ready for her?"

"Sure," I said, unwrapping the bib-length smock draped around my neck. "Hey, that night you all went to Club Nitro, did you hitch a ride with Tessa King?"

If she thought my interest was strange, she didn't show it. Sadness settled on her face. "No, we were supposed to go together, but Phoebe needed a ride and Tessa only had a two-seater, so Fred gave me a lift. He works publicity."

I went in search of Phoebe and found the action star warming up by marching in place. "Ariel's ready for you," I said.

"Thanks."

Before she could leave, I asked, "You don't know where Tessa's car is, do you? I understand you rode to Club Nitro with her Tuesday night. Did she take you back to the hotel, too?"

Phoebe gave me a wary look. "What's it to you?"

"Stacy's investigating Tessa's death," Nigel broke in. "I think it'll be ratings gold."

Wincing, I turned to see him come out of the ball-room, trailed by the camera guy who had clearly filmed my short interaction with Phoebe. She looked from me to Nigel, a frown gathering on her brow. "What the hell for? Wasn't it an accident?"

Wishing I could strangle Nigel, and wishing I'd been more discreet, I fumbled for an explanation. "The cops don't seem to think it was an accident," I said, "and I wanted . . . well, after Rafe was shot here . . ."

"Who? What? Someone was shot here?" Phoebe pointed to the floor, her face a mask of astonishment.

I nodded. "My former partner, Rafe Acosta, was shot to death in the ballroom. The police suspected me because we'd had some business arguments and recently broken off our engagement, so I had to find the real killer."

"Did you?"

I nodded again.

"Damn, girl," Phoebe said admiringly.

"And is only little whiles since Stacy is finding who killed Corinne Blakely," Vitaly added, emerging from the ballroom in time to hear the end of our conversation. "Stacy is bull on scent of the murderers."

Phoebe, Nigel, and Larry looked puzzled, but Zane guessed, "Bulldog?"

"*Da.* The bulldog."

"Isn't it dangerous to go looking for killers?" Phoebe asked.

"I don't—"

"She is getting shooted by Rafe's murderer," Vitaly put in. "And the studio was arsoned. Poof!" he threw his arms over his head to indicate the flames.

"Damn, girl," Phoebe said again.

"Rafe's killer didn't set the fire," I said, anxious to get away from this discussion. "Look, you can still see some of the charred boards." I led them into the ballroom and pointed out some of the blackened spots. I'd asked the floor refinisher to keep as many of the singed planks as he could since they were original to the house, historic, and I liked to imagine various Founding Fathers and their wives doing a Virginia reel the length of this room, their feet sliding and clomping on these very boards.

Ariel appeared then, looking for Phoebe, and everyone went back to doing their jobs. I heaved a huge sigh of relief, beginning to regret I'd ever asked question number one about Tessa's death. Beginning, in fact, to regret I'd ever signed on to do *Blisters*. I crossed to the stereo to slot in the CD that held our music, shoving it in a bit more forcefully than necessary. The machine spit it out. I growled low in my throat and Zane took the CD from my hand, inserting it gently.

"What was—" he started.

"Let's just dance," I said, too mindful of the camera rolling and Nigel lurking. We worked for two hours without more than a five-minute water break and I eventually relaxed, caught up in the music and the challenge of teaching a neophyte so much in such a short time.

"You've got to be conscious of your lines, our lines," I told Zane. "Look how your hands flop. The line extends through your hands, through your fingers." Bracing his wrist, I told him to extend his fingers like he was reaching for the far wall. He tried it, stiffly.

"Exactly! See how when I extend my leg, like so"— using my core to stabilize myself I raised my right leg to above head height and pointed my toe—"and you grab it, we form an inverted 'V'? The judges are looking at our lines. Let's try the whole dance again."

Zane groaned. "Do you practice this long every day? My quads are sore, my glutes are sore, and my shoulders are so sore from holding this damn frame that I won't be able to lift my hands over my head tomorrow." He ran his fingers through the damp strands of hair sticking to his forehead. "Be careful, or I'll get rid of you on Trade Day."

Blisters had a gimmick where the celebs could swap partners after the first night of competition but before they knew how the viewing audience had voted. They were allowed to offer any incentive they wanted—cash, a percentage of their audience votes, an onstage appearance at their next concert or walk-on part in their next movie—to persuade a competitor to trade pros. What was grossly unfair about the process, in my humble opinion, was that the pro didn't get a say in it. If the celebs wanted to swap, it was a done deal; the pro had no more voice than if the stars were trading earrings or timeshares. What was really, really unfair was that on Saturday night's kickoff, if the celeb was voted off, his or her new partner—not the original one—went, too.

"Oh, please." I dismissed his whining with a wave of my hand. "I teach a couple of group classes every day and usually have at least six or seven private lessons with my competitive students. Vitaly and I practice maybe ten to twelve hours a week and spend another couple hours with coaches. We'd do more, except it costs us two-fifty for a forty-five-minute "hour" of coaching. Then, I weight train, do jazz and ballet classes, and try to work in a yoga class or two for flexibility." I ticked the items off on my fingers. "Running the studio—scheduling classes, payroll, enticing new students, cleaning, getting the floors refinished, and more—is separate from the dancing and training. On top of that, we compete in twenty or twenty-five competitions a year, which means we're on the road, dancing, almost every other weekend."

"I had no idea a ballroom dancer worked so hard," Zane said.

I smiled. "It's not all false eyelashes and sparkly dresses. I'm an athlete and a small businesswoman in one; it's hard work."

"You make me feel like a slacker," Zane said, pulling me closer than the dance required and smiling into my eyes. "Although when I hold you like this, I feel—"

A tingle danced through me, but I put the proper distance between us. "Concentrate," I demanded, in a mock-stern voice. We went through the dance another three times and Zane's frame was becoming more consistent and he had learned the choreography when a loud thud came from the small studio where Phoebe and Vitaly were practicing. Looking at each other, Zane and I hurried down the hall. We slid to a stop at the open studio door.

Vitaly and Phoebe lay side by side on their backs, breathing hard. Larry stepped in close with the camera to film their expressions while Nigel clapped. "Excellent!"

"What happened?" I asked Vitaly.

He got to his feet, brushed off his slacks, and gave Phoebe a hand up. "We is trying lift, but Phoebe is not trust Vitaly, so she fall, *splat*." He looked wounded by Phoebe's lack of trust.

"You dumped me on my nose," Phoebe said heatedly, "so I returned the favor."

When Zane and I looked puzzled, Nigel explained delightedly, "She swept his legs out from under him. Brilliant! Larry got it all. That's a wrap, Lare." He and the cameraman walked out, discussing potential setups at Take the Lead later that day.

At my horrified expression, Vitaly leaned in close to whisper, "We is stage it all. Nigel wanted us to have fight, so we choreograph, just like dance. Is not much real about this reality TV, I am thinkings." The thought didn't seem to trouble him. His eyes sparkled and his long face was lit up the way it was on the dance floor, with the kind of vibrancy that made him stand out, even though off the floor he usually faded into a crowd.

Phoebe scrambled to her feet and winked at me. "Vitaly's a good sport and he is *strong*." She turned to him. "How'd you like to come to Hollywood for a small part in my next film? It's called *Flashback* and we can rewrite one of the scenes so me and my costar, Chuck Norris, are taking ballroom dance lessons from you when the villains burst in, trying to kill us, and we have an amazing fight scene—sort of *Crouching Tiger* meets *The Matrix*."

"I will stick with the dancing," Vitaly said firmly. "I cannot leaving Lulu for a Hollywood career. She will miss me too muches."

"Lulu? I thought you were gay."

"Lulu's his boxer pup," I explained, laughing.

"See?" Vitaly brought up a photo of the dog on his smartphone and Phoebe and Zane made the appropriate noises.

"I've got a German shepherd—Max," Zane said. "He's staying with my sister while I'm out here. I wish I could've brought him."

"I'm a cat person," Phoebe announced.

Zane and Vitaly squinted at her with distrust, then Zane looked enquiringly at me. "No pets," I said, evoking the kind of "what's wrong with you?" looks that made me explain, "When I'm gone practically every other weekend for competitions, it wouldn't be fair to kennel a dog that often. I've got kind of a part-time dog, though." I told them about Hoover.

Zane said he was meeting his mom and agent for lunch, but would be back in the afternoon for more practice. Phoebe said she had a conference call, and Vitaly had errands to run. Left on my own, I decided to demonstrate forgiveness, be the bigger person, and call my sister. Kicking off my shoes, I padded barefoot into the office and picked up the phone. When I asked Danielle if she wanted to meet me for lunch, her first question was, predictably, "Is Zane coming? We had such a lovely time at lunch the other day."

I rolled my eyes, glad she couldn't see me. "Zane's meeting his mom," I said. "She's a piece of work."

"He introduced you to his mother already?" Danielle's screech made me hold the phone away from my ear.

Heaving a sigh, I explained about Kim Savage stopping by the studio.

"Oh." Silence emanated from her end of the line.

I could hear part of a conversation in the background—her coworkers at the union office, I assumed. "Do you want to lunch or not?" I asked testily.

"Have you seen Zane outside the ballroom?" she asked. "I mean, other than the night you were photographed at his hotel?"

My momentary hesitation was the same as an admission.

"Not." Danielle hung up.

Grrr. Why did God make sisters the most frustrating species on the planet? She didn't want to accept my olive branch? Fine. She could make the first move now. Her combative attitude made me want to marry Zane only so I could ask her to be my maid of honor. I'd make her wear a puce-colored gown because it would look dreadful with her red hair. Hah!

Recognizing that my own response was less than mature—although totally justified!—I was on the verge of descending to my living quarters for an exciting lunch of Greek yogurt, strawberries, and leftover bulgur wheat when Maurice and Hoover came through the door.

"Come walk this mutt with me, Anastasia," Maurice said, looking a bit less dapper than usual with a strand of white hair on his forehead and a smudge on his loafer. "I need moral support. He nearly dislocated my shoulder earlier when he saw a cat. Ripped the leash right out of my hand! Then, he almost caused an accident when he dashed across the street after the poor thing. He made an almighty ruckus when the cat went up a tree. He leaped up it, barking his damn-fool head off; you'd have thought he'd treed a bear. One man threatened to call the police about 'noise pollution' if I didn't make him stop. Not ten seconds later, when I hauled him away from the tree and scolded him, a woman said she was calling the SPCA to report animal abuse."

Laughing so hard tears came to my eyes, both at Maurice's story and Hoover's innocent expression, I fondled the dog's ears, asked Maurice to wait while I put on walking shoes and sunblock, and met them out front. Maurice willingly handed over Hoover's leash when I offered to take it, and strolled beside me toward the waterfront. Hoover, welcoming the opportunity to expand his territory, lifted his leg on almost every tree we passed. He must have a bladder the size of an RV's gas tank. The Great Dane wanted to check out the hot dog vendor when we arrived at the river's edge, but I hauled on his leash and pulled him toward the path that paralleled the Potomac.

The water smelled fresh, warmed by the sun. Boats with colorful sails floated on the calm surface and a flock of seagulls scuffled for half an ice-cream cone left on the pathway. Encouraged by Hoover's barks, they took to the air when we approached. A mix of tourists and workers on their lunch break ate sandwiches or drank smoothies from benches or on the grass. Clouds on the horizon hinted at a thunderstorm later in the day. With Hoover settled down a bit and prancing by my side, I told Maurice about Club Nitro and what Zane and I had learned from the bartender.

Maurice wrinkled his brow. "If Tessa wasn't purchasing drugs, as Zane insists, what could she possibly have wanted from a drug dealer?"

"No clue." Tugging on Hoover's leash, I dissuaded him from investigating a dead fish at the water's edge. "No one seems to have seen her since then, so I kind of think—"

"Something happened to her in the park, or wherever she went off to with the dealer."

I nodded. "Oh, and that's not the worst. Well, Tessa dying is the worst, but Nigel figured out that I'm kind of investigating and he wants to get it all on film. He caught me asking Phoebe about that night and had Larry record it."

A pained expression settled on Maurice's face. "That feels . . ."

"Scummy. Exploitative. Like I'm prying into her death out of ghoulish curiosity."

Maurice cocked his head in agreement.

Sucking in a deep breath, I said, "I'm done asking questions. I don't care if Nigel thinks it would be 'ratings gold' for me to get involved, or if he's offering a reward of fifty thou. I'm going to concentrate on winning that Crystal Slipper and leave the detecting to the police." Decision made, I felt like a weight had dropped off my shoulders.

A bevy of parochial schoolgirls in plaid skirts and white blouses went giggling past and Maurice gave them a courtly half bow that made them giggle harder. Two of them stopped to pat Hoover's head and he wagged his tail hard enough to flatten the grass. When they moved on, I looked at my watch and realized I was going to be late getting back to the studio. Wishing I could spend the afternoon lolling by the river, watching the boats drift past and the bees nosing into the clover, I reluctantly tugged on Hoover's leash and we headed toward Graysin Motion.

We arrived just as a Jaguar swooped in to steal a parking spot from the van that had been preparing to parallel park in it. Kim Savage got out, completely ignoring the dirty looks the van's driver gave her, and marched toward the outer staircase. Wearing a leopard-print skirt with a black blouse, she looked disgustingly chic and sexy for a woman old enough to be a grandma. She paused when she drew abreast of me, Maurice, and Hoover, and announced, "I thought my input at rehearsal would be helpful so I'll be sitting in this afternoon. I'm allergic to dogs." She curled her lip in a disdainful way and Hoover curled his lip, too, accompanying it with a low growl.

"Not to worry, Ms. Savage," Maurice began, "we were just leav—"

"Oh, too bad," I said, resisting Maurice's attempt to take the leash from me, "because Hoover's the studio mascot and he'll be spending the afternoon with us." I smiled brightly, won the wrestling match for the leash, and led the happy Hoover into my house. "Tell Zane I'll be up in a few minutes," I called over my shoulder.

Feeling a bit ashamed of my animosity toward Kim Savage—what had the woman ever done to me?—I blotted my flushed face with a cold washcloth and bolted a banana and a quick cup of yogurt (letting Hoover lick the empty container). I used the interior stairs to return to the studio. The Great Dane settled at his usual spot under the front windows, well away from Kim Savage, who perched on a chair just inside the ballroom door, next to Maurice. Zane greeted me with a big smile and we picked up where we'd left off, ignoring Nigel, Larry, and the sprinkling of crew members who did a good job of staying out of our way as we circled the floor.

"No, don't lead with your heel," I was telling Zane an hour later when a change in the air currents made me look toward the door. Detective Lissy stood there, his gaze fixed on us, and I faltered. Zane stepped on my toe.

"Sorry, Stacy," he said when I winced.

"Not your fault," I said. I broke away from him. "I think we need to take a break." I nodded toward the door.

Detective Lissy tromped toward us, polished wing tips squeaking on the wooden floors. Ignoring everyone else in the room, he addressed Zane. "New information has come to light in the matter of Tessa King's death," he said. "You'll need to come down to the station with me."

"Why, you pompous—" Kim began, jumping to her feet.

"What information?" I asked.

"I'm not coming unless you tell me why," Zane said.

With a barely perceptible shrug that said it was Zane's business if he wanted to be embarrassed in front of his colleagues, Lissy said, "We have a witness who overheard you arguing with the victim in her room the evening she was killed. You 'slammed out of the room in a rage,' is how he put it."

Someone gasped and I heard Nigel mutter, "Are you getting this, Larry?"

Kim Savage shouldered her way between her son and Detective Lissy. She threw her shoulders back, a well-endowed leopardess defending her cub. "My son is not going with you. It's absurd to think he could have hurt that woman. The press . . . I don't want to think about how the press will play it if word gets out." She actually paled.

"And you are?" Lissy raised an inquiring eyebrow and Kim Savage introduced herself.

"It's okay, Mother," Zane said, putting her gently aside. "I don't mind going to the station to answer a few questions. The detective's got to do his job, and I've got nothing to hide."

Lissy gave Zane a skeptical look as he ushered him toward the ballroom door. I wondered if Lissy had been born cynical, or if his time with the police force had made him that way. Maybe a little of both.

"I'm coming with you," Kim Savage said.

"No," Zane and Detective Lissy said in unison.

She halted, looking frustrated, and pulled out her phone. "Don't say a word until I get a lawyer there," Kim

Savage called after her son. Her stiletto heels tip-tapped as she hurried into the hall after them, already talking to someone named Mort. Maurice followed her and I heard him offer to drive her to the police station. He knew the way, having been arrested a mere month ago.

"My God, this is fabulous," Nigel crowed.

I shot him a disgusted look, ripped off my mike pack, handed it to the sound technician, and hurried to the window. Hoover rose at my approach and we both looked down in time to see Detective Lissy's car pull out and watch Maurice open the Jaguar's door for Kim Savage, slide into the driver's seat, and flip a U-ey to follow.

"Woof." Hoover laid his chin on the windowsill, apparently sad that he hadn't been invited to go.

Stroking his head, I said, "They'll be back soon, boy." I hoped I was right.

Chapter 12

Staring out the window, it occurred to me that it would be hard for Graysin Motion to win on *Blisters* if my partner was in jail, or so distracted by worry about being tried for murder that he couldn't concentrate on promenades or spin turns. I ditched my new-made resolution to stop investigating; I needed to clear my partner's name so we could continue to compete. Part of me wanted to head for the police station, but instinct told me Zane wouldn't like a crowd of people hovering in the waiting area, ready to grill him again when he emerged from his interview with Detective Lissy.

Nigel Whiteman took the option away by throwing a chummy arm around my shoulders and saying, "Well, luv, with your partner gone, it looks like we'll have to switch up our schedule a bit. How's about putting on some street togs and we'll do the 'out and about' interviews with Kristen this afternoon. You can take the dog," he added, his gaze falling on Hoover. "He's a photogenic bloke." Hoover sat up straighter at this praise.

The "out and about" portions of *Blisters* were supposedly unscripted segments where one or another of the dancers who lived in the area strolled around local attractions with Kristen Lee. They were designed to help viewers get to know both the professional dancers and the city and I'd enjoyed them when watching the show in previous seasons. A stylist went downstairs with me to help choose street clothes that would photograph well while Nigel summoned Kristen back from the spa where she was spending the afternoon.

The show's hostess arrived just as the stylist finished outfitting me. Her streaky blond hair done up in a topknot, flawlessly made-up and wearing a green linen jacket that contrasted pleasingly with the yellow sundress the stylist had put me in, Kristen Lee grumbled about the change of schedule as she climbed into the van that was to take us to our filming sites. A second van held crew members and equipment.

"I don't think it's asking too much to be allowed to get a facial," she said, patting her smooth, virtually unlined face. "It's part of my job to look good. I can't help it if Zane went and got himself arrested—that's no reason to upend everyone else's plans."

"He wasn't arrested," I said, shifting Hoover over to make room for Kristen. "It's just an interview. You don't need a facial," I added. "You've got beautiful skin."

She shot me a look, apparently trying to decide if I was being sincere, and settled onto the seat. "Thanks. You're sweet. So, this is how it will work."

With a no-nonsense manner that was more Barbara Walters than Joan Rivers, she took me through the drill and outlined the questions she would ask me. I was surprised by her professionalism, since I'd always thought she was kind of fluffy. Her on-screen persona for *Blisters* was relentlessly upbeat and a little ditzy, and I'd made the mistake of assuming that was what she was really like. I began to think there was more to Kristen Lee than I'd expected.

"Keep it short and simple," she directed, as the van pulled over at Union and King streets where the Old Town trolley began its route. "Think sound bite, not dissertation. Viewers have short attention spans." She stepped gracefully down from the van. When I followed her, Hoover tried to nudge past me and almost sent me sprawling. I noticed with a resigned sigh that at least two cameras recorded my klutzy moment.

We started our tour by taking the trolley the length of King Street. The conductor was inclined to argue about Hoover's presence, but Nigel drew him aside for a conversation (and a bribe, I suspected), and Hoover was allowed to board. The production company had coordinated with the Chamber of Commerce or some such and we had the trolley to ourselves. The camera guys took photos of Kristin and me from several angles, but mostly with us gazing eagerly out the open windows at the historic buildings, the breeze fanning our hair back. The director instructed me to point several times, as if indicating sites of interest, and said the edited version would show appropriate footage of City Hall and Market Square, Ramsay House where the Visitor's Center was located, and famous restaurants and shops. I wondered if the latter had had to pay a product placement fee like in the movies.

The van picked us up at the end of the line near the Metro station and hauled us to the George Washington Masonic Memorial a block to the west. The earlier clouds had thickened and the wind had freshened. It tugged at my skirt as Kristen and I walked along the path wending through manicured lawns sloping upward to an impressive-looking edifice. The memorial was a huge, tiered stone building, nothing like the slender Washington Monument on the Mall. I'd been inside the Masonic Memorial only once, for a wedding reception, and I'd been more interested in flirting with the best man than inspecting the archives and historic art. The building housed a grand hall, several smaller meeting rooms, and a theater; in fact, Saturday night's debut of *Blisters* was being filmed here. The building was currently closed to tourists as the production company built the set for the first broadcast.

"Did you know they filmed part of the second *National Treasure* movie here?" Kristen asked. I shook my head, and she launched into the questions she'd prepared. I never had any trouble talking about how I'd become a dancer and my love of ballroom, so the time went quickly as I described my early dancing efforts as a preteen with my first partner, and my fifth partner and I being selected as Rising Stars just before my seventeenth birthday.

Standing in front of the memorial, conscious of the diesel fumes emanating from a tour bus in the parking lot, I was hoping we were almost done when Nigel strode up.

"Okay, Stace, now you ask Kristen something about the murder, like where she was when Tessa was killed."

"What the hell?" Kristen's eyes hardened.

Nigel gave her two sentences about my investigation while I squirmed.

"I don't think—" I started.

Nigel rolled his hands in a "get on with it" motion. "Hurry. We're losing the light." He backed off a couple of steps.

"Uh, Kristen, so I hear you went to Club Nitro Tuesday night with Zane and Tessa and everyone," I said, feeling incredibly awkward. "Did you happen to see her leave?"

She batted her eyelashes in a parody of innocence, although I could see the anger in her eyes. Rain began to spit on us. "Why, no, Stacy. I had one club soda and left waaay early. I was tucked up in bed, getting my beauty rest, well before eleven o'clock. Alcohol and late nights are *fatal* for one's skin, so I don't indulge." She gave the camera a sugary smile.

I didn't know if it was because she wanted to protect her squeaky clean image, because she was pissed at Nigel and me for putting her on the spot, or because she had something darker to hide, but the way she held my gaze without blinking and the way the cords on her neck suddenly stood out told me she was lying. Before I could ask a follow-up question, the rain began in earnest and we scrambled back to the van. Whether by accident or design, Kristen ended up in the second van and Hoover and I rode back to the studio with a chatty lighting technician and the stylist.

The odor of wet dog pervaded the van and our damp clothes steamed up the windows. I could hardly wait to leap out when we reached Graysin Motion. Hoover beat me to the door, dashed inside when I unlocked it, and shook himself vigorously, spattering me, the walls, and the hardwood floors with water. Just perfect. A knock sounded and I hurried to open the door, hoping it was Maurice coming to retrieve Hoover.

Phoebe Jackson stood on the doorstep, a red raincoat with a hood keeping her dry.

I gaped at her.

"It's damn wet out here. Can I come in?" Phoebe's smile brightened the gray afternoon.

Stepping back, I let her in. Hoover sniffed her thoroughly, decided she wasn't a threat, and padded into the kitchen. I could hear him nosing around my cupboards.

"You're probably wondering what I'm doing here," Phoebe said as we stood awkwardly in the hall. Raindrops slid from her slicker to plop on the floor. "Vitaly and I just finished our practice—that man is a pistol—and I got to thinking about what Nigel said earlier about you looking into Tessa's death. Is that true?" Her brown eyes searched my face.

"Sort of."

Not asking me to clarify, she nodded decisively. "I want to help. Tessa was my friend."

I had the feeling that things were snowballing out of control. "I'm not— I don't—"

Phoebe interrupted my blathering. "Zane told me you and he went back to Club Nitro last night."

"He did?" Zane had a big mouth. It took me only a split second to recognize the hypocrisy in that when it was my big mouth that had let Nigel know I was looking into Tessa's death. Maybe Phoebe could help . . . "What kind of car was Tessa driving?"

"A green Mercedes, a two-seater, just like Nigel's. Rented, of course. Look, how about I make us some coffee while you get dry?"

I realized I was wet and shivering. "Okay. I'll just be a minute. Coffee stuff's in the cabinet to the left of the range."

Ducking into my bedroom, I shucked off my sodden sundress and tossed it over the shower rail. I rubbed my chilled skin briskly with a towel, wrung out my hair and combed it, and scrambled into a pair of striped capris and a light pink sweater. Feeling a thousand percent better, I followed the aroma of coffee back to the kitchen to find Phoebe feeding Hoover bites of cheese from a hunk of cheddar. His tail thumped.

"I hope you don't mind," she said, spotting me. "He looked so hungry and I couldn't find any dog food."

"He's not mine," I said, and explained.

We sat at the table with our coffees and Phoebe glanced around the kitchen. "It doesn't quite feel like you," she said, nodding toward the turquoise-tiled counter with its crumbling grout, the mismatched appliances, and the stained linoleum.

A little impressed by her sensitivity, I explained about inheriting the town house from Great-aunt Laurinda. "I sold a lot of her old furniture recently and now I'm trying to figure out if I want to tackle the kitchen first or redecorate the front room."

"When I got out of prison the second time," Phoebe said, "I ditched everything from my former life—and I mean *everything*. I gave the furniture and household crap to the Salvation Army, kicked my worthless boyfriend to the curb, and donated my clothes to a women's shelter. I even cut my hair." She ran a hand over her shapely skull. "Out with the old, in with the new," she said with a wide grin. "I didn't know what the new was, which sounds kind of like what you're going through. I haven't looked back. Tessa encouraged me. I got clean in prison and the warden gave my name to Tessa when she came around looking for some 'pull yourself up by your bootstrap' stories for a documentary she was doing. We met, and clicked, and next thing I know I'm one of three women featured in Tessa's documentary *Two Strikes and*

Starting Over. A producer saw it, likcd what he saw of me doing a martial arts sequence, and next thing I know I've got a part in a movie. That was nine years ago." She shifted in her chair and the overhead light cast a golden glow on her cocoa skin.

"What happened to the other women in the documentary?"

Phoebe sobered. "One of them's back in prison for good and the other's dead. Killed by her boyfriend."

The stark words kept me silent for a moment. "So, did you and Tessa keep in touch all that time?"

"Off and on. When my agent mentioned *Ballroom with the B-Listers*, I jumped at the chance to work with her again. And now she's dead." Sorrow sounded in her voice. She got up to place her empty mug in the sink, and I wondered if she was hiding tears from me; Phoebe struck me as a private person, despite her openness about her former life.

"You and she rode together to Club Nitro," I said, "which is the last place any of you saw her."

Phoebe turned and if she'd been crying, the tears were gone now. "Uh-huh. We parked on the street about a block and a half from the club—Tessa had a thing about not giving her keys to valets—and walked in together. I saw her a few times after that—we weren't in the same booth, but I saw her dancing and talking to people—but when it came time to leave, I couldn't find her. I even walked back to where we'd left the Merc, but it was gone."

"What time was that?"

"Two thirty? I was more pissed than worried. I snagged a taxi, planning to give her some grief the next morning for ditching me."

"Did you tell Detective Lissy all this?"

She nodded.

Realizing I'd barely touched my coffee, I took a long swallow, thinking. "What about drugs?"

Her eyes hardened. "What about them? I've been clean for twelve years. I don't even take aspirin."

I shook my head rapidly. "No, no, not you. Tessa. Did she ever do drugs that you know of?" I explained about Zane's and my conversation with the bartender in the park.

Phoebe looked both puzzled and thoughtful. "She could've done a recreational line or two, like most folks in Hollywood," she said. "I don't think she was into the hard stuff. She didn't act coked up."

I trusted Phoebe would know. I thought through the timeline. Tessa arrived at the club with Phoebe, danced and drank until about one when she wandered over to the park—on the spur of the moment, or for something prearranged?—and met a drug dealer. Sometime between then and two thirty, she returned to her car and drove off. Or, maybe someone killed her and stole the car.

"You know," Phoebe said, interrupting my thoughts, "she was worried about something."

I perked up. This was new information. "Really? What?"

"I'm not sure. I got the feeling she was involved with a new man and that maybe things weren't going the way she'd hoped. She was also kinda frustrated with *Blisters* and Nigel. It seemed like she was ready to move on. She said she was tired of manufactured drama, feathered costumes, and third-rate talent. I told her I hoped she wasn't referring to me." The ghost of a smile flitted across Phoebe's face. "She said that if the shoe fits . . ."

We chuckled and then jumped as Hoover scrambled to his feet and gave a deep "Woof" a split second before someone knocked on the kitchen door. From the way Hoover's tail was wagging, I knew he liked whoever was there. I peered out, and seeing Maurice, opened the door.

"I've come to take the hound off your hands—" he started, but then caught sight of Phoebe leaning against the stove. "Excuse me, I didn't mean to interrupt." He wore an off-white shirt and striped tie with his usual blazer and was newly shaved. He was obviously headed out, if his air of anticipation was anything to go by. I was dying to ask him what had happened at the police station.

"No problem," Phoebe said. "I'm leaving. I need to rest up before the show tomorrow night. I'm petrified at the thought of forgetting the steps in front of a national audience. I dreamed about it last night. This ballroom dancing stuff wears me out. I thought martial arts was tough, but this—" She shook her head in a bemused way, collected her red jacket from the back of her chair, and started down the hall. I walked her to the door, and then returned to where Maurice was leashing Hoover in the kitchen.

"What happened at the police station?" I asked.

Maurice looked up from clipping the leash to Hoover's collar. "Nothing much. Zane was with Detective Lissy for perhaps forty-five minutes. When he came out, reporters were waiting, so he 'no commented' his way out of the station. He didn't even stop to talk to his mother, who was understandably anxious." Maurice frowned disapprovingly.

"What—"

"I'm sorry, Anastasia, but I've got to go. I'm meeting Kim in twenty minutes."

I blinked at him. "You have a date? With Kim Savage?"

He smiled. "I do, indeed. So, if you'll excuse me . . ." He led Hoover out the door and I closed it slowly after them.

Well! I determined to be in the studio as early as possible in the morning, to get the full scoop from Zane himself.

Chapter 13

I hadn't realized that prepping for the live shows would take all day. With our first show set to air Saturday night, the day was a tornado of activity. Final costume fittings were followed by spray tans airbrushed on by Ariel and her cohorts. The tans were just dark enough to add some color to our skin under the television lights. For Latin dances later in the season, we'd get darker tans. Then vans transported us to the George Washington Masonic Memorial where the first show's filming was taking place. We did run-throughs on the dance floor, working with the live band for the first time. Cables snaked across the floor and stage, a table was set up for the judges, and dozens of people scurried to and fro. Nigel was everywhere; I heard him even when I couldn't see him. Counting steps for Zane as we waltzed, I looked out into the empty room with its plush, stadium-style seats, envisioning it filled with more than three hundred spectators that night. The thought didn't trouble me; an audience ringed the dance floor at every ballroom competition.

I squeezed Zane's hand as we finished our run-through.

"You're totally ready for this, Zane. Sure you don't want to give up that acting thing and concentrate on ballroom dancing? You'd be winning competitions in no time." I was laying it on a bit thick, but getting amateurs into the right frame of mind before a big competition is one thing that sets successful pros apart.

"I don't think so, Stacy." His smile seemed forced and I wondered if he was suffering from stage fright or if he was fretting over the police interview. I didn't get a chance to ask him about it as a production assistant appeared to whisk him off to speak to a reporter with the other celebs. I had to hang around for a rehearsal with the other pros for an exhibition number we were doing to close the show.

Nigel had come up with the idea of doing a dance memorial for Tessa and tasked Solange Dubonnet with choreographing the number. The redhead taught it to us quickly, looking decidedly un-memorialish in orange leggings and long tank top that should have clashed with her hair but didn't. Marco Ingelido was there, as were the married couple, Tonya and Nikolai Grishenko, and me and Vitaly. The choreography was flashy but simple, kind of like Solange, I thought cattily, and we picked it up easily. It was a relief to be dancing with Vitaly, to give myself over to his strong lead and gliding step, after the weeks spent rehearsing with Zane.

"Is good, no?" Vitaly said, as he helped me up from the death drop that ended the number.

"Is very good," I agreed, returning his smile.

Ariel came to fetch me not long after that. Walking to the room set aside for makeup, we passed on one side of the velvet curtain that veiled the stage and dance floor from the backstage area. Angry voices drifted from behind the curtain and Ariel and I exchanged embarrassed glances.

"I'm not going to play it that way." Kristen's sugary accents were decidedly more strident than usual. "My contract—"

"Don't think that just because Tessa's gone, your job is safe." Nigel's British accent clipped the words short. "We're still in talks with Hannah's people. Play the game, luv, play the game."

The sound of stiletto heels receded and I wondered what game Nigel wanted Kristen to play. "What was that about?" I whispered to Ariel as we moved into the hall.

She glanced over her shoulder before saying, "Tessa told me she was considering replacing Kristen with Hannah Malik, the comedienne who did so well on the show two seasons ago. She thought a more comic vibe during the post-dance interviews might go over well with the audience, and figured Hannah could keep the audience warmed up during commercial breaks, too. I didn't know she'd actually been in touch with Hannah's agent, though. Why don't you have something to eat while I get set up?"

We stood in a long, narrow lodge room that had the makeup counter, chairs and mirror set up at one end, and a table laden with food at the other. Carpet patterned in wine and beige would hide most any spills, and matching draperies along the far wall made it look as if the room had windows, when I knew it didn't. Taking Ariel's advice, I noshed on veggies and the tiny sandwiches arrayed on a table while Ariel laid out her brushes and cosmetics. I finished with a protein drink, knowing I needed to keep my energy level up, but not wanting a full stomach to spoil the line of my dress. I wished I'd remembered to give Zane a few tips on eating for the best performance. When students didn't eat properly before a competition, they frequently fizzled out, not realizing how much energy the adrenaline drained out of them.

"I'll be right back," Ariel murmured, disappearing through the door and calling, "Kiko, what did you do with my Bobbi Brown eyeliners?"

I tossed my empty bottle into the recycling bin, and when I turned around, Mickey Hazzard was standing at the table. I figured the disgraced evangelist had come to fuel up before he and Solange took the floor as the first couple to dance tonight. He was already in costume, a powder blue tux with a ruffled shirt that made him look like he'd gotten lost on his way to a 1980s prom.

"Hi," I greeted him. We'd been introduced at the press conference, but hadn't exchanged more than three sentences previously, so I was surprised when he gave me a narrow-eyed stare.

"Is it true?" His deep, smooth voice would have been mesmerizing from the pulpit, I suspected.

"Huh?"

"That you're investigating Tessa King's death?"

"I—"

He took two long steps toward me and grabbed my upper arm. "Because you've got no business poking around in my private life."

"Let go of me!" I wrenched my arm away and glared at him.

"You take note. Look what sticking her nose where it didn't belong got Tessa King." He leaned in close enough that I could see a trace of red in his eyes and smell licorice on his breath.

"Are you threatening me?" I drew myself up, almost as tall as he was in my heels.

"Tessa King got what she deserved. 'As ye sow, so shall ye reap.'" Turning on his heel, he snatched a handful of celery sticks from the food table, bumping into Ariel on his way out the door.

I stared after him, wondering what Tessa had ever done to him. His threat and his agitation, not to mention his hatred of Tessa, made me wonder who else involved with this show might have had a grudge of some kind against the dead producer.

"Why's Mickey got his panties in a wad?" Ariel asked as I seated myself in her chair. She brushed foundation over my face and neck.

I told her what the man had said and a serious look settled over her face. "I've been wondering why he agreed to do *Blisters*," she said. A delicate floral scent wafted from her cleavage as she leaned in to set the foundation with powder. "I figured he didn't realize Tessa was the coproducer until he'd already signed up."

"Do he and Tessa have history?"

Ariel gave me a pitying look, the kind of superior look that even a young Hollywood insider can give a nearing-thirty ignorant outsider. "She's the one that outed him."

My crinkled brow must have betrayed my puzzlement, because she added, "*Pastors of Hypocrisy?* Don't you watch movies?"

"I dance."

She chuckled and swiped a glittery shadow across my eyelid. "That's the documentary Tessa did two years ago about hypocrisy in the evangelical Christian community. It's got footage of supposedly teetotaling preachers slugging down the booze at a conference, proof that one minister built his seventy-five-hundred-square foot home with funds out of the offering plate, and—"

"—and video of Pastor Mickey with underage girls," I said. "I heard about it. I didn't know Tessa was involved."

Nodding, Ariel said, "It was nominated for an Oscar, but lost to a Michael Moore film that wasn't nearly as good. Anyway, I guess he blames Tessa for breaking up his marriage and for his getting fired by his congregation. Times have been tough in Mickey-world since *Pastors of Hypocrisy* came out. I think he only signed on with *Blisters* for the money—he probably needs it to pay his divorce lawyers."

Wow, she was cynical for someone barely a quarter century old. Before I could ask her any more about Mickey Hazzard's relationship with Tessa, several dancers and crew members flooded in and surrounded the food table, including Zane. Catching my eye in the mirror, he flashed me a smile and came over to us. A certain rigidity in his stride revealed his tenseness, although he was hiding it well.

"You look stunning." His gaze swept over my blond hair in its smooth chignon and down the drift of pale pink satin and chiffon that was my dress. I had tested every seam several times to make sure Nigel hadn't booby-trapped it in some way. "Ariel is gilding the lily." He placed a warm hand on my bare shoulder and I felt the tingles all the way to my toes.

"You look pretty dashing yourself," I said, standing so his hand fell away. In a stark black and white tux that would have passed muster with judges at an actual waltz competition, he had his hair brushed back and wore a pink bow tie that matched my dress.

An assistant stage manager poked her head in and called, "Places." I took a deep breath, held it for a moment, and then place my hand on Zane's arm. "Shall we?" he asked.

"Absolutely."

The show both whizzed past and lasted longer than the most recent ice age. Time went quickly during the dances, which we watched on a monitor from a holding room. I couldn't help mentally critiquing the other couples as they danced, and agreed with the judges' scores more often than not. In addition to Carmelo, there were two female judges, one of whom had competed as a professional dancer. The other came from Broadway and had worked as a choreographer. I felt a pang, remembering that Corinne Blakely was supposed to have been a judge this season, but her murder had forced the substitution of the choreographer. Time crawled during the commercial breaks and the post-dance interviews that Kristen Lee conducted with the sweaty but relieved couples. Mickey Hazzard, I was pleased to see, danced with all the elegance of a two-by-four, although I was forced to admit Solange's choreography did a good job of hiding his gracelessness.

Then it was our turn, second to last, and I was whispering encouragement and "relax" to Zane as we took our positions in the middle of the floor. Adrenaline coursed through me, as it always did before a big competition, and I took three deep, slow breaths. This is what I lived for. I never felt more alive, more *me* than on the dance floor, competing. The whisper of chiffon against my ankles, the music's caress, the energy flowing from the audience—this was home. I was ready to win.

The lights blazed, the band struck up "My Heart Will Go On," and I led Zane into the first gliding movements, expertly making it look as if he were leading me. I counted "*One*, two, three," through my smile, and whispered "lines" when we struck our first pose. Heat from the lights warmed my bare arms and I was aware of the faint chemical scent from our spray tans. Midway through the dance, during a haunting French horn solo, the magic took hold and, for a few bars, we moved effortlessly together, becoming the doomed lovers Jack and Rose, waltzing on the deck of the *Titanic*. Then Zane put in an extra step and I came back to reality and guided him through the last measures. It wasn't until Zane braced me for my back-arching final pose and swept me into an excited hug when the last note died away, that I had the chance to survey the audience.

Tav, blazingly handsome in a dark suit and white shirt, sat in the second row. He smiled proudly and threw me an air kiss. Danielle sat beside him and I had to bite my lip to keep tears from welling up. I hadn't realized how afraid I was she wouldn't come. Her red curls spilling around her shoulders, my sister was applauding hard. As I watched, she put two fingers in her mouth and whistled. I winced, but grinned. I'd never been able to do that. I gave them both a little wave, and blinked when I spotted Detective Lissy watching impassively from a seat on the aisle. What was he doing here? I wondered, trailing Zane to where Kristen stood waiting to talk to us. She directed most of the questions to Zane and then the judges displayed their scores, complimenting Zane on his lines—I pinched him surreptitiously—and his frame, but saying his footwork needed work, as did his musicality. True.

At the show's end, the memorial dance silenced the

crowd. Kristen was supposed to ask for a moment of silence for Tessa, but she didn't need to. We dancers stood with our heads bowed on stage, hands clasped, and I made a mental note to congratulate Solange on the effectiveness of her choreography. After a suitable pause, Nigel surprised everyone—including Kristen Lee, it seemed—by walking out onto the set and taking the microphone from the hostess. I leaned forward, anxious to hear what he had to say. When the audience's rustling had died away, he spoke.

"We all feel the loss of Tessa King, me most of all," he said. "Her death was a tragedy and I want to announce tonight that *Ballroom with the B-Listers* and my production company are offering a fifty-thousand-dollar reward to anyone with information about her death. The individual or individuals responsible must be brought to justice."

Gasps sounded from the audience and I wondered if Detective Lissy knew in advance about Nigel's reward idea. Judging by his reaction—stiff shoulders and a poker face—it didn't seem so. I couldn't help but think again about how the studio could use that kind of money. We could pay off the back taxes and maybe even have some left over to put toward a parking lot. The band struck up the closing music and we beamed at the cameras for eight seconds until one of the directors yelled that we were clear. The judges' scores put Nanette the pet psychic and Marco Ingelido in first place, with Vitaly and Phoebe right behind them. Zane and I were in third and Calista Marques was last, several points below Mickey and Solange. Calista's partner, Nikolai, had lost his grip during a death drop and she'd landed on the floor. Although she'd scrambled up and they'd finished the number strongly, they still trailed in the judges' ratings. Nigel and the director looked pleased with how the show had gone, calling us together for a brief meeting.

With all the dancers circled around, Nigel said, "Good show, everybody. We're off to a great start. We'll keep things moving next week with nightclub dances: hustle and East Coast swing."

There was an even mix of groans and excitement when he named the next dances. I was more of a ballroom purist and would have preferred a foxtrot or a cha-cha, but I could get into the nightclub dances as well. Vitaly looked disgusted, while Solange clapped her hands.

"Even better," Nigel continued, "is that we've gotten permission to broadcast the competition from Club Nitro on Saturday." He looked around as if expecting applause.

I was appalled. Club Nitro? The last place Tessa King was seen alive? It seemed like an insensitive, even callous, choice.

Apparently, Zane agreed. "Nigel, doesn't that seem a little sensationalistic, like the show's exploiting Tessa's murder?"

"Exactly!" Nigel said, pointing a finger at Zane, as if he thought Zane had complimented him. "Ratings gold, baby." Nigel clapped his hands to get our attention again. "Don't forget that Monday is Trade Day." He grinned evilly. "Some of you might want to think about your options." His eyes lingered on Calista, who was rubbing her flank, which probably hurt after her fall. Thanking the crew and the dancers again for a great show, Nigel and the director marched off to schmooze with some bigwigs who had attended.

Zane and I exchanged glances. "So, are you still looking to trade up on Monday?" I asked.

Hugging my waist, Zane grinned down at me. "There is no *up* in this competition. You're the top."

"Aww." I kissed his cheek.

"Phoebe better watch out, though," Zane said, nodding discreetly to where Calista Marques was clutching at her partner Nikolai's arm, tears of disappointment or anger in her eyes. "Our young Disney phenom didn't like being dropped on her tutu."

We were dissecting our performance on our way to the dressing rooms when Tav and Danielle caught up with us. My sister looked fabulous in a green satin jacket and slim black pants, and I couldn't blame Zane for returning her hug enthusiastically when she congratulated him.

"Let's all go out and celebrate," she said, giving me a hug, as well. The tightness in my throat eased, even though her gaze lingered on Zane. I hugged her back hard enough to make her squeak.

"Celebrate third place?" Zane asked.

"Celebrate not falling on your keister on live television," Danielle said, smiling.

"Well, when you put it like that . . . let me get this makeup off." Zane disappeared into his dressing room.

"I cannot make it tonight, Danielle," Tav said. "I must catch an early flight tomorrow."

My gaze flew to his face. "Oh? I didn't know you had a trip planned."

"My father will be in New York City for the day. I am going to see him." Tav looked like he had mixed emotions about the prospect.

His father was an obscenely wealthy Argentinean

rancher. I'd never met him, even though he was also Rafe's father and we'd been planning to marry. Rafe and I had ended our engagement only a couple of weeks before we were due to fly to South America for me to meet his family. At the time, I'd been relieved that I didn't have relationships with them that I'd have to sever, as well.

"I guess we'll be a threesome, then," Danielle said with forced cheeriness. "How cozy."

The thought of a threesome didn't make me any happier than it made my sister. "I'm going to beg off, too," I heard myself say. "It's been a long week. You two go and have fun." I felt a twinge of jealousy at the thought of Danielle and Zane partying together, but not as much as I'd have thought. Truth was, a light dinner and a long soak in the tub before bed sounded more appealing than a high-octane evening out.

Danielle tried to hide her pleasure, failing miserably, and Tav gave me a look I couldn't read. "I will wait while you change and give you a ride home," he said to me.

Smiling my thanks, I ducked into the dressing room all the women shared. It took me the better part of half an hour to get out of my costume and return it to the wardrobe mistress, de-makeup my face, pry rhinestone-encrusted bobby pins out of my hair, and slide into the comfy warm-up pants and airy top I'd worn to the Masonic Memorial what seemed like days ago but was only this morning. I found Tav waiting for me in the Grand Hall, studying the portraits and historical artifacts. A few people associated with *Blisters* milled about, but I didn't see Danielle or Zane.

"They left a few minutes ago," Tav said, correctly interpreting my head swivels. "Savage said to let you know

they would start at the bar across the street from his hotel if you changed your mind about joining them." His
eyebrow moved up a questioning fraction.

"Nope. Let's go."

We accomplished the short ride back to my town
house in near silence. Tav parked at the curb. "Do you
need a ride to the airport?"

"I will take the Metro," he said, "but thanks." His fingers tapped on the steering wheel and he half turned to
face me. "Would you like to come with me? I would enjoy introducing you to my father."

Wham! His offer took me by surprise. "To New York?
Tomorrow?"

Tav nodded, his dark eyes holding mine.

"Why?"

"We are in business together. Arturo would enjoy
meeting you."

Hm. I wasn't sure about that. Rafe's description of his
father had made the man sound intimidating. "The
show . . . my students . . ."

"We can catch the first flight back Monday morning
and you will be in time for all your commitments."

I was tempted. But if we were overnighting in New
York, what would the sleeping arrangements be? I
peered into Tav's face, trying to read his expression.
What would his father think at having me sprung on
him? Tav and I weren't even dating—we were business
partners—but his father would certainly think we were
more than that. He knew that Rafe and I had been *way*
more than that, and not that long ago. I couldn't do it.

"I'd love to meet your father sometime," I said,
"but—"

"I understand." Not giving me the chance to explain

further, Tav got out of the car, and came around to open my door. He walked me up the front steps and waited while I unlocked the door. I gave him an uncertain look, hoping I hadn't offended him or hurt his feelings.

"I *do* understand," he said. He bent and kissed me gently on both cheeks. "I will see you when I get back. Do not do anything foolish—like tackle a potential murderer—in my absence."

Before I could reply, he was halfway down the walk, the ghost of a laugh drifting back to me.

Chapter 14

Soaking in the long, claw-footed bathtub half an hour later, I relaxed into the scent of lavender from the expensive bath salts Mom had gotten me two Christmases back. I didn't take baths very often; I guess I didn't slow down long enough to savor them. Warm water covered me almost to my shoulders and it felt heavenly. I needed to build more relaxation into my schedule, I decided, letting my head fall back against the rim. The water's heat kneaded knots out of my tense muscles and worked magic on my sore feet. I tried to turn the tap on with my toes, but the old fixtures were stiff and I couldn't budge them. I was wondering if more hot water was worth the effort of sitting up when a crash, like splintering glass, jerked me upright.

Water sloshed onto the tiled floor and I grabbed automatically for the thick white towel I'd laid out. This wasn't the grinding crash of cars colliding that I heard from the street occasionally; this was much closer, in the house. Goose bumps appeared on my arms. Wrapping the towel snugly around myself, I hurried out of the bathroom, my wet soles leaving footprints on the wood floors. I really wished I had the gun Uncle Nico had given me, but it resided in a police evidence locker since it had been used to shoot Rafe. Maybe I should buy another one. I inched into the foyer and the slight play of air over my damp skin made me shiver, despite the day's lingering warmth. Flipping on the hall light, I saw nothing amiss. The front door was closed and locked, the narrow windows on either side intact. I peered through the closest one. Nothing but a woman walking a small dog half a block down and a few cars driving by at normal speeds.

I crossed into the parlor, and light from the hall winked off shards of glass sprayed across the floor. Conscious of my bare feet, I reached around the doorjamb and hit the light switch, illuminating the room. In addition to the glass, a rust-colored brick teetered half on and half off my new ottoman. As I watched, its weight pulled it over and it fell with a heavy thud to the floor, making me jump. Someone had thrown a brick through my window! A white splotch showed on its underside; it looked like a piece of paper rubber banded to the brick. Hurrying back to my bedroom, I put on my slippers and returned to the parlor, picking my way through the minefield of glass.

Gingerly, I hefted the rough brick in my hand and tugged at the piece of paper. The rubber band snapped, popping my wrist, and I almost dropped the brick. The paper fluttered to the floor. "Ow," I muttered, stooping to retrieve it. Unfolded, it was a two-inch-by-two-inch square with hand-printed capital letters: LET SLEEPING DOGS LIE. I crinkled my brow. What the hell did that mean? I wondered if it could be a bad joke of some kind, like kids calling random phone numbers and whispering "I know what you did." I leaned forward to look through the broken window. Nothing moved on my small patch of real estate. No teenagers giggled in the tree's shadow. Growing up, our trees and shrubs had been toilet-papered once by teens who mistook our house for the house of one of their friends. . . . Was this a similar event?

I didn't like the only other explanation that occurred to me: Someone was warning me away from investigating Tessa King's death. Suddenly becoming conscious that I was wearing nothing but a towel and must be spectacularly backlit by the parlor's lights, I crunched my way out of the room to my bedroom, where I set the brick on my dresser and slipped into a robe. Not one of my slinky peignoirs, which seemed too insubstantial right now, but Great-aunt Laurinda's tatty old flannel robe that whispered along the ground when I walked. She'd been a very tall woman for her generation. Marching to the kitchen, I found the dustpan and broom and returned to the parlor to deal with the glass.

Ten minutes later I had most of it swept up, although I wouldn't be walking barefoot in this room anytime soon. The bigger problem was the hole in the windowpane. Thank goodness it wasn't the dead of winter so I didn't have an icy wind blowing in. I couldn't call a glass installer at near midnight on a Saturday night, so I unearthed an empty cardboard box, flattened it, and duct taped it to the window. There. Not perfect, but it would do for the night. I checked all the lights again and retreated to the bedroom, closing and locking the door, which I never did. When I crawled into bed and pulled the covers up, the brick glared at me from the dresser. With a sigh, I got out of bed and tossed a towel over the brick. The note fluttered to the floor and I left it there.

Only after I was in bed again with the lights turned off did it occur to me that I might have called the police. Nah, I dismissed the thought. The police had more important things to do on a Saturday night than worry about who had heaved a brick through my window. It's not like they would fingerprint the place or canvass the neighborhood. They'd give me a report for my insurance company, and that would be that. I'd report it in the morning, and maybe mention the note to Detective Lissy next time I saw him, even though I suspected he'd scoff at me. Either that, or chew me out for asking questions about Tessa's murder. With that happy thought, I drifted into an uneasy sleep.

Sunday afternoon found me sitting in a Laundromat with Zane Savage, watching his tighty-whities go around in a sea of soapy foam. He'd called shortly after the glass installer presented me with a bill for twice his normal charges since he'd come out on a Sunday. I was wondering if I should give up eating for the rest of the month, or air-conditioning, in order to pay the bill, when the phone rang and Zane asked me to meet him.

"I thought Hollywood stars sent their laundry out," I greeted him when I arrived at the Laundromat. It was a cheery space with lots of windows, but it smelled wet and linty.

"Do you know how much that costs?" Zane asked, kissing my cheek. "I might've been a star once, but no longer." He didn't sound bitter. "The furnished apartments we're in don't have washers in the units, and a pipe burst in the laundry room, so I'm reduced to this." He gestured to the Laundromat.

"So what's up?" I was pleased he'd called.

"Maybe I just wanted company while I did my laundry." He smiled, crinkling the skin around his eyes.

"Danielle not available?"

His smile broadened. "Jealous much?"

"Not." I moved magazines off a chair so I could sit, transferring them to the white melamine table that fronted the row of chairs.

"Your sister's fun. We had a good time last night, but we didn't have breakfast together." He sat kitty-corner to me, his knee bumping mine.

"None of my business." Resisting the urge to ask what he and Danielle had done together, I blurted, "Someone threw a brick through my window last night. With a note." I handed it to him.

A line appeared between his brows as he read. He looked at me. "You think this is about Tessa?"

I shrugged. "I can't imagine what else it would be."

"What did the police say?"

"I didn't see any point to calling them." I explained my reasoning.

"This is good," Zane said, waving the paper square.

"Really? My wallet doesn't think so."

"No, think about it. This means we're getting somewhere."

"'We,' Kemosabe? Did I miss the bit where someone tossed a brick through your window?"

"You're cute when you do indignant."

"I'm not 'doing' indignant." I tried to get annoyed with him, but couldn't pull it off, not with him giving me that mischievous smile I remembered so clearly from

Hollywood High. "Fine. Tell me what Detective Lissy wanted."

That sobered Zane up. "He thinks I did it, that I killed Tessa."

I gave him a skeptical look.

"No, really. The man next door to Tessa told the police he heard us arguing Tuesday afternoon and that I slammed out of her room. Which is true."

"What did you argue about?"

His gaze drifted past me, fastening on a pregnant woman coming through the door with an overflowing laundry basket and a toddler by the hand. Zane jumped up to take the basket from her and put it on a table. When he came back, he looked me square in the eyes. "You."

"Me?" My voice squeaked.

"She wanted me to pretend to be hot for you, seduce you, have a few steamy moments for the camera. She thought a romance would be good for the ratings."

A slow burn crept through me. "What did—?"

"I told her to forget it, that I wasn't going to play that kind of game with you . . . or anyone." He must have read doubt in my expression because he leaned closer. "See any cameras?" Before I could answer, he kissed me, pulling my head forward with a hand at the back of my neck. The scruff of goatee and whiskers along his jaw were soft against my skin. After a good thirty seconds— and I mean *good*—he pulled away. "If I'd been going along with Tessa's plan, there'd have been a camera around to catch that, and a camera the other night on your doorstep."

I sucked in a deep breath. "So, Lissy accused you of killing Tessa because you argued with her?"

"Tessa might have said something about kicking me off the show if I didn't cooperate," Zane admitted. "Detective Lissy called that 'motive.' Little does he know that I don't give a snap"—he snapped his fingers—"for this show. It means a lot more to my mom than it does to me. If it doesn't reignite my acting career, I can go back to teaching drama at UCLA and coaching kids going on auditions. That's what I've been doing the past three years."

I'd quit listening after the bit about his mom. Was Kim Savage capable of killing someone—a producer, for instance—who jeopardized Zane's return to TV stardom? She was fit, tough, determined.... I could hardly ask Zane where his mom had been Tuesday night. The pregnant woman pulled a box of dryer sheets out of her hamper and the mountain fresh scent drifted to me.

Zane rose to remove one load from the dryer, and schlep the other from the washer into the dryer, giving me a chance to think. He'd said he didn't care about doing well on *Blisters*, but his intensity during practices and his edginess last night told me otherwise. A wisp of a girl dropped a handful of change, and quarters clinked against a washer and rolled across the floor. I stopped one with my foot and handed it to her. I still hadn't come up with a subtle way of finding out about Kim's whereabouts Tuesday when he plopped down beside me, depositing a load of warm clothes on the table, and said, "Fold. It's the car that's giving them fits."

I looked a question at him, and plucked a golf shirt from the pile. It had that slightly burnt smell clothes get in a commercial dryer sometimes. I smoothed the collar.

"The police. Tessa's car being missing is what convinced them that this is a murder and not an accident."

"I can see that." If Tessa had walked away from Club Nitro for some reason, her car should still be parked on the curb where she and Phoebe had left it. If she'd gone back to the apartment, it should be in the parking lot. If she'd broken down along the road and tried to walk for help, the police should've found the car on the roadside. It'd be too much of a coincidence—wouldn't it?—for her car to get stolen on the night she died. "Finding her car could be key to finding out what happened to her." I sorted socks, leaving the underwear for Zane to fold.

Zane nodded. "The police are looking for it, believe me."

"Maybe it went into the river. She swerved to avoid a deer or another car, and her car plunged into the river. The impact broke her legs, but she managed to get out of the car." Only to drown because she couldn't get to shore. The thought made me queasy.

"I know where she went into the river."

His words startled me. My look invited him to explain.

"There was a map on the bulletin board in the conference room at the police station. It had a photo of Tessa tacked up, some tide charts and papers I couldn't read, and a map of the area. There was a mark along the Potomac where they found her body, and another mark, on the Anacostia, which had to be where she went in. We probably drove past it Thursday night."

I shivered at the thought. "What else did the police ask you?"

Zane ran his fingers through his hair. "Did Tessa have any enemies? How long ago and why did we break up? Had she been acting strangely, differently? Was she involved with someone?"

That triggered a memory. "Phoebe thought she was dating someone new."

He gave it some thought, his gaze seemingly tracing a crack in the linoleum. "Could be. It's not like she would have come running to me with news about a new lover. We didn't have that kind of relationship. We were friends in a 'we have history' way, but not a 'share everything' way."

I understood the distinction. We folded clothes in silence, me laying the socks one on top of another and rolling them into a neat ball, Zane folding T-shirts, jeans, towels, and underwear alike: once over horizontally and once vertically. It felt domestic, cozy, and I was suddenly glad we were in a public place, listening to an annoying cartoon on the television now, and getting a whiff of dirty diapers from the toddler who was busy following a fly as it buzzed against a window. I was glad I hadn't offered to let Zane do his laundry at my place . . . it would have felt too intimate.

An unwelcome thought struck me and I dropped a pair of socks. Fishing them out from under the chair (where I spotted drifts of lint and dust suggesting no one had used a broom in here for quite some time), I had a thought. "The brick. The note. Someone from the show killed Tessa. No one else knew I was investigating but, thanks to Nigel, everyone involved with *Blisters* knew."

Zane gave me a troubled look. "Damn. Who?"

I found myself telling him what I'd overheard between Nigel and Kristen, and about Mickey Hazzard's threats. "There might be another dozen people with grudges against Tessa, for all I know," I said. "I haven't chatted much with a lot of the crew, the camera guys and wardrobe folks, for example, or the band members . . .

for all I know one or more of them has worked with her before and hates her for some reason. It would help if we knew where everyone was Tuesday night, but that's not going to happen. People aren't going to tell me where they were or what they were doing, especially now that Nigel has 'outed' me."

Zane grinned at my description. "Maybe I could find out. We all live together in that complex—most of the b-listers and some of the crew, anyway. Even Nigel's there. Kristen's invited me over for drinks. I'll start with her."

I'd just bet a glass of wine or a G&T wasn't all Kristen had in mind, but I stifled the thought. "Why are you doing this?"

"Are you kidding? The police think I did it. That's so far off base it proves to me they're not likely to catch the real killer. Tessa meant a lot to me at one time." He stuffed the folded clothes into a laundry sack and gave the cord a tug.

"Could I get your autograph, Hayden?" A woman about my age stood beside Zane, what looked like an old receipt and pen in hand. From the hungry way she looked at him, I knew she'd been a huge *Hollywood High* fan and would have bet my last nickel she'd had his poster up in her room, too.

"Sure." Zane gave her a tight smile, not bothering to correct her about his name, scribbled his autograph, and handed the receipt back.

"I voted for you last night," she said. "As many times as I could."

"Thanks." Zane angled his body away from her, clearly dismissive, and after a moment she took the hint and drifted off. "It's a hard line to walk," he said, reading my expression. "I appreciate the fans and want to be kind to them because they keep me employed, after all, but I hate it when they act like they know me, or like they have a right to my time because they watch my show. Problem is, I like acting and I like eating, and fans come with the territory when you've got a hit show."

"It's a catch-22," I agreed. I checked my watch. I'd scheduled three students for this afternoon, knowing Sunday was the only chance I'd get to work with them. "Sorry I can't keep playing laundry wench," I said, "but I've got students."

Zane's lips brushed mine. "I'll let you know if I get anything from Kristen. About the case, I mean."

I rolled my eyes and left, planning to get something from, or on, Kim Savage. I couldn't grill Zane about when his mom arrived in town or her dislike of Tessa, but I knew someone else who'd be happy to talk about her.

Chapter 15

After sessions with my three students, I called Maurice, feeling a little sneaky about offering to help walk Hoover when what I really wanted was to grill him about Kim Savage.

"Thank you, Anastasia, but I've already walked the brute," Maurice said, exasperation in his voice. "I took him to Cameron Run. He rolled in a dead fish by the pond and now he stinks to high heaven. Mildred's coming home this evening and I've called three grooming parlors, none of which is open on a Sunday." He sounded about ready to tear his hair out . . . or do away with one rambunctious Great Dane.

"I'll help you give him a bath," I said, thinking that most of my day was being devoted to cleaning something or other. "On my way."

I stopped at a Giant en route and bought three 64-ounce containers of tomato juice since that was supposed to work on skunk smell. At least, I remembered Mom using it when her beagle got sprayed, and hoped it would work on other odors. While I was there, I got bottles of cheap shampoo and conditioner, too, figuring Maurice might not have enough on hand to wash Hoover. As an afterthought, I tossed a packet of dog treats in my basket. Bribes.

Pulling up at Maurice's small house with its elegant eggplant-colored door and ivy covered front lawn area, I didn't bother knocking. The barks and curses coming from the back told me where Maurice and Hoover were. Following the brick footpath along the side of the house, I found myself in a small backyard with a brick patio just big enough for a grill and a bistro table, a patch of grass about the size of my bedroom that smelled newly mown, and a dogwood sapling. Maurice, with damp spots on his shirt and yellow shorts, held a hose that he aimed at a barking Hoover. The dog did a play bow, wagging his tail furiously, and danced out of the way of the stream of water.

Maurice hailed me with relief. "Thank goodness you're here. I can't both hold him and wash him. Grab his collar and I'll hose him down. Hoover, come."

The big dog cocked his head, considering.

"Look what I've got," I said, tempting him with a treat.

He trotted over and snarfed it down; the stench of rotting fish nearly knocked me down. "Pee-yew! Hoover, you reek," I said, reluctantly grabbing his collar to keep him in place. "Do you think we just dump the tomato juice over him, or do we have to rub it in?"

"I'd rub it in some," Maurice said after a moment's thought. "Just a minute."

He disappeared into the house, letting the screen door bang shut behind him. Emerging a moment later carrying a toilet bowl brush, he said, "Bought this yesterday. This wasn't how I was planning to use it, but needs must . . ." He handed it to me. "I'll pour. You scrub."

While I held Hoover's collar, Maurice poured the first container of tomato juice over the dog's back and haunches. Hoover immediately shook himself, spattering red droplets all over me. Thank goodness I'd changed into my scruffiest pair of denim shorts and a T-shirt before coming.

"Hoover! Sit." I pushed down his rear end, and scrubbed at his back with the plastic brush. "How was your date last night?" I asked casually since Hoover seemed to like the scratch of the toilet brush on his back and shoulders and wasn't squirming to get away. "I'll bet Kim Savage isn't spending her day dousing a putrid-smelling dog in tomato juice." I congratulated myself on how subtly I'd brought up her name.

Smiling, Maurice said, "Undoubtedly not. She has a bichon frise, but Layla has a standing appointment with the groomer."

"You met Layla?" Not quite as monumental as meeting the parents or the kids, but it was interesting.

"I think we're ready for the hose."

I held Hoover's collar with both hands and Maurice drenched him, rinsing off the tomato juice. I gave the pooch a sniff test. "Smells better. A little shampoo ought to do the trick." I squirted half a bottle of the coconut-lime-scented shampoo into my hand and began massaging it into Hoover's coat. It smelled a lot better than *eau de rotten fish*. He slurped my face with his tongue.

"How long's she been in town?"

"Since last Sunday. She wanted to come out with Zane, but she had commitments in California."

Bingo. She'd been here before Tessa died. I tried to

think of a tactful way to ask where she'd been Tuesday night, but couldn't come up with one, so I asked bluntly, "I don't suppose you happen to know where she was Tuesday night?"

Busy soaping Hoover's hind legs, I couldn't see Maurice's face, but his voice held surprise and disapproval. "Surely you don't suspect Kim had anything to do with Tessa's death?"

I peered over Hoover's flank. "I wouldn't rule her out. She's"—*obsessed, desperate*—"intent on restarting Zane's career and Tessa stood in the way. Potentially." I explained about Tessa threatening to remove Zane from *Blisters*. "She's also smart and looks strong. If she saw Tessa as a threat to Zane . . ."

"Kim Savage is a lady," Maurice said. "She's educated and talented and a loving mother. She raised Zane and his sister alone after their father left, you know."

As if that made her an instant candidate for sainthood. She'd threatened to get me booted from *Blisters* because I didn't let her into the studio fast enough. What would she do to someone who *really* got in her way?

"I thought you were through with investigating. I know I got you started, but you need to call it quits. Implying that Kim is capable of murder . . ." He shook his head as if disappointed in me.

His tone stung. "You'd rather see Zane arrested?"

"I'd rather let the police figure it out. Poking around in people's private lives feels sneaky, underhanded."

Trying not to sound as hurt as I felt, I said, "Rinse."

Turning the hose on Hoover, Maurice managed to get as much water on me as on the dog and I wondered if it was an accident, despite his contrite-sounding, "Sorry, Anastasia!"

"I'm covered with tomato juice, dog hair, and fish scales—a little water isn't going to hurt anything." I released Hoover and the giant dog dashed around the yard in circles, stopped to shake himself vigorously, and resumed running. He dropped to the ground and lay panting. Then, before we could stop him, he rolled onto his back, paws waving in the air, and proceeded to coat himself with grass clippings.

"Hoover!" Maurice and I yelled.

He scrambled up, shook himself again, and looked at us expectantly. Blades of grass stuck off him at funny angles, making him look like a chia pet on steroids. We couldn't help it: we laughed.

Mildred Kensington was pulling up to reclaim Hoover when I left, and I eyed her in this year's Cadillac sedan, wondering if the leather seats would be grass-coated and coconut-lime scented by the time she got Hoover home. We exchanged cordial greetings and I told her she'd find her pet in the backyard.

"I do hope he's been a good boy," she said in the doting tones of a woman who thinks her pet isn't capable of being anything else.

Waving good-bye without answering, I headed for home. Despite Maurice's disapproval, I intended to find Tessa's killer. Keeping Zane out of jail and earning a reward that would pay off half the tax debt were worth it, even if I had to be a teeny-weeny bit sneaky. Okay, Maurice's words had hurt more than I wanted to admit. A plan formed in my mind. Zane had stopped me from approaching the drug dealer Tessa talked to before she disappeared, but I'd bet he hung out in the same spot every night. Drug dealers didn't take Sundays off, did they? It crossed my mind that even if the police had interrogated the man, he might have been reluctant, given his line of work, to be totally honest with them. Maybe if someone who wasn't a police officer talked to him—someone like me, say—he would reveal something that would help me figure out if Tessa left the club on her own or if someone was with her. Of course, there was always the possibility that the drug dealer had, for whatever reason, killed Tessa himself and dumped her body in the river, disposing of her car later, although I didn't know how he could figure out which one was hers. So, it would probably be smart not to go to the park alone. I dismissed the thought that it might be smarter not to go to the park at all.

I envisioned asking Danielle or my mom to visit a D.C. park with me to confront a drug dealer and grinned at the thought. Vitaly would do it, happy to expand his circle of American acquaintances, but he was in Baltimore with John and Lulu. Maurice was clearly not a candidate. Tav was out of town. Who else . . . ? The answer came to me in a flash and I didn't know why I hadn't thought of Phoebe Jackson immediately. Why, she'd undoubtedly dealt with dozens of drug dealers over the years and was probably fluent in drug dealerese. I didn't know how to get hold of her, though. I was sure she had an apartment at the same complex that Zane did, but I didn't know what unit she was in. I glanced at the sky. It was barely six o'clock and the sun would be up for another two and a half hours at this time of year. I suspected drug dealers, like vampires, didn't come out until after sundown, so I had plenty of time to find Phoebe, even if I had to knock on every door in the complex to do it.

*   *   *

By the time I showered and changed—choosing "meet the drug dealer" clothes took time—and located Phoebe, it was pushing eight thirty. I'd knocked on random doors at the apartment complex, starting with the units near Tessa's, until I found a crew member who knew Phoebe's unit number. Luckily, the action star was in and looked pleased to see me.

"Stacy! What're you doin' here, girl?" She invited me into an apartment that was a duplicate of Tessa's, right down to the same cheesy print over the sofa. Three sets of dumbbells and an exercise ball sat beside a yoga mat against the wall. Miscellaneous items of clothing and most of the Sunday *Post* were draped over the sofa and easy chair. Multiple pairs of shoes peeked out from under the love seat. It took me a moment to place the song playing from an iPod docking station: "Cell Block Tango" from *Chicago*.

"Margarita?" She gestured toward the blender and half-full glass on the counter.

"No, thanks," I said, although it was tempting. "I'm actually here about drugs."

Phoebe's dark brows snapped together. "I don't—"

"I know you don't." I explained what I wanted.

Phoebe was still frowning when I finished. "Zane had the right idea," she said, moving to the counter with two long strides. She swallowed some margarita and eyed me over the glass's rim. "You don't want to go messing with no drug dealers. They are not nice people." Bad memories shadowed her face.

"I know, but listen. I had a thought on the way over here. What if we told him about the reward? Nigel's reward for information about Tessa's death."

Phoebe considered, absently licking salt from the

glass. "That might work," she admitted. "I still think it's a dumb-ass idea. Let the police brace him."

"Right. Like he's going to tell them anything."

Her eye roll conceded me that point. "What are the chances the dude saw anything, Stacy? It's not worth it."

"That's okay. I understand." I headed for the door, hoping she'd stop me.

She did. "Where're you going?"

I turned and gave her a look that said she knew.

"Damn, girl." Phoebe worked her lips in and out. "That's blackmail. You know I can't let you go down there by your damn-fool self."

I didn't say anything. With a sigh, she slung a large purse over her shoulder. "Don't blame me if we wake up tomorrow at the bottom of the river."

Chapter 16

Darkness draped the southeast end of Pennsylvania Avenue. No lights shone from Club Nitro and I realized uneasily that the club must be closed on Sundays. I'd been counting on the presence of dozens of people in line outside the club to make us fccl lcss isolated in the park. I pulled into the empty valet parking lot and parked my Beetle. I hesitated, looking across the street at the seemingly empty park.

"Second thoughts?" Phoebe asked.

"No." Still, I didn't open the door.

"Let's get it over with." Phoebe got out and I followed suit. "Where does this dude hang out?"

"He was over there Thursday night," I said, pointing to the spot on the sidewalk that had seemed like the drug dealer's territory. A kid who couldn't have been more than ten or eleven leaned against the fence, arms crossed over his chest. A dinged-up pickup slowed at the curb as we watched and the boy exchanged a few words with its occupants, then vanished into the park.

"That kid works for your dealer," Phoebe said, watching as he reappeared and passed something to the pick-up's passenger. "A bagboy. We'll start with him." She stalked across the street, ignoring the van bearing down on her and forcing the driver to stand on his brakes.

I scuttled across the street in her wake, making "so sorry" gestures at the van's driver. He took off with squealing tires and the odor of exhaust. I didn't catch what Phoebe said to the kid, but he darted away as I drew even with them.

"I told him his boss—the kid says he goes by Li'l Boni—stands to make some money by talking to us. We'll see if that gets him. If not, I'm going home. I am not crashing around this park hollering for Li'l Boni."

"He's not 'little' anything," I said. As I finished speaking, the man I'd seen Thursday night materialized from the shadows and studied us from ten feet away. He seemed even bigger up close, with a heavy brow, bald head, and a cold stare. His black leather coat sagged down on the right, and I imagined he had a gun in the pocket. I backed up two steps but Phoebe held her ground.

"Rashid tell me you wan' talk 'bout money." His voice was a bass rumble that fit with his appearance.

Phoebe looked at me as if to say this was my show. "I'm Stacy," I said, holding out my hand.

Li'l Boni didn't even look at it and I let my arm drop to my side, feeling foolish. "There's a reward for information about Tessa King. I know you talked to her Tuesday night."

"You don' know nothin'." His expression didn't change.

He was probably right about that. "Um, well, this is Tessa." I held up the photo from the newspaper that I'd tucked into my pocket. "She was a producer for *Ballroom with the B-Listers*."

"I watch dat. I voted for d'other chick."

I didn't bother asking him which one, although Phoebe exclaimed, "Why you didn't vote for me, bro?"

His eyes cut to her, then returned to me. "The money?"

"If you watched the show last night, you know. Nigel Whiteman, Tessa's partner, offered a reward to anyone with information about her death."

Li'l Boni took a step forward and a shadow moved behind him. I wondered uneasily if he had lieutenants ready to back him up if things went south. "I din' kill the bitch."

"But you talked to her?"

After a moment, he nodded. I stayed quiet, hoping he'd be more forthcoming. "She wanted to make a documentary about dealers, pimps. 'Strect capitalists,' she called us."

As soon as he said it, I knew he was telling the truth. I mentally hit myself for not having guessed it earlier. Tessa had made several gritty documentaries—the fluffy dance show wasn't her only project. "She wanted to film you?"

He nodded and a large diamond stud on his ear winked. "Me and my bomb squad."

"You said?"

"Show me the money."

For a moment I thought he was asking me for the reward money, but then I realized that's what he'd said to Tessa.

"And?"

"Bitch said she was still gettin' the deal put together.

She'd get back to me. I tol' her she knew where my office was at." He pointed to the sidewalk and suddenly grinned, lighting up the night with a mouthful of gold and small diamonds on each of his front six teeth.

"Then what?"

He shrugged. "She left." He pointed down the street toward where Tessa had parked her Mercedes. "Got into a car with a dude and drove off." Now, he pointed to the southeast, the route Zane and I had taken Thursday night.

"A guy? She left with a guy? Who? What'd he look like?" I moved closer to Li'l Boni in my excitement and he slipped a hand into his pocket. I backed away quickly. "Sorry. No offense, Mr. Boni. Can you describe the man?"

Shaking his head, he said, "Too far."

It was about two blocks to where Tessa's car had been parked and impossible, in the absence of street lights, to see much of anything beyond the vague shape of two cars, one parked on either side of the road. I felt deflated. "Well, thanks anyway."

"I saw dat other bitch out here, the one from the show," Li'l Boni offered. "Same night."

Phoebe stiffened beside me, as surprised as I was. My eyes widened. "Who?"

"Chelsea."

I crinkled my brow. There was no Chelsea on the show.

"What'd she look like?"

Li'l Boni gave me a look. "Chelsea. Skinny blond ho." He held his hand, palm down, at about midchest. "Short, but with attitude."

The other women on the show were all brunettes or

redheads. I was the only blonde, except . . . "That sounds like Kristen Lee," I said slowly, "but—"

Phoebe cut in. "Kristen used to play Chelsea Irving on *Irving Crescent*," she said.

"Right. What I said. Chelsea Irving." Li'l Boni nodded. "Bitch was here Tuesday night, looking for Carrie."

Who the heck was Carrie and why would Kristen be looking for her *here*?

Seeing my confusion, Li'l Boni put a finger to the side of his nose and jerked his head back as if snorting. "Carrie."

To say I was dumbfounded was putting it too mildly. I couldn't imagine Kristen Lee traipsing around this park in the dead of night, looking to buy cocaine. Still, what did I know about Kristen? Nada. I'd bought in to her "one club soda and early to bed" routine. "What time? Before or after you talked to Tessa?"

"Early."

Before I could probe further, an SUV that had already been around the block once cruised by again. "I got bidness to tend to," Li'l Boni said, his gaze following the SUV.

Phoebe and I were dismissed.

"Thank y—" I started, only to gasp when Li'l Boni's big hand flashed out to grab my wrist. His thumb overlapped his thick fingers by at least two inches, making me feel like he could snap my bone with no more effort than breaking a toothpick.

"The reward." His eyes had narrowed and his nostrils flared. He didn't look angry, but menace flowed off him and Phoebe's words about drug dealers not being nice guys came back to me.

"I don't have it yet. I'll tell Nigel. He—"

"We're leaving now." Phoebe's voice was flat and surprisingly calm. It took Li'l Boni about as long as it took me to spot the gun that had appeared in her hand.

Two men stepped out of the shadows behind Li'l Boni and I scrunched my eyes closed, waiting for bullets to rip into us. This was not going the way I had planned. Opening my eyes again, I saw the emotionless way Li'l Boni measured Phoebe. Reaching into my pocket, I dug out the money I had put there earlier and thrust it toward the dealer. My hand trembled.

"A hundred dollars. For your time. I will make sure Nigel knows how helpful you've been and I'm sure . . . when he gives out the reward . . ."

Phoebe nudged me off the curb as Li'l Boni took the money and released my wrist. "You got balls, bitch. I might even vote for you this week," he told Phoebe as she backed into the street. His laughter followed us across the street.

We scrambled into the car and I peeled out, making it about half a mile before pulling over to the roadside to take a deep breath a still my shaking hands. "Damn, girl," I repeated Phoebe's favorite phrase to her. "I didn't know you had a gun."

She patted her purse. "Every smart woman has a gun."

I guess I knew what that made me.

"I thought you were a martial arts star and could kung fu your way out of anything." I was babbling, still keyed up and shaky from the encounter with Li'l Boni.

Giving me a disbelieving stare, Phoebe said, "Kung fu doesn't work against guns. I don't do kung fu anyway. I started with tae kwon do and I've been getting into krav maga lately." When I looked a question at her, she added, "Israeli. You know what we need now?"

I looked at her blankly.

"Pie. Any Village Inns around here? Diners?"

Laughing weakly, I wilted forward so my head rested on the steering wheel, then straightened and started the car.

Over slices of pic at a Silver Diner, Phoebe and I discussed the evening. It wasn't yet eleven o'clock, but I felt like I'd been up for three days. A woman alone reading a fat paperback was the diner's only other customer, and one of the servers ran a rug sweeper. An oldies station played softly in the background. Forking up a bite of cherry pie, I let the tart and sweet flavors mingle in my mouth before swallowing.

"Hits the spot," Phoebe agreed with my unspoken comment, eating the last morsel of her pecan pie. "Just like Nana used to make. Hell, probably still does. I haven't been back to Atlanta in ten, twelve years."

"That's sad."

Phoebe leaned back against the red vinyl booth, not following up on my comment. "Let's not do that again, girlfriend. I am too old for that kind of excitement."

I knew she wasn't talking about the pie. "Agreed. Do you think Boni was telling the truth?"

"Man's got no reason to lie."

"Coffee?" The server appeared and refilled Phoebe's cup. I shook my head; caffeine at this hour would keep me up all night.

Leaning forward, I whispered. "What about Kristen? Do you think she does drugs? Was she really in the park, or was it maybe some other blonde from the nightclub?"

Phoebe's eyelids closed halfway and she gave me a look I couldn't interpret, a mix of world-weary cynicism and maybe disdain for my naïveté. "Ain't no big deal if Kristen does a line now and then. Everybody does. Well, except me, now that I'm clean, and maybe Robert Downey Jr."

"I've never—" I cut myself off, not wanting to sound like Priscilla Perfect, or like I was judging her. "So you think it's coincidence that Kristen was in the park near the time that Tessa disappeared?"

Phoebe emptied a packet of sugar into her coffee and stirred it thoughtfully. "Probably. Li'l Boni probably gets a lot of business from Club Nitro. I'm sure he pays some of the staff to point potential customers his way."

I bit back the "Really?" that sprang to my lips, tired of looking so clueless. "Who was the man, then? The man Tessa left with?"

"That's the question, isn't it? No way to know, I guess. Dude could be anyone—a hot bod she picked up for the night, another source for her new documentary, Zane."

"Zane?"

She shrugged. "They used to have a thing."

"Used to."

"And he left earlyish."

"To get some sleep before rehearsals."

"If you say so." Phoebe sipped her coffee.

I drew in a deep breath and held it for a moment, fighting back the urge to defend Zane. It had to be someone from the TV show, I reminded myself, thinking about the brick through my window. As much as I wanted to think Tessa had met another slimy character—a pimp, maybe—to interview for her new documentary and he'd killed her, I knew better. Zane had argued with Tessa earlier that day. . . . Knowing it was too abrupt, I slid out of the booth. "We'd better get going. Early call tomorrow."

We travelled the short distance to the long-stay complex in silence, Phoebe yawning twice. "Thanks for going with me," I said as she opened the door to get out.

Swinging her long legs out, she grinned. "Don't you know Nigel would be sick if he knew he'd missed the opportunity to film you and me mixing it up with a drug dealer?"

The thought made me grin as I drove off.

Chapter 17

Vitaly was waiting for me Monday morning, Trade Day, when I staggered up the interior stairs to Graysin Motion. We'd agreed to meet at six thirty to get in a rehearsal before our *Blisters* commitments got in the way. He gave me a comprehensive look, and said, "Well, looking what the cat dragged in."

"I didn't sleep well." I'd tossed and turned until almost two, and then had nightmares where I was dancing with Li'l Boni and he was going to shoot me if we didn't win.

"Dancing will make you feels better," Vitaly announced. "Come." I took his extended hand and let him pull me into the ballroom. We stretched and marched in place for fifteen minutes to warm up, then Vitaly turned on the CD player. "Cha-cha first."

The steady beat of "Corazon de Melon" came through the speakers and Vitaly drew me in. He took a checked step toward me on the second beat of the bar and I stepped back, keeping the ball of my foot in contact with the floor. Rosemary Clooney's voice transported me to an open-air bar where Spanish phrases tangled with the music. Imagining a sultry Havana night got me into the mood of the dance that originated in Cuba, and my hips swayed to the beat. My free leg remained straight and our cha-cha-cha chassé was rhythmic and effortless.

Vitaly was right: after an hour of dancing, I did feel better. It always worked that way. I kissed him on the cheek when we finished. "Thanks. See you in five." I ran downstairs to shower before the TV crew arrived.

When I returned, the studio bustled with activity and I almost bumped into Zane when I turned the corner to my office. He steadied me with his hands on my upper arms and his smile was warm. "Hey."

"Hey," I said.

With a peek down the hall to ensure no one was there, he bent his head and kissed me. I leaned into the kiss for a moment, but pulled away quickly at the sound of a footstep. I glanced over my shoulder. No one.

"It wasn't near as much fun doing my laundry after you left." He smiled down at me.

"Let's get going, people." Nigel's voice sounded from inside the ballroom. "Time is money. Chop-chop."

"Have lunch with me," Zane whispered as we moved toward the ballroom. "I took Kristen up on her invitation last night."

"Can't," I said. "Appointment." We entered the ballroom before I had a chance to tell him I had made an appointment with Detective Lissy to tell him what Phoebe and I had learned last night. He'd sounded less than thrilled to hear from me, but had agreed to a lunchtime meeting.

The sight of Calista Marques in the middle of the ball-room floor drove all thought of Detective Lissy from my mind. Oh, no! Hip cocked, she was texting, bobbing to music coming through earbuds, jaw working on a piece of gum. She didn't look up when I came in. My gaze flew to Vitaly where he stood talking to Phoebe. She gestured widely, apparently trying to convince him of something, but he shook his head. Nigel and two cameramen got it all. Vitaly strode toward me and Zane, and Phoebe fol-lowed.

"What's Calista doing here?" I asked in a low voice, afraid I knew.

"Phoebe is tossing me aside like the used Kleenex," Vitaly said, giving her a hurt look.

"I did not tell the girl I would trade," Phoebe said, exasperated. "I agreed to let her practice with you this morning, take you for a test drive, if you like. She's mak-ing a ten-thousand-dollar donation to my foundation just to dance with you for an hour. Don't go getting all sulky on me."

"I am not BMW," Vitaly said.

I could see his feelings were truly hurt. I hugged him. "Maybe Calista won't like dancing with you," I said.

"All the womens like dancing with Vitaly," he said glumly.

Phoebe punched his arm. "You're my main man," she said. "Just dance with the skinny child for an hour and then we can get down to practicing. You and me are go-ing to the top of the leaderboard this week."

"Not a chance in hell," Zane said. "That spot's re-served for me and Stacy."

Calista walked up then, pulling one earbud out of her ear. "I am so excited to dance with you, Vitaly," she said, flipping her dark hair over her shoulder with the back of her hand. Her light olive complexion glowed with good health and youth and I thought enviously of the days when I didn't have to spend more money on moisturizer than makeup. Her brown eyes, fringed with the lashes that had landed her a mascara ad, smiled into his.

"Me, as well," Vitaly said. Shooting a darkling look at Phoebe, he offered Calista his hand and led her to the middle of the floor. One camera tracked their progress and the other focused on Phoebe's face. Nigel came to stand beside us.

"They move well together, don't you think?" he asked.

I knew he was trying to needle Phoebe, so I didn't say anything, but he was right. Calista followed Vitaly's lead like she'd been dancing with him for years. Her every gesture, the way she held her head, her dainty steps, made it seem as if she had music rather than blood in her veins.

"She and Nikolai were at the bottom of the leaderboard," Nigel murmured, gesturing to the new cameraman to move to a spot near the windows.

Was he implying that Calista had been voted off? I was sure he already had access to the voting results from Saturday night. If the viewers had kicked off Calista, and she ended up with Vitaly, he would go with her and that would halve our chances of winning *Blisters* and receiving the prize money. Zane draped an arm across my shoulder, as if aware of my thoughts, and squeezed. "I wouldn't trade you for anyone," he whispered.

It didn't take Calista the full hour to make up her mind; she walked up to Phoebe before the last note of the foxtrot died away. "I so want him," she announced.

I tensed and watched Vitaly, who was pretending disinterest by rooting in his gym bag.

Phoebe pursed her lips. "Sorry. I don't want to trade."

"I'll give you ten percent of my viewer votes." Calista Marques hadn't reached the pinnacle of fame so young without having more determination than the average bear. And she was clearly determined to finish the *Blisters* season with Vitaly.

Phoebe shook her head.

"I'll get my agent to sign you."

Zane's brows disappeared under his hair and I gathered Calista's offer was a good one.

"I'm happy with Ari."

Calista's expression said she doubted it. "I'll headline a fund-raiser for your girls' club."

For the first time, Phoebe hesitated. Her gaze went to Vitaly and a line appeared between her brows. Then she nodded decisively and stuck out her hand. "Deal."

Calista beamed, shook hands, and rushed over to Vitaly. She hugged him and his expression reproached Phoebe over Calista's shoulder.

"Didn't slave auctions get outlawed after the Civil War?" Zane asked in an undertone.

"Tell the viewers why you traded Vitaly, Phoeb," Nigel said, beckoning one camera closer.

I suddenly wondered if he'd offered either of the women incentives to trade, knowing that a partner switch would up the drama and increase viewer interest. This show was making me cynical.

"It was too good a deal to pass up," Phoebe said. She spoke to the camera, but I knew she was really explaining herself to Vitaly. "With Calista Marques singing at our fund-raiser, we'll raise millions. *Blisters* is just a TV show. Girls who need a leg up, who need help getting themselves back on track, are *real*."

I supposed I couldn't argue with that. Vitaly approached and gave her a bear hug, lifting her off her feet. "I understands," he said. "You are the good person, and a good dancer. Too bad you are now losing the competition."

Phoebe grinned in relief and socked him on the shoulder.

I arrived at the police station off of Mill Road, in the Beltway's shadow, at noon. An admin type walked me back to Detective Lissy's office after branding me with a visitor's badge. Lissy didn't appear to be in the office, but when I knocked tentatively on the open door, his head appeared above the desk. "A moment, Ms. Graysin." He disappeared again, but stood up seconds later with a creak of his knees, holding up a pen. He settled himself in the chair behind his desk and looked impatiently at me where I hovered in the doorway. "Sit."

I sat. I'd been here before and it didn't look like anything had changed. Photos of his grandchildren still marched in descending height order along the credenza. File folders, which probably weren't the ones that he'd had out when I'd been here last, but which looked the same, were precisely aligned with the edges of his desk. His inbox and outbox were both empty. I suspected the garbage in his trash can was organized by size: bigger items on the bottom, smaller ones on top.

"Well?" His impatient voice broke into my thoughts.

"Phoebe Jackson and I talked with a gentleman named Li'l Boni last night and got some information about Tessa King."

"You said as much in your phone call," he said with a "get on with it" motion.

I crossed my legs, refusing to be hurried. I told him about last night, leaving out only Phoebe's speculation that Zane was the man who left with Tessa and the bit about Phoebe's gun. I didn't know if it was legal for her to carry it around in her purse and I didn't want to get her in trouble.

"You do realize that it was extremely foolish of you to confront a criminal like Boni on his turf?" Lissy's voice and expression were sour.

I'd realized it as soon as he grabbed my arm, but I wasn't going to admit it to Lissy. I remained silent.

"We spoke with Li'l Boni, after the bartender pointed us to him." Lissy tapped his pen on his desk. *Tick, tick, tick.* "His real name is Levon Bonine."

I didn't say anything, suspecting that if he had learned as much as Phoebe and I, he'd already have kicked me out of his office.

Finally, he drew a steno pad toward him and pulled a sharpened pencil from his desk drawer. "What did Bonine say the man looked like, and exactly when did he see the person he identified as Kristen Lee?"

"He didn't get a good look at the man with Tessa, and he actually identified the blonde as 'Chelsea,' but Phoebe said that was the name of a character Kristen used to play on a television show."

"Irving Crescent," Lissy supplied, surprising me. "My wife watched it," he explained, clearly anxious to distance himself from the nighttime soap. "I'm a *Jeopardy!* man myself. That and *Hoarders.*"

The thought of this precise, compulsively neat man watching *Hoarders* tickled me. I'd caught part of an episode once and it almost made me ill.

He allowed himself a half smile at my amusement.

"It's a train wreck," he said. "It is beyond my comprehension how people live like that, surrounded by all that ... clutter."

The way he said "clutter," it sounded like a sin on par with mass murder. I gave him the information he wanted, and a hopeful look. "So I helped?"

Before he could either acknowledge my contribution to his investigation or, as I suspected would happen, read me a lecture about sticking to dancing, a tall man with reddish hair and a gun at his waist poked his head in. "The hit-and-run vic's come around, Marv. I'm headed over there." He named a nearby hospital.

"I'm done here," Lissy said, rising. "Give me thirty seconds." The other man nodded and exited with only a cursory glance at me.

I knew my cue when I heard it and I rose, too. "I know the way out," I said.

Lissy gave a curt nod, pulled a suit jacket from the coat rack behind his desk, and accompanied me to the office door. I started down the hall, but turned when he called, "Ms. Graysin."

He was going to thank me, I thought, keeping the smile off my face and lifting a gently enquiring eyebrow.

"In future, leave the investigating to professionals. Stick to dancing."

Without replying, I turned and flounced toward the exit, wishing I was wearing a full skirt that would flounce better than the linen slacks I had on.

Chapter 18

Back at Graysin Motion, the first person I saw was Kim Savage. Zane's mother wore a gray silk pencil skirt and a white blouse that displayed her curves. A leopard-print belt defined her waist and matched her platform pumps. She'd clearly been lying in wait for me because she pounced as soon as I came through the door.

"Stacy, there you are."

I stared at her warily, mistrusting her sudden friendliness. "Hello, Mrs. Savage."

"Kim."

"Okay, Kim."

I brushed past her to get to the ballroom, intending to collect the choreography notes I'd made earlier. She followed me. Larry the cameraman trailed behind her. Uh-oh. I found my spiral notebook and picked it up. "Can I help you with something, Mrs. Sav—Kim? Zane's not here. We rehearsed this morning." I didn't mention that I expected him in about an hour; he was going to tell me what he'd learned during his evening with Kristen. I hadn't yet made up my mind what I'd tell him about Li'l Boni and his assertion that Tessa had left with a man.

"I understand you're helping the police find Tessa King's murderer," Kim said.

I knew my "uh-oh" instincts were right. "I wouldn't put it that way." And I knew darned well Detective Lissy wouldn't put it that way.

"I want to help. After all, it's my son who's a suspect. I want to clear his name."

Her voice oozed sincerity, but the calculating look in her eye (not to mention Larry's presence) told me this encounter was staged . . . for whose benefit I wasn't yet sure. I clutched my notebook to my chest, as if that would ward her off. Nothing short of garlic and a crucifix was likely to slow her down. "Did Nigel put you up to this?" I asked, suddenly sure the producer had egged her on to talk to me, thinking it would make good TV.

She blinked but recovered quickly. "Of course not. It's important to me to see justice done, for Tessa's sake."

Oh, please. The soulful look that went with the words almost made me gag and I wondered if my throwing up would boost the ratings. Well, two could play her game. "Okay, then. Where were you Tuesday night?"

"Me?" She widened her mascara-fringed eyes.

"You."

"I don't see what . . . I thought I could give you the scoop on Tessa and some of the cast members, as a Hollywood insider. Did you know Nigel was almost indicted for what happened on his last reality show, for instance? The network managed to keep it hush-hush, but—"

"I'd rather hear where you were Tuesday night, more like early Wednesday morning. Say, after midnight?"

Kim stiffened and she pointed a red-tipped finger at me. "I don't like what you're implying."

"What am I implying?" I gave her an innocent look. "I asked a simple question."

Her gaze flitted from me to the camera. "I was in my hotel room, asleep."

"Got any witnesses?"

It took her a moment. "Of course not!"

"That's too bad." I shook my head sadly, beginning to enjoy this, channeling some combination of Columbo and Cagney. All I needed was a trench coat. "As I see it, you had several reasons for wanting to get rid of Tessa King. You disapproved of her relationship with Zane, even though it was over, and she might've been going to boot him from *Blisters*, which would have brought his comeback—a comeback you engineered—to a screeching halt. So I can see why—"

She slapped me. Her palm struck my cheek and rocked my head to the side. I stared at her openmouthed for a moment, the sting flaring until it felt like the whole side of my face was on fire. Her features contorted with anger, and she raised her arm again. I put my foot out at hip level, just to keep her away. She bumped against it with her stomach, stumbled backwards, arms going around, and fell on her fanny, skirt rucking up to reveal a glimpse of thigh and Spanx.

"Stop the camera," she cried, pulling the skirt down and straightening her neckline. When Larry merely moved in for a close-up, she scrambled to her feet, kicking off her pumps, and went for him. I dropped my notebook and grabbed her around the waist. This close, the scent of her heavy perfume almost made me sneeze. Larry shuffled backwards, a grin on his usually impassive face.

"Brilliant!" Nigel's voice cut in on the action. "Fabulous, Kim-darling."

She froze and shook herself free of my restraining embrace, turning to face Nigel in the doorway. I saw the moment she decided to go with the out he offered her. Or maybe it wasn't an out—maybe they'd planned the whole encounter. I couldn't tell. Pasting a smile on her face, she glided toward him, saying, "Thank you, Nigel. Even though I gave up my acting career for my children, it's still in my blood."

"I'd like to shed your blood," I muttered under my breath. My face hurt like the dickens and I saw in the mirrors that a red hand-shaped mark marred my cheek. Larry zoomed in for a close-up of it and gave me a thumbs-up. I wasn't sure why. Because I'd taken on Kim Savage? Nigel strode up and tossed an arm around my shoulders, like we were old pals.

"What's going on?" Zane spoke from the doorway.

"It was brilliant," Nigel said, a grin spreading across his face. "Your mum and Stacy got into it and Kim walloped her." He mimed a slap.

Zane frowned and crossed to me. Taking my chin in his hand, he turned my face gently to inspect the mark on my cheek. "Let's get you a cold cloth for that," he said softly. All hint of softness fled his face as he turned toward his mother and said, "I can't believe even you would stoop to assaulting my dance partner."

Kim threw her hands up dramatically, somehow managing to look both outraged and hurt. "It wasn't assault! It was . . . method acting. I got into the emotion of the moment. She practically accused me of killing Tessa."

"Did you?"

The words hung in the air.

Kim stared at her son, openmouthed, and then spun on her heel. "You know where to find me when you want to apologize," she said. She stalked from the ballroom, hips swaying.

"Bravo!" Nigel clapped.

Zane, a little ashen-faced, turned to me. "Come on, Stacy, I'll get you a washcloth." We entered the hall together and he turned left to dampen a washcloth in the bathroom and I went into my office, collapsing onto the love seat. Kicking off my shoes, I put my feet up and leaned my head back against the cushions. This was so not what I had signed up for.

Zane returned and knelt beside the love seat, pressing the cloth against my cheek. The cold relieved the pain and I sighed.

"Look, Stacy, my mom's a passionate woman, and sometimes she—" He took a deep breath and tried again. "My succeeding in Hollywood is extremely important to Mom, maybe because she grew up without many advantages and she's always wanted financial security for me and my sister. I'm sure she didn't mean—"

I just looked at him and peeled the cloth back so he could see my swollen cheek.

"Oh, hell," he muttered. "Did you really ask her if she killed Tessa?"

"Don't try to make this my fault," I said, struggling to sit up higher.

A firm footstep sounded in the hall and then Tav's voice said, "Hello, Stacy. The plane arrived—" He broke off. "Excuse me. I am interrupting." His voice had gone flat.

I tried to imagine what the scene looked like from his perspective with me lying on the love seat and Zane kneeling beside me, leaning close. Oh, no. I jerked myself upright, letting the washcloth fall. Zane reared back, startled, as I swung my feet to the floor. "No, Tav, it's not what it looks like."

His gaze had fastened on my cheek and he wasn't listening to me. He strode forward, hands bunching into fists at his sides. "Did he strike you?" He looked from me to Zane who had scrambled to his feet. Tav's face had gone rigid and cold in a way I'd never seen before.

"I've never struck a woman in my—" Zane started angrily. He looked like he might hit Tav for suggesting it.

I stood, separating the men. "Of course not," I said. "It was his mother."

Tav looked from me to Zane, some of the anger fading from his eyes, and his hands relaxed. "I think you had better explain."

I told both men what had happened, with Kim prodding me to go into "investigator mode" and me asking her where she'd been. "I didn't say I thought she killed Tessa," I said. "I only asked her where she was Tuesday night. I got the feeling Nigel goaded her to ask me about the investigation."

"He probably told her to slap you, too," Zane said.

Knowing he wanted that to be the case, I didn't say anything; however, I was pretty damn sure hitting me had been Kim's spur-of-the-moment idea. The woman clearly had anger management issues.

"I think it is time I had a talk with Whiteman," Tav said, surprising me with his grim tone. "This foolishness has gone on long enough." He headed for the door.

"Wait, Tav—" I didn't think it was a good idea to alienate Nigel. He was in a position to make me and Vitaly and Graysin Motion look very, very bad. We'd have trouble winning if Nigel was against us.

Zane grabbed my arm before I could stop Tav. "Let him. It'll do Nigel good to learn he can't steamroller everyone."

As if by mutual accord, we followed Tav, hoping to overhear what he and Nigel said to each other. When we got to the ballroom, Larry burst out as if shoved, looking flustered, and the door shut firmly behind him. All three of us leaned in, but I couldn't make out the words through the thick walls and door, built in an era when houses were meant to last. I could hear Tav's stern tones and Nigel's more excitable voice, but the words were lost. Larry, Zane, and I gave each other questioning looks, and I got an urge to giggle, thinking we looked like a Three Stooges routine with each of us semihunched over, ears hovering near the door. I pressed my lips together to hold back the giggles and tiptoed halfway down the hall. Good thing I did, because the door opened moments later, giving Larry and Zane only a split second to distance themselves from it before Nigel and Tav came out. Larry bent over as if looking for something and Zane wiped his hands down his slacks, as if he'd just emerged from the bathroom. The giggles burst from me, causing Nigel and Tav to look my way. Shaking my head, I clapped my fingers over my mouth and hurried to the stair door, making it halfway down the stairs before collapsing in a fit of laughter.

Laughing made my cheek hurt and I continued downstairs and checked it out in my bedroom mirror. Fading somewhat, but still red. Oh, well, at least I wasn't going to be on TV tonight. *Blisters* used to have a results show that aired on Monday nights, but they'd gone to announcing who was getting kicked off at the start of the Saturday broadcast. That was kind of harsh on whoever got eliminated because it meant they'd worked all week for nothing.

Letting my hair out of its ponytail so it partially hid my cheek, I returned to the studio. Everyone was gone except Zane. Too bad—I'd been hoping to ask Tav what he'd said to Nigel. Zane was practicing our hustle choreography in front of the ballroom mirrors. "Keep the upper body still," I corrected automatically.

He turned and gave me a rueful smile. "Some day, huh?"

"I could use a break."

"Let's go for a drive and I'll tell you about my evening with Kristen."

I looked at my watch. No one drives anywhere in the D.C. area without calculating whether or not they're likely to get caught in rush-hour traffic. "Okay."

Chapter 19

When Zane crossed the Woodrow Wilson Bridge I figured out where we were going and I clasped my hands together in my lap. I wasn't sure I wanted to see the spot where Tessa had died. Past Bolling Air Force Base and Saint Elizabeth's Hospital, he pulled off the Anacostia Freeway and parked along a service road north of Anacostia Park that paralleled the river and the highway. We got out of the car in silence.

"It was right around here," Zane said, spreading his arms. "This is the spot the cops had marked on the map. I'm sure they don't know precisely where she went into the water, but it was around here somewhere."

We were north of the Pennsylvania Street Bridge, so either Tessa had gotten turned around or she hadn't been headed to the Eakins Extended Stay after leaving Club Nitro. The city had started "reclaiming" the Anacostia River area in the last ten years or so, adding parks and a river walk that were a vast improvement over the previous unwelcoming landscape. The area we stood in was still awaiting its turn at a makeover. The low tide exposed a short expanse of glistening mud that stretched from the shore to the water. It emitted a rank smell of decomposing fish and oil. Small crabs scuttled for cover when our shadows fell on them and I wondered if they thought we were herons looking to pluck them up with our long bills. Coarse grass grew on the slight slope that fell away from the road to the river's edge, and it was clogged with soda bottles, fast food trash, flimsy plastic grocery bags, and cigarette butts. From the number of the latter, I wondered if this was a popular fishing spot. A black man stood a hundred feet upstream, casting a line into the water.

If this was where Tessa went into the river, there was no evidence of it. I don't know what I'd expected to see, but numerous tire tracks imprinted the mud on both sides of the road and the trash could have come from fishermen or people tossing litter from their cars, or been washed downstream by the river. The only thing that struck me was that the slope was gentle enough and the current slow enough that anyone with two functioning legs would have been able to climb out of the water to safety. "So sad," I murmured.

Zane didn't say anything. He stared out over the Anacostia as if expecting Tessa's ghost to rise from the depths and tell us what had happened to her, to point a spectral finger at her murderer. "There's nothing here," he said finally, and turned to walk upstream.

I fell into step beside him, slipping my hand into his. He squeezed it hard and gave me a grateful smile. "So," he said, deliberately throwing off his somber mood. "Kristen. She makes a mean G&T."

"I'll bet." I nudged him with my hip and he laughed.

"She and Tessa had a little history I didn't know

about," he said. "Tessa was an assistant producer on *Irving Crescent* when Kristen was playing Chelsea Irving."

"Interesting."

"Kristen blames her for her character getting killed off. She said Tessa convinced the producers and the writing staff that her character was played out, that they needed to jump-start the show by bringing in a new 'bad girl.'"

"I can't see anyone killing over that, at least not this long after the fact," I said.

"No, but what if it was about to happen again? After her third drink, Kristen began to cry, and said that Tessa had it in for her, that she was trying to get her fired from *Blisters* so that Hannah Malik could take over as host. They were also considering going to a two-host format, reuniting Donny and Marie Osmond."

I cocked my head. That actually sounded fun. A great blue heron exploded into the air a few feet in front of us. I hadn't noticed the bird until the heavy wing flaps alerted me. We watched him gain altitude, and then continued walking, flipping our hands in greeting to the fisherman when we passed him.

"Any luck?" Zane asked.

"Not biting today," the man answered with a philosophical shrug.

Navigating the uneven terrain was challenging and I was getting grit in my sandals. Zane's hand tightened on mine when I stumbled. "We should go back," he said.

I didn't argue and we began to retrace our steps. "So what did Kristen have to say about Tuesday night?" I asked.

"That she danced with a couple of guys from the crew, drank one club soda, and left early."

"Someone saw her in the park before midnight, the one where we met the bartender," I said. I'd given it some thought, and decided I didn't want to spread what might be untrue gossip about Kristen, so I left out what Li'l Boni had said about her buying drugs.

Zane's brows soared. "Really? I wonder what she was doing there?"

I shrugged as if I had no idea, but then he answered his own question. "Probably looking to score some coke."

Now it was my turn to be surprised. "Did you know she—"

"She hinted that we could do a line or two last night," he said. "When I didn't jump on it, she let it drop." He didn't sound shocked or appalled like I would have been if I'd been having a cocktail with a friend and she trotted out the drug stash. Zane studied my expression. "I don't do drugs, Stacy. I tried them when I was young and into the partying scene—marijuana, E, a little coke—but it didn't take me long to realize how stupid I was being. I haven't snorted, swallowed, or smoked an illegal substance since *Hollywood High* was canceled."

I was relieved, but tried not to show it.

Apparently, I didn't succeed. "Not everyone in the movie industry gets high every night," he said, half amused. "It's a business. People need their wits about them. I know some actors who think drugs get their creative juices flowing, makes it easier for them to 'enter into the character,' but most people in Hollywood are just like the folks you'd meet on the streets of Podunk, Oklahoma, or some Ohio burb."

"Only with better boobs and tans."

Zane laughed and gathered me in for a long kiss. Our

bare, sweat-filmed flesh stuck together, but I didn't mind. "I like you, Stacy Graysin," he whispered against my ear. "A lot." He gave my sore cheek a gentle kiss.

I didn't know how to respond. "We need to go or we'll get stuck in rush hour," I said, pointing to the freeway where the cars were beginning to stack up.

Zane had a pile of scripts to read through and was meeting an up-and-coming director for dinner, so he dropped me off and zoomed away. Climbing the exterior stairs to the studio, I heard swing music from the ballroom and peeked in to see Vitaly and Calista rehearsing with no camera in sight. Vitaly had his hands on Calista's slender hips and was trying to show her the motion the dance required.

She rolled her hips experimentally. "How's that?" Her eyes met Vitaly's in the mirror.

"Put a little more sexy in it," Vitaly said, standing back. "Let your inner"—he used a Russian word—"loose."

From the way he wiggled his hips on the Russian word, I translated it as "vixen," "pole dancer" or "girl being attacked by Africanized bees."

Calista let loose, rotating her hips in a way that would have done a burlesque dancer proud. She looked a lot older than seventeen, especially when she sent Vitaly a heavy-lidded look over her shoulder, her dark hair falling over one eye. "Like that?"

"That's the ticker," Vitaly said, clapping.

" 'Ticket.' "

Smiling, I backed away. I missed having Phoebe around, but we had a better chance of winning the Crystal Slipper with Calista; she was a better dancer and she had a bigger fan base than Phoebe. Retreating to my office, I eyed the papers piled on my desk. I'd been planning to organize my receipts from the last competition, for tax purposes, but I caved into temptation and logged on to the computer to see what the blogging world had to say about Saturday night's competition. I knew that in addition to the official *Blisters* site, there were several Web sites that posted comments about *Blisters* competitors and their dances. I had skimmed a couple, noting with relief that people seemed to like Zane and me (mostly Zane)—when an article caught my eye. The headline read BALLROOM OF DEATH?

I skimmed it, getting madder and madder as I read. It was about Graysin Motion. Some reporter had done what Maurice and I had feared: she'd caught on to Graysin Motion's involvement—peripheral!—in the three recent ballroom dancing murders: Rafe's, Corinne's, and Tessa's. My studio's connection with Corinne's death was only tangential and pretty much limited to the fact that Maurice was having lunch with her when she keeled over. Okay, he also got arrested. But to say that Graysin Motion itself was involved was pretty near libel, and I contemplated suing the pants off the reporter. She hadn't even had the courtesy to come to me for a comment. I clicked away from the article without finishing it to demonstrate my disdain for the shoddy reporting practices. That would show her, all right.

Just as I was getting really worked up, a photo on another site snagged my attention. It was clearly shot in a dim room, and a bit out of focus—probably taken by a cell phone. It featured Zane looking very cozy with a woman, his arm around her shoulders and their heads tipped toward each other. Their lips were close, not quite touching, as if they'd just separated from a kiss. From the background, it looked like they were in a piano bar. The woman's face was a bit fuzzy and only shown in profile, but I'd recognize those red curls anywhere. My sister Danielle.

I pushed away from the computer, disturbed by the spike of jealousy that stabbed through me at the sight of Zane and Dani looking so . . . entranced with each other. It must have been taken after the show Saturday night. Unable to resist, I scrolled through the site, looking for other photos, but that was the only one. A cut line off to the side said only: "*Blisters* hopeful Zane Savage enjoys the local attractions in Alexandria, Virginia." Hmph. So now my sister was a "local attraction."

Without pausing to think, I dialed my sister's number at work. "I see you and Zane had a *very* good time Saturday night," I said, not bothering with "Hello."

"What are you talking about?"

I gave her the URL and waited a few moments for her to find the site. Keyboard clickings and the sound of phones ringing filtered to me. Then came a faint squeal. "I'm famous!"

"Too bad the picture's so blurry no one can tell it's you."

"You knew."

"Do you want to be famous?" I was genuinely curious.

There was a brief pause while she thought about it. "Probably not. Too annoying having those rude paparazzi following you around and gloating when you put on five pounds or have a bad hair day."

What she said made sense. Before signing on with *Blisters*, I'd thought it would be fun to be famous. But being scrutinized every minute of the day, having your private moments interrupted or your screwups posted on the Internet . . . I was revising my opinion of fame.

Danielle went on. "This is still fun. Me and Zane Savage! I need to e-mail the link to Jennifer and Heather and Tony and—"

"And Coop?"

That shut her up. I pictured her twining a red curl around her forefinger. "Coop thinks we should see other people," she said. Even though she kept her voice even, I could hear the sadness underneath.

"Oh, Dani, I'm so sorry. I didn't know."

"There's nothing to be sorry about," she said in a falsely cheery voice. "We haven't broken up or anything—we're just redefining our relationship a little bit."

"And does Coop have someone in particular he's 're-defining' with?" I knew darned well what "we should see other people" meant in relationship-ese. It meant, "Sayonara, baby, only I'm too chicken to spell it out for you."

"Tricia Holstein," Danielle whispered.

"A cow? Really? He's seeing a woman named after a cow?" I knew I shouldn't make fun of the unknown woman because of her name, but Danielle was my sister and no one had the right to steal her boyfriend away, especially not Heifer Girl.

Danielle gave a watery chuckle. "She even kind of looks like one—big brown eyes and a very . . . solid build. She plays chess."

I rolled my eyes. Coop competed at chess tournaments and volunteered to coach a local school's chess team. Danielle frequently complained that his online chess habit got in the way of conversation in the evenings. "Look, how about I come over this evening and take you out for Chinese and ice cream?"

"You don't eat ice cream."

True. Dessert was not part of a dancer's usual menu. "I'll watch you eat the ice cream," I said.

"That's sweet of you, sis, but I'm busy tonight."

Was there a tinge of guilt in Dani's voice? My sisterly suspicions aroused, I asked, "Oh? What do you have planned?"

"Um, well, Zane and I are going to dinner with a director who's in town to give a speech at one of the universities. He's done a couple of films Zane really respects and he's putting together a new project, so . . ."

Oh. My. God. Zane and Dani were going on a date. A real date, not a "let's cruise by a murder scene" sort of outing, or a "let's do laundry" get-together. Dinner. A fancy dress. And who knew what they had in mind for dessert, but I'd bet it wasn't Ben & Jerry's.

"Oh," I said, trying to keep the hurt and surprise out of my voice. I'd thought Zane really liked me. He'd said so not two hours ago. "You can have a rain check, then." I fiddled with a paper clip.

"Great!" Danielle's response was too hearty, too eager. She knew I was pissed and/or hurt about her date with Zane, but she was going to pretend she didn't so we didn't have to talk about it. Pretense of ignorance was the time-honored sisterly way of avoiding fights and unpleasant confrontations. "Let's do it tomorrow night, okay?"

"Sure," I said, twisting the paper clip until it snapped in two. "That'll be fun."

We hung up and I clinked the paper clip pieces into the trash, fighting back the tears that threatened to spill over. I was not going to cry, damn it. I had no reason to. I liked Zane okay, but we'd known each other only three weeks, for heaven's sake. It's not like I wanted to marry him and have his babies; I'd been considering a fling, a little post-Rafe rebound, a temporary liaison that would end naturally and without angst when Zane returned to Hollywood. I didn't need to go getting all melodramatic because he and Danielle obviously enjoyed each other. I did kind of wish, though, that he'd mentioned he was going out with my sister tonight. Granted, it was none of my business who he dated, but it felt a teensy bit ... not straightforward. I didn't want to call it dishonest.

I didn't feel like sitting on my fanny all evening. I was feeling restless, antsy. My thoughts drifted back to the article I'd been reading before seeing the photo of Zane and Dani. Clearly, Graysin Motion was going to continue to get bad press until Tessa's case was resolved. Well then, it behooved me to see that it got resolved sooner rather than later.

Trouble was, I didn't know how to do that. As I was pondering my options, Vitaly stuck his head in the door. "Calista is gone. Maybe we should working on the Viennese waltz?" He strolled in with his lanky grace and stood, hip cocked, waiting for my answer.

I made a face. "I really don't feel up to it, Vitaly." I told him about the article, the unexpected tax debt, and my fears for the future of Graysin Motion.

"We are going to win the *Ballroom with the B-Listers*. The new students will come floodings in."

"Not if they think they're going to get rubbed out while they rumba," I said morosely.

"Is not happenings." Vitaly shook his head so his hair flopped. "Of all the murdered peoples, not one is student. We can telling them this."

That would reassure them. "If we only knew who

killed Tessa. The police could close the case and all the speculation would go away. Not to mention, we'd earn Nigel's reward."

"Then let us finding out," Vitaly said, throwing his arms wide.

"I'm out of ideas," I admitted.

"We should searching Tessa's home," he said. His face lit with enthusiasm. "John and I are seeing this on DVD last night. Private eye Remington Steele, who is really Pierce Brosnan, breaked into the house of the victim and the murderer is popping out of the pantry." He took a hop forward. "Poof! Case solved. John does not find Pierce Brosnan so hot, but I am liking," he confided.

Me, too. "I don't know . . ." I'd been in Tessa's small apartment, but only for a couple of minutes. The police had probably searched it already, so it was unlikely we would find anything useful. I remembered where Zane had found the key and wondered if it was still there. For all I knew, the apartment's contents might have been boxed up already and sent to Tessa's next of kin, whoever they were. It was probably a wild-goose chase. . . .

"We go now," Vitaly said.

"It's not even dark," I objected, "and isn't John expecting you?"

"John is at a convention in Milwaukee," Vitaly said, putting the emphasis on the final syllable. "And Lulu is at the vet clinic because she is having spaying. Is better if not dark so we can observe the clues."

It dawned on me why Vitaly was so eager. His job was at stake, too, if Graysin Motion went under. He'd find somewhere else to teach, maybe near his home in Baltimore, but he'd be starting over with a new student base, since most of his current students wouldn't want to trek to Baltimore to continue with him. His income would take a big hit, for a while at least. I didn't know how he and John split living expenses, but I didn't imagine he wanted to be totally dependent on his partner.

"What the hell." I was suddenly filled with recklessness, the desire to do something—anything—trumping my reservations. "Let's do it, Remington."

Chapter 20

It was dusky when Vitaly and I arrived at the long-stay hotel. We'd walked the half mile from Graysin Motion. A sprinkling of cars dotted the parking lots and lights glowed in some of the windows. I smelled sausage and onions as we neared the building, and my tummy rumbled. I'd had to dissuade Vitaly from dressing in ninja black from shoes to face mask and now I dragged him into the lobby and toward the elevator instead of letting him skulk around back looking for a fire escape.

"That is how Remington Steele got in," he whispered.

"The elevator is less conspicuous," I said, pushing the button for the fifth floor. "We don't want to attract attention. We're just two residents coming home from work or a busy day of house hunting."

A woman stuck her arm through the elevator doors as they were closing and got on, poking the third floor button. We rode up in silence, all of us watching the panel's lights, until the doors opened at the third floor and the woman got off. I began to feel jittery as we started upward again and I was having second thoughts when the doors dinged open and we faced the empty hallway. "I don't know if this is—"

"Which way?" Vitaly started down the hall without waiting for an answer, and I hurried after him. A rattle from my left startled me, but it was only the ice maker in the vending machine nook. I sucked in a deep breath and blew it out, deciding I wasn't cut out for a career as a private investigator, a la Remington Steele and company. I tried to dredge up the name of Stephanie Zimbalist's character from that show, but couldn't. I'd been only six or seven when it went off the air, but I remembered watching it with my dad who'd had the hots for Zimbalist. Vitaly had passed Tessa's door and I called him back. No crime scene tape barred entry, and I didn't know whether or not to be grateful; no way was I going to violate a police barrier to get into the apartment.

I felt along the top of the doorjamb, as I'd seen Zane do, and cringed at the gritty feel of dust beneath my fingertips. Clearly, the cleaning staff didn't dust up there often. Just as I was saying, "Maybe the key's gone," my fingers grazed the key and it plunked to the floor.

Vitaly picked it up. "Too bad we is not needing to kick the door open," he said, lifting his leg as if measuring where to plant his foot.

"Yeah, that would be inconspicuous. Open it."

Giving me a wounded look, he fitted the key in the lock and turned it. It yielded with a tiny click and the door inched open. A mechanical hum from down the hall told me the elevator was returning and I pushed Vitaly into the room and closed the door.

"His partner is not shoving Remington," Vitaly complained.

"Ssh." The room's utter darkness told me the draperies were still closed, so I slid my hand up the wall to find the switch, confident the light wouldn't be seen from the parking lot. My eyes flinched closed against the light's glare and I blinked them open to a scene of utter chaos.

"My graciousness," Vitaly said.

That was an understatement. The room looked like a tornado had swept through. The bedclothes were jumbled on the floor and the closet's contents were strewn atop them and on the furniture. File folders that had been neatly piled on the desk were now on the floor, their contents scattered. All the dresser and desk drawers hung open and empty. Even the microwave oven and freezer doors were open and a wave of cold air wafted from the kitchenette. The laptop was gone.

"What a mess," I murmured, wondering if the police could possibly have wreaked this havoc in their search. I didn't think it likely, but if not them, then who? Thieves, maybe? That didn't seem likely, either—the timing was too coincidental.

"Someones has had the idea like us," Vitaly said. He took a step toward the bathroom, nudging a drift of papers aside with his foot. "What are we looking for?"

Good question. I'd had a vague hope that some clue or piece of information would leap out at us, practically shouting, "This is why Tessa was killed." I thought about her meeting with Li'l Boni, and her documentary. "Something about her current projects," I said. "Notes, a date book. Anything that would tell us what she was working on and who she might have been meeting." I suddenly wondered if she'd filmed any of her interviews. I hadn't thought to ask Li'l Boni if she'd recorded their conversation. I headed toward the kitchen, scanning for a video camera, but didn't see one. I'd ask Zane if Tessa used one. If so, maybe the police had confiscated it. Or maybe the person or persons who had ransacked the room ahead of us had made off with it.

The kitchen held nothing of interest. The open fridge displayed a couple of yogurts, some baby carrots, and four diet sodas. The freezer held nothing but a tray of tiny ice cubes, the kind that melted within seconds of putting them in a glass of water. Cupboards and drawers held a bare minimum of plates, glasses, and silverware. No papers. No camera. I trod on a piece of paper and my foot slipped. Catching myself with a hand on the fridge, I bent to pick up the page.

I found myself staring at Calista Marques' birth certificate. It had probably drifted in here when whoever searched the place upended all of Tessa's files. Wondering if Tessa had done research this detailed on all of *Blisters*' contestants, I noticed Calista and my mom shared a birthday. Different years, of course. Huh. Small world. I set the page on the counter.

Vitaly emerged from the bathroom, saying, "Nothing but makeups and the shampoos smelling like grapefruits." He wrinkled his nose. "I will checking the closet."

I was only half listening. Something about the kitchenette bothered me. The ice cubes! If the freezer door had been hanging open for hours or days, shouldn't they have melted? We'd assumed the intruder had come and gone, but— "Vitaly!"

He spun and looked a question at me. I beckoned him closer, then pointed at the closet door, the only closed door or drawer in the apartment. "I think there's someone in there," I whispered, standing on tiptoe to speak directly into his ear.

Vitaly's eyes got big. *"Da?"*

"We need to get out of here and call the police."

"But then he might gettings away."

I motioned frantically for him to keep his voice down, and then chopped my hand toward the door we'd come in. We could discuss how to keep the break-in artist from escaping when we were safely out of the apartment. We tiptoed single file toward the door, but as we drew level with the closet door, it burst open, clipping Vitaly's shoulder. A tall, bulky figure bulled his way out and lunged for the door.

"Yow." Vitaly reeled back, clapping a hand to his shoulder. "Is just like Remington Steele!"

Instinctively, I stuck out a foot and the fleeing figure tripped and fell forward, landing heavily on his knees. Before he could scramble up, Vitaly pounced on him. I whipped out my phone and started to dial 911.

"You might not want to do that." The man's voice was muffled from where Vitaly had his face pushed into the carpet. "How are you going to explain being in Tessa's apartment?"

The voice was familiar. Vitaly let up on the pressure and the man turned his head to look at me. I gasped. Mickey Hazzard. I regained my composure. "Vitaly and I were walking past the apartment, on our way to visit ... Phoebe, and we noticed the door was open. We came in and found you burgling the place."

"Is good story," Vitaly said, nodding his approval.

"I'm not a burglar," Hazzard objected. "The place looked like this when I got here. I hadn't been here more than a minute when I heard you guys in the hall and shut myself in the closet."

I gave him a disbelieving look and finished dialing. The emergency operator wanted me to stay on the line, but I hung up after giving her the details and suggesting she let Detective Lissy know.

"What was you lookings for?" Vitaly asked, easing himself off Hazzard so the man could sit up.

"None of your damned business."

I considered him. The way his mouth turned down at the corners, I knew he wasn't going to answer. Was it possible he was telling the truth? "If you didn't make this mess, who did? And what were they looking for?"

Hazzard stayed mulishly silent, refusing to speculate. He didn't make any move to get away, perhaps figuring that it was two against one, or realizing that it was fruitless since we knew who he was. It was ten minutes before two uniformed officers showed up, guns drawn, and ordered all three of us to show our hands. Before Vitaly or I could say anything, Hazzard spoke. "Thank goodness you're here, officers. I'm staying in this hotel and was walking past this room when I noticed the door was open. My poor friend Tessa was killed last week and I peeked in, wondering who could be in her apartment. I found these two ransacking the place."

I glared at him, outraged, and he smirked, smugly pleased about having stolen my story.

"He is lyings," Vitaly said, waving his hands in a way that made one of the officers caution him to hold still.

The other officer, a man younger than me, looked from Hazzard to me and Vitaly, clearly uncertain what to do. "Maybe we should take them all down to the station," he suggested to his partner. "Sort it out there."

In silent agreement, the taller cop motioned us toward the door.

"This is not happenings to Remington Steele," Vitaly said sadly.

* * *

Detective Lissy and I faced off in an interview room two hours later. It was full dark now, past nine o'clock, and Lissy was clearly peeved at having his evening interrupted. I hoped his peevishness wouldn't erupt into a full-blown Lissy-fit. I was equally edgy: worried about Vitaly, tired, thirsty, and aware that I was on thin ice legally. If Lissy chose to believe Hazzard over Vitaly and me, we were in deep trouble. I was especially concerned about Vitaly since I didn't know what would happen to his legal immigrant status if he got convicted of breaking and entering.

"Ms. Graysin, why does it feel like you're meddling in my case again?" Detective Lissy asked, his tone more weary than aggressive. He removed his black-framed glasses and polished the lenses with a small cloth he pulled from his pocket. Despite the late hour, he was dressed as always in a spotless suit, shirt, and tie. If I hadn't seen him once at a Little League game, I'd have been convinced he didn't own any other clothes.

"Hazzard was in the room when—" I started hotly.

Lissy interrupted me with an upheld hand. "The desk clerk—a university kid—admits that Hazzard gave him two hundred dollars for the key to Tessa King's room."

Relief made me limp. "Well." I couldn't think of anything else to say. "Can Vitaly and I go then?"

"We released Mr. Voloshin an hour ago," Lissy said.

"Oh. That's good." I gazed at him uncertainly.

"Don't think I believe that story about you and Voloshin happening to walk by and finding the door open."

I kept my mouth shut.

"Since the door wasn't damaged and I don't think you've got a set of picklocks, where'd you get the key?"

I considered saying "What key?" but then caved in the face of his certainty. "Top of the doorjamb. I knew it was there because when Zane and I checked on Tessa before we knew she was killed, that's where he got it."

Lissy held out his hand. I dug the key out of my pocket and placed it in his palm.

"Thank you. Now, you say Ms. King was in the habit of keeping a key on the lintel and this was common knowledge?"

"I don't know how common. Zane knew. Probably others." Even though I was mildly annoyed with Zane for being out with my sister while I was being grilled at the police station, I didn't want him arrested.

"So any number of persons could have been through that apartment in the week since her death," Lissy mused, thinking aloud.

I suddenly remembered I'd never told him about the brick. We'd been interrupted last time I was here ... something about a victim waking up. "I've been meaning to tell you ..." I started, and proceeded to fill him in about the brick and the note.

He listened politely and I couldn't read his thoughts. "Do you have the note?"

"Not on me. It's at home."

"I'll want to see it."

I nodded. A burst of masculine laughter came from the hall, followed almost immediately by the scent of popcorn. My tummy rumbled embarrassingly and I realized I was starving.

"If, as you say, this brick came through your window last Saturday, why didn't you tell me sooner?" The look he bent on me was frankly skeptical.

"I was going to," I said, half rising, "but your partner

or someone came in and you rushed off to the hospital to interview someone."

"Ah, yes. Mr. Figueroa." Lissy steepled his fingers. "Unfortunately, although he regained consciousness, all he could remember was that it was a Dodge that hit him."

I was uninterested in Lissy's difficulties with other cases. "Don't you see what the note means?" I said, reclaiming his attention. "It means someone involved with the show killed Tessa. No one else knows I'm investigating her death."

"Funny," Lissy said in an unamused voice. "And here I thought it was my job to investigate her death."

"Well, yes," I admitted, "but I was asking a few questions—"

"As you're wont to do."

"—because the papers are making a big deal out of my studio being involved with—associated with—three murders. That's not fair."

"Life isn't—"

"Oh, spare me." I pushed to my feet and glared at him. "Can I go?"

He made a sweeping gesture toward the door. "Please."

I made a point of walking gracefully and unhurriedly to the door, even though I felt like running pell-mell for the exit. I had entered the hall but was still within earshot when he called, "Don't forget to bring in that note you said you got."

Said I got? Grrr. My graceful walk turned to stomping and I resolved to fax him the note the moment I got home so it would be waiting for him when he arrived in the morning. I occupied myself on the taxi ride home with composing a few scathing lines to accompany the note.

It wasn't until I was in bed half an hour later, note already faxed to Detective Lissy, in that relaxed state halfway between waking and sleeping, that my brain spit out a number it must have been working on since I saw Calista's birth certificate at the apartment. I sat up. Given the year on the certificate, Calista Marques was no dewy, seventeen-year-old ingénue—she was twenty-three.

Chapter 21

Twenty-three, twenty-three, twenty-three. The number bounced in my head Tuesday morning. I'd mulled it over last night and realized Calista must have lied about her age to get the Disney role that shot her to fame. Being sub-twenty was her ticket to playing Lisa for a couple more years. I found it somewhat ironic that Zane was doing all he could to convince directors to give him meaty adult roles while Calista was apparently doing the opposite. Hollywood: a topsy-turvy place. Did Calista know Tessa was in on her secret? Could she have killed to protect her secret and her Disney career? Only one way to find out.

I knew Calista started each day with a run along the Potomac. She'd mentioned it when Vitaly commented on how fit she was. Today, she was getting a running partner whether she wanted one or not. Jogging wasn't really my thing—it's hard on my knees, which get enough abuse from dancing—but I dug out my Nikes and headed toward the river shortly before six. I was by no means the only exerciser out and about this early and I exchanged greetings with a handful of runners, dog walkers, and Rollerbladers before reaching the river.

Mist hung over the water even though the day was clear. A sense of peace settled on me as I looked over the Potomac. It stretched like a sheet of gray-green glass today, seemingly frozen, although I knew currents surged beneath the surface. I marched in place, letting the river work its magic, unknot muscles still tight from the break-in and visit to the police department. I should get down here more often. Twenty or more walkers and joggers passed me before I spotted a woman running with a high knee action, landing on her toes. Sunglasses covered her eyes and she had her dark hair pulled back in a ponytail that swished from beneath a baseball cap. A shapeless gray T-shirt drooped to midthigh, hiding most of her figure. I didn't recognize Calista Marques until she had passed me; not the most dedicated paparazzo would have IDed her in that getup.

I fell in beside her, soon realizing that her pace was deceptively fast. "Hey, Calista," I said.

She turned her head, startled. "Oh. Hi, Stacy. I didn't know you were a runner." She didn't sound thrilled to have a running buddy, but she didn't tell me to get lost either.

"Since high school," I said. If she took that to mean I was on the cross-country team, that was fine by me. In reality, I'd run only one semester as a sophomore, in a required PE class, where Coach Zelvetore had insisted we run a sub-thirteen-minute mile to get a passing grade. "What about you? Did you run track in high school?"

"I was homeschooled," she said, foiling my plan to ask what year she graduated. "The show, you know."

The sun was beginning to make itself felt and perspiration beaded under my jogging bra. A soaring osprey suddenly dove toward the river and fought for altitude again with his talons sunk into a fish. The sight made me yearn for breakfast; I wanted to get this over with. "So, I happened to see a copy of your birth certificate," I said, eschewing subtle for point-blank, "and it says you're twenty-three, not seventeen."

She turned her head to face me and her brows rose above the rim of her sunglasses. "You *happened* to see? You mean Tessa told you."

Bam. Just like that—the information I was looking for. I felt like letting out a big "Yeah!" but I didn't have enough breath for it. "So . . . you knew Tessa . . . had your birth certificate?" My words came out in gasps.

"Of course. Who do you think gave it to her?"

I stared at her, and tripped over a lone shoe on the path because I wasn't watching where I was going. I didn't fall, but it took me a moment to regain my stride and I had to sprint to catch up with Calista again. "Color me skeptical, but why would you give something like that to Tessa King?"

"It's so not your business," she said, "but I gave it to her to prove my age." She stopped abruptly and swiped the hem of her shirt across her barely damp face. "Look, I don't want to play a dingbat teen for the rest of my life. 'Oh, Daddy, it's *so* not fair. You can't take away my phone just because I got a D,'" she trilled, dropping instantly into character. "Yeah, I'm grateful for the chance Disney gave me, but I'm ready to move on. Unfortunately, my contract runs another two and a half years. And my paycheck is pathetic."

Hm. I suspected her definition of "pathetic" and mine were galaxies apart.

She jogged in place. "I was a virtual unknown—I'd only had two small parts in movies that went straight to video—and they locked me into a long-term contract worth peanuts when they signed me for *It's a Double Life*. I can't get out of it without a huge legal battle that would cost me millions, not to mention the hit to my reputation. But . . . they'll dump me in a hurry when the public finds out my true age." Her lips curving upward, she added, "My tweenage fans won't be able to 'relate' to me anymore. So sad." She gave a mock pout.

"Tessa was going to publicize your actual age?"

Bending at the waist to stretch, she said, "Brilliant, isn't it? *Blisters* will get a huge ratings bump, I'll get 'fired,' and the show will be the perfect platform for me to show viewers that I'm not a kid anymore." She straightened and did a mini bump and grind, looking very adult, indeed. A passing jogger whistled. We both gave him "drop dead" looks. "Tessa—Nigel, now, I guess—is going to 'confront' me with the information next week when I'm scheduled to dance the rumba, and I'm going to dance the hottest, sexiest rumba the FCC censors have ever seen. Pure brilliance."

If she was telling the truth, she didn't seem to have a motive to kill Tessa. Hands on my hips, I surveyed her for a moment, wondering if a woman who had lived a lie for the last ten years was capable of being truthful. Her openness niggled at me. I asked, "Why are you telling me this?"

She shrugged. "Now that Vitaly and I are partners, you'll see us rehearsing our dirty dancing rumba, and it's next week anyway. Just don't tell anyone else before then, okay?"

"What if you get kicked off Saturday night?"

With a secretive smile, she said, "Not going to happen. In fact, I'd say Graysin Motion's chances of winning *Blisters* went up about a thousand percent when I joined your team."

Was she hinting that the fix was in, or was she so conceited that she assumed she'd win the Crystal Slipper? That spurred my competitive instincts and I vowed Zane and I would give her a run for her money. "Whose idea was it to 'out' you on *Blisters*, yours or Tessa's?"

"My agent's, actually." Calista laughed. "She and Tessa shared an apartment when they first came to Hollywood. She knew Tessa would go for it." Glancing at her platinum watch, she said, "Speaking of my agent, I'm having breakfast with her in thirty, so I've got to dash. See you in the studio later."

She ran back the way we'd come and I followed more slowly. Kicking at a pebble, I watched it bounce erratically down the path. I'd come here expecting denials and fear from Calista, but she'd completely turned the tables on me. I felt disgruntled at having my theory so completely blown up. If Calista was telling the truth, she had no reason to murder Tessa. If she wasn't . . . that thought made me wonder where Calista had been the Tuesday night Tessa got killed, and I kicked myself mentally for not asking. It was a good thing I made my living as a dancer and not an investigator.

An hour later, I had to face Zane in the ballroom. Knowing he'd been out with Danielle the night before, and wondering if they'd spent the night together, I found it impossible to behave as usual. I adopted a brisk, nononsense teaching method and knew I was criticizing his dancing more than usual. Midway through the morning, he shook his hair off his face, took a pull from his water bottle, and asked quietly, "Is something wrong, Stacy?"

"Of course not." I brushed past him to get a bottled water from the mini fridge in the bathroom. Returning to the ballroom, I didn't meet his eyes, but pretended to fuss with the CDs atop the stereo cabinet.

"What's got you so tense?"

Without my hearing him, he'd come up behind me and when I turned I found him mere inches away. His nearness flustered me. I leaned back as far as I could, trapped between his broad chest and the stereo. "Tell you later," I said, giving a tiny nod toward Larry. "Let's get back to work."

After a moment of scrutinizing my face, he backed away and we resumed our hustle practice. Since the hustle had originated in the Hispanic communities of New York and Florida, and was a mishmash of mambo, salsa, and swing steps, I'd tried to evoke a Latin feel with my choreography so it wasn't quite the *Saturday Night Fever* vibe many would be expecting. Zane had no trouble with the rock step, but he kept losing contact with me on the side break. We ran through it several times and couldn't help but think about performing it at Club Nitro. I thought it was a little creepy, and definitely in poor taste, to be filming the second show at the last spot anyone saw Tessa alive. It felt a little like dancing on her grave, but all of that only made Nigel more keen on the idea.

The producer came bouncing into the ballroom as Zane and I were wrapping up, papers clutched in his hand. "Saturday night's ratings were our best ever for a kick-off show—we got a thirty-two percent share—and the Google and blog traffic are off the charts." He smiled his sharky smile. "The news this morning has the blogosphere going wild. I was gobsmacked. I knew casting Hazzard was a brilliant move the minute Tessa suggested it."

Zane's brow wrinkled and he wiped the sweat off it with a hand towel. "What news? Did something happen to Mickey?"

"The prat got arrested for breaking into Tessa's apartment last night," Nigel crowed.

He was so wound up I was convinced he'd have been skipping around the ballroom if we weren't there.

"He *what*?"

I pretended to towel my face, hoping my expression didn't betray anything, and praying that Nigel's source, whatever it was, hadn't mentioned me or Vitaly.

"Yeah. There was a paragraph on some news site about him getting taken up by the coppers. My assistant caught it through Google alerts and texted it to me."

"Does this mean he's off the show?" A teensy part of me was prepared to rejoice if Solange lost her partner.

Nigel looked at me as if I were insane. "Are you insane? Off the show? This'll drive millions of viewers to our next broadcast. As long as the coppers don't keep him locked up, he and Solange will close Saturday's show."

"I should have known," I muttered under my breath as Nigel bustled out to do something important and producery. I tried to slip away in his wake, but Zane caught my arm.

"So, tell me what's eating you."

He clearly wasn't going to let me duck his question, so I slumped down against the ballroom wall, and he joined me. We had the place to ourselves now that Nigel and the crew had moved on to one of the other studios. Vitaly and Calista weren't due for another hour. "Vitaly and I were there last night," I said.

"There?"

"At Tessa's. We caught Mickey Hazzard."

"You what? What were you doing at Tessa's?" He inched away from me along the baseboard.

I fed him the lie about me and Vitaly going to see Phoebe and seeing Tessa's door open.

"Phoebe's apartment isn't even on that floor," he said.

Oops. "We were confused." To distract him, I said, "So we ended our evening at the police station. How was your dinner with the director?"

"Great." Zane's face lit up. "Darren invited me to audition for his next picture, said he thinks I'd do well for the part of the assassin."

"That's a compliment?"

He laughed. "That's a potential paycheck. Your sister was great, by the way. Charmed the socks off Darren and his wife."

"You didn't mention Danielle was going with you." I bent over my extended legs to stretch my hamstrings, hiding my face in my knees.

"I figured she would tell you."

I sat up, a bit embarrassed by my cowardice. "It would have been nice to hear it from you," I said, gazing at him straightly.

He stood and pulled me to my feet. "Stacy, I got the call from Darren after the show Saturday night, when Danielle and I were out together. I was excited about meeting with him and mentioned it to Danielle. She said it sounded like fun, that she loved Darren's movies, and I invited her to go with me. There was no more to it than that. It wasn't like I deliberately invited her instead of you; it just fell out that way. Right place, right time. C'mere." He tugged me into his arms and kissed my forehead. "I like Danielle, but I . . . *really* like you."

I let him kiss me, still not totally convinced, but coming around. A scritch of sound by the door made me pull away and look over Zane's shoulder. No one was there, but after a moment I thought I heard the door leading to the outside stairs close.

"What?"

I didn't answer. "Vitaly? Maurice?" I walked to the door and looked down the hall. No one. I wondered if a prospective student had come in . . . sometimes we got walk-ins. I had an itchy feeling between my shoulder blades.

"What?" Zane asked again, catching up with me.

"I thought I heard someone," I said. "Tessa's death, the warning note, the police station last night . . . it's all making me paranoid."

"Just because you're paranoid doesn't mean they're not out to get you," Zane said.

I socked his shoulder. "I'm going to hit the shower."

He nuzzled my neck. "Is that an invitation?"

"Not hardly." I wriggled free, still feeling a bit uncomfortable about his dating both Danielle and me, despite his explanation. "I've got students this afternoon, and you need to run through our hustle routine about a hundred times until you've got the choreography down cold."

He took it with good grace, planting a noisy kiss on my cheek, before slinging his gym bag over his shoulder. "Am I allowed to stop practicing long enough to take you to dinner tonight?" he asked.

"Thanks, but I've got plans." I didn't tell him that my

plans were with Dani, or that I wanted to get her take on their date before deciding whether or not I wanted to see more of him outside the ballroom.

"Later in the week, then." Not waiting for an answer, he smiled in a way that almost made me rethink the shower offer, and left. Only then did I realize I'd forgotten to ask him if Tessa habitually had a videocam with her.

Chapter 22

With twenty minutes to spare between my shower and when my first student would arrive, I called Kevin Mc-Dill in his office, figuring I owed the reporter an update since he'd gotten the autopsy data for me. He growled something into the phone when he answered, and I decided to take it as a greeting.

"I'm having a lovely day, thanks," I said. "How about you?"

"Graysin. I'm on deadline."

"I'll keep it brief." I told him about surveying the spot where Tessa supposedly went in the water, the brick and threatening note, Nigel's reward offer, finding Mickey Hazzard in Tessa's apartment, and my conviction that the killer was somehow associated with *Ballroom with the B-Listers*.

"All very interesting," McDill said, "but I don't smell a story. The bit with the brick has potential, but readers don't get wound up unless there's blood involved. Call me back if someone kneecaps you." He hung up.

I stared at the phone, half annoyed and half amused,

then hung up and skedaddled back to the studio to meet my student; I'd heard him come in while I was on the phone. Calista and Vitaly had arrived and were rehearsing in the ballroom. After forty-five minutes with my student, a heavyset man in his mid-forties who had taken up ballroom dance to lose weight and fallen in love with it (even though he hadn't lost a pound), I returned to my office to work on choreography for another pair I coached.

Calista and Vitaly were still at it three hours later when I left the office to get ready to meet Danielle.

"You must be related to Ivan the Terrible," Calista moaned as I walked past the ballroom. "I should have let Phoebe keep you."

Vitaly responded with a simple, "Again," and I grinned to myself. I kept my fingers crossed that the voters had retained me and Zane, Vitaly and Calista, and Phoebe and her new partner. I guessed that the reality star obsessed with his biceps would go first. He danced like a whirling dervish on speed and was self-absorbed and obnoxious, to boot. Still, his show was hugely popular, so that might translate into viewer votes. I'd seen mediocre but high-profile dancers beat out good dancers on this show in earlier seasons. No one was safe, as Kristen delighted in telling viewers.

Danielle and I had agreed to meet at a restaurant we liked in Shirlington. I got on the Jeff Davis Highway headed north, intending to cut over on Glebe. I was running a little bit late since I'd spent some extra time on my hair and makeup, not because I wanted to outshine Dani—we weren't *competing* or anything—but just because I felt like looking my best. Really. Traffic headed toward the city wasn't too bad, although the southbound lanes were choked. I pushed down on the Beetle's accelerator until I was doing over sixty miles per hour, wanting to make up some time, but a light turned red ahead of me and I tapped on the brake with a muttered, "Drat."

Nothing happened. Thinking my foot must have slid off the pedal, I pressed the brake again, but the car didn't slow. I stomped on it with both feet, almost subconsciously noting my limited options with rising panic. A steady stream of traffic to my right made it impossible for me to slide off onto the shoulder and hope the car halted before plowing into anything. The median to my left was narrow and I was afraid that if I aimed for it, the car would jump it and plunge into the oncoming lane. Not good. I prayed that the light would turn green.

Without my foot on the accelerator, my speed bled off somewhat, but the car was still doing forty as I neared the intersection. The light remained stubbornly red with an intermittent flow of cross traffic in and out of the intersection. A hundred feet away, I saw a teenager start across the street in front of me. Hands tucked into his pockets, he bobbed his head in time to the music apparently blaring through his earbuds as he slouched across the intersection with all the haste of a teenage boy who gets a mild kick out of making cars wait for him, who knows he's the master of the universe and that cars will always stop for him, even when he's crossing against the light. Oh, God, no. I was going to hit him.

I simultaneously leaned on my horn and leaned back as far as I could against my seat, as if the backward pressure would slow the car. *No, no, no . . .*

The boy looked up, maybe because someone yelled,

or maybe because he sensed impending danger. He paused for a fatal second, and I saw his eyes get round. He sprinted. My Beetle slid into the intersection, missing him by a hair. I hardly had time to think a prayer of gratitude, or note the kid's upraised middle finger, before I was in the middle of the intersection. I was going to make it, I thought, willing the car to slow more. I was going to—

Wham! Something slammed into the rear passenger side of the car, whipping my Beetle around until it faced the oncoming traffic, which had stopped now that the light had finally—*finally!*—turned. My left shoulder slammed against the door, hard, and then my head bounced backwards, thunking against the headrest, and the airbag deployed. It was several moments before I realized the car had stopped moving and I was alive. I coughed and felt pains in my chest, arms and neck. The airbag wilted around me and I batted at it, feeling claustrophobic. People appeared at the driver's side door and were opening it. Warm, exhaust-scented air flooded in, and I blinked at the variously concerned and angry faces.

"Are you okay?" "What the hell were you doing?" "You almost killed me!" "Is she drunk?"

The words buzzed around me, intertwining until they made no sense.

"Give her some air," a voice said and the crowd backed away from the door. An ambulance's siren split the air, drawing nearer. Honking horns almost drowned it out.

"I'm okay, I think," I croaked, then coughed again. There was a powdery white residue coating me and floating in the air. Rational thought returned. "The driver who hit me! Is he all right?"

"She's fine," someone said. "She was driving a florist's van and it's barely got a scratch."

Sagging with relief, I didn't even want to think what my precious Beetle looked like. I knew it had more than a scratch. I took a deep breath and felt an ache in my chest. Ow. Maybe I'd broken a rib. Holding on to the steering wheel, I made a stab at swinging my left leg out of the car. With one foot resting on solid ground, I managed to get my right leg out, too, so I was facing the crowd of onlookers. Strangers looked in at me and one man offered me a hand just as an ambulance and a fire truck pulled up and the EMTs came trotting over.

"My brakes didn't work." I know I repeated that phrase upward of fifty times as I spoke to the EMTs (who decided I was bruised and shaken up, but not seriously injured), the florist, the onlookers, my insurance agent (by phone), the tow truck driver, and the police. After my breathalyzer test was negative, the cops began to take me a bit more seriously. When the tow truck driver had my poor Beetle hooked up, one of the officers asked him to take a look underneath it, see if he spotted an obvious mechanical cause for the accident.

The wiry, middle-aged man reappeared in minutes, wiping greasy hands along his overalled thighs. "Sure do," he told the cop. "Someone doesn't like this young lady."

"What's that supposed to mean?" the policeman asked.

The mechanic gave me a look. "The brake line's been sliced clean through. No way it's an accident."

I'd been feeling a bit better, calmer, but at his news I felt faint. The embroidered letters spelling out "Dave" on his chest wavered and I blinked. "Someone cut my brake line? I could've killed someone." Images of the teen dashing across the street would stay with me forever.

"Or been killed." The cop eyed me, a hint of suspicion in his gaze again, clearly wondering what I'd done that would make someone want to kill me.

I took several deep breaths through my nose, trying to calm myself. The air smelled of roses and carnations. Even though the florist had long departed, the flowers that had fallen from the back of her van still littered the street, most of them now crushed by the traffic siphoning by as a cop directed traffic through the intersection. One white rosebud lay at my feet, slightly bruised. I stooped to pick it up and cradled it in my hands. Lifting my cupped hands to my nose, I sniffed. The delicate scent made me want to cry and I blinked rapidly.

I signed some forms for the police and Dave, and took the card he offered, which told me where my car would be. "Can I go now?"

Before the officer could answer, a voice hailed me from the far side of the street. "Stacy!"

I looked over to see Danielle hurrying toward me, weaving her way through the slowly moving traffic, red curls bouncing, worry on her face. I'd called her as soon as I got my wits about me. I couldn't hold the tears back any longer. They streamed down my face, making me snuffle. Danielle wrapped her arms around me in a way that hurt and comforted at the same time.

"Are you okay?" she asked.

I blotted my eyes and blew my nose. "No permanent damage," I said, letting her lead me to her car.

"I can't believe they didn't take you to a hospital." She

opened the passenger side door for me and waited patiently while I maneuvered myself onto the seat with lots of winces and groans.

"I refused to go."

She slammed the door harder than necessary.

Chapter 23

Danielle insisted on taking me back to her apartment for the night after I told her what happened. "I'm not leaving you alone with a homicidal maniac trying to do away with you," she said. "Besides, someone should check on you tonight, make sure you don't have a concussion or something." She held four fingers in front of my face and steered with one hand. "How many fingers am I holding up?"

"Twelve."

"Ha-ha. Very funny." She shot me a look. "Any idea who would want to kill you?"

We pulled into her parking lot before I could answer, and what with her helping me into the condo, running me a hot bath, easing me out of my clothes, and gasping at the seat belt bruise running diagonally across my chest, it was forty-five minutes before I got around to answering.

"Same person who lobbed a brick through my window," I said, relaxing in the steaming bathtub, letting Danielle's eucalyptus-and-mint-scented bath oil soak the pain out of my abused body. She sat in the hall outside the small bathroom, wanting to be nearby in case I needed help or passed out. She was a good sister.

"And that would be . . . ?"

"Probably whoever killed Tessa."

There was silence for a moment from the hall. "Oh, great," she finally said. "You've managed to piss off a homicidal maniac."

"Would you stop saying that? There's no homicidal maniac running around." At least, I didn't think there was. The body count seemed a bit low for that, although if I ended up dead, that would double it.

Feeling somewhat looser, although still achy, I maneuvered myself out of the tub, dried off, and wrapped myself in the fluffy robe Danielle had draped over the toilet. Tan. I shook my head. My sister's whole wardrobe consisted of tans, beiges, and grays, "neutral" colors that wouldn't offend anyone. I'd rather go nude than wear beige.

"I'm getting you a green robe for your birthday," I announced as I tied the sash and emerged from the bathroom. "It'll go great with your hair."

She looked at me with disbelief. "Someone tries to kill you and you're critiquing my wardrobe?"

I shrugged and my shoulder twinged. "Ow."

She gave me a "serves you right" look. "Are you hungry?"

I realized I was. It was now almost nine o'clock and we'd never made it to the restaurant. I sat at the kitchen counter, drinking a glass of white wine, while Dani heated some frozen burritos in the microwave. I was almost hungry enough to eat them without mentally counting the fat grams and calories in each one. They went surprisingly well with the wine. When Dani got out a box of brownie mix and dumped it into a bowl, I didn't say a word about my diet or needing to keep my weight down so Vitaly could lift me; I passed her the egg carton.

With the aroma of baking brownies drifting from the oven, Dani and I moved into her living room. "The wallpaper looks good." I noticed the photo of her and Coop that used to sit on the bookcase next to a photo of Danielle and me was gone.

She shot me a look to see if I was being snippy. "Thanks."

"I'm sorry." I didn't need to spell out for what.

"Me, too."

We smiled mistily at each other and then looked away in embarrassment. "So," Danielle said briskly, "who killed Tessa and why, and why is he or she trying to kill you?"

We batted around theories for half an hour, until the timer dinged, but didn't arrive at any answers. By the time we'd each eaten two warm brownies with glasses of cold milk, Danielle knew everything I did about *Blisters'* cast, Phoebe's and my conversation with Li'l Boni, Mickey Hazzard breaking into Tessa's apartment, and anything else I could think of.

"We need to figure out who Tessa drove off with," I said, setting my plate on an end table, "but I don't know how to do that. Obviously, no one's going to admit to it. It could be any of the men from *Blisters*—Zane, Mickey, Larry, other crew members—"

"What about Nigel? From what Zane says, he seems like a real piece of work."

I nodded. "Oh, he is, but he wasn't at Club Nitro that night."

"So he says." Dani infused the words with sinister meaning.

I thought about it. "Well, no one saw him. He said he was eating dinner with a friend."

"Doesn't mean he couldn't have come by the club after dinner and picked up Tessa, either by prior arrangement or not."

"Why would he want to kill Tessa?"

Dani shrugged. "Maybe they had a torrid affair and he didn't like it when she dumped him."

"He told me they were lovers." Of course, the same rationale might apply to Zane. I pushed the thought away and certainly didn't say it aloud.

My sister nodded as if that were proof. "Or, she was his partner—she probably knew where all his bodies were buried, so to speak. Did you know he was almost indicted for that death on *Race around the World*? Zane told me. When that contestant fell from the balloon, there were all sorts of accusations that the producers— Nigel and some other guy—hadn't paid enough attention to safety, that they'd encouraged the guy to do dangerous stunts, even though he was so not qualified for them. His wife sued them and they gave her a bunch of money to settle out of court, Zane heard."

I wasn't discounting the possibility that Tessa might have known things about Nigel he'd rather keep quiet, but since there was no evidence he was even at the club, I wanted to concentrate on more likely suspects. Even as I tried to articulate why I thought Kristen might have wanted to kill Tessa, I yawned. Seeing it, Danielle sprang up. "Bedtime for you."

I didn't have the energy to object. Giving her a long

hug in the hallway outside the guest bedroom, I said, "Thanks, Little."

"Anytime, Big."

Danielle was long gone to work by the time I awoke in the morning. A glance at her kitchen clock told me I should've been long gone, too. My muscles had stiffened up overnight and shrieked as I forced my arms and legs into the clothes I'd worn yesterday. I found some ibuprofen in Danielle's medicine cabinet, took three of them with a big glass of juice, and hurried outside, only then realizing I had no transportation. I stared around the parking lot with frustration for a moment, before pulling out my cell phone to call Maurice.

He arrived in record time, and drove me to the rental car office, exclaiming at the bruise that had bloomed on my temple overnight from where my head had banged against the car door. "My dear Anastasia! Will you be able to dance?"

I gave him a wry smile, not a bit offended at the question. It was what any dancer would ask. "I think so," I said. "No bones broken or internal organs punctured—just bruised and stiff and achy."

He waited until the agency assigned me a car and then said he would see me at the studio. "Four of my students are coming in," he said. "We'll use the small studio to keep out of your way."

"Don't worry; they're not filming us today. I think Nigel and his posse are over at Take the Lead, harassing Solange and Marco Ingelido and their partners. We get a break, although Zane and I will be practicing, of course."

As I said the words, I realized that Danielle and I

had steered clear of talking about Zane last night and I still had no idea what had happened on their date and how she really felt about him. I drove very slowly and carefully to Graysin Motion, earning honks from annoyed motorists. Leaving the rental car in my carport where it looked like a usurper, I went in through the kitchen and brushed my teeth and hair and made a pot of coffee before heading upstairs with my brimming mug.

Tav was sitting at his desk when I came into the office and he sprang up. "My God, Stacy, where have you been?"

There were equal parts anger and concern in his voice and I gave him an uncertain look. "I—"

Noticing the bruise on my temple, he came over and grabbed my upper arms, making me wince and jolt coffee onto my shirt. "Ow. Now look what you've done."

Tav studied my face, and then brushed aside the collar of my shirt to peer at the livid bruise that peeked from the neckline. "What happened to you? I know you were with Savage. If I thought he—"

"I wasn't with Zane! What's gotten into you?" I wrenched myself away and bit my lip with pain. I doubled over for a moment, setting my coffee cup on the floor before I could spill it again. When I caught my breath, I raised my head and peered at him through the hair that was falling over my face. "I was in an accident."

"*Por Díos*, Stacy. Sit down."

All tenderness now, he led me to the love seat, accidentally kicking over my coffee. "*Mierda.*"

I'd never heard him cuss and I started to giggle, despite the pain and my confusion over his behavior.

"I will be right back." He hurried out and returned

with paper towels from the bathroom, using them to sop up the coffee. When he had done that, and fetched me another cup of coffee from downstairs, he sat beside me. "Tell me."

I gave him the short version, finishing with, "The tow truck driver says the brake line was cut. I expect to hear from Detective Lissy later today."

"Cut!" Concern etched his handsome face. He smacked his fist onto his thigh. "This is because you are asking questions about Tessa King's death. You must stop."

"But the studio—"

"The studio is not worth your life. If you do not promise me you will stop investigating, I cannot continue as your partner."

I gaped at him. "But—"

"So you would lose the studio anyway, or have to share it with someone like that Solange."

She had tried to buy Rafe's half of the studio after his death and only Tav's intervention had saved me from having to become partners with her or give up Graysin Motion entirely. "I'm only trying to earn the reward so we can pay off the taxes."

"Really?"

I furrowed my brow. What did he mean by that? "Yes, really. You wouldn't—"

He looked implacable, full lips drawn into a thin line, dark eyes fixed on mine. "If it is the only way to keep you from getting killed, then, yes, I would."

"What about Rafe's legacy?" I said, hoping that playing the half brother card would change his mind.

"I did not take on this partnership because of Rafe," he said. "I did it because of you, because I could see how much the studio meant to you, and because—" He cut himself off and got up and walked to his desk, standing with his back to me.

I was too angry at his tactics to appreciate his reasoning. "You're not being fair."

"I will not stand by and let you get killed."

Something in his voice gave me pause. "Why did you think I was with Zane last night?" I asked finally.

Tav turned around, crossing his arms over his chest. "I saw you kissing him yesterday."

I winced. It had been Tav I heard. "A kiss is a long way from . . ."

"But you like him." He made it a statement.

"I like lots of people."

"Please. Do not be *poco sincero*—disingenuous, Stacy."

Biting my lip, I said, "Fine. I like him, but I'm not in love with him. I hardly know him. It's none of your business who I date, any more than it's Vitaly's or Maurice's or . . . or Hoover's!" I felt close to tears and I willed them back, knowing they were the product of pain, the lingering shock of the crash, and confusion. How had we gone from his forbidding me to investigate to an argument about my love life? "There hasn't been anyone since Rafe," I whispered.

Tav came back to where I sat and his hand caressed my hair briefly. I closed my eyes. "I will give you my brother's share of the studio; you will own it outright. But do not ask me to stay and watch you encourage a murderer to kill you. I cannot do it." The anger had left his voice, and now I heard only finality and a trace of sadness.

I wanted to cry out that I didn't want him to give me

his share of the studio, that he couldn't afford to do it, that I'd quit investigating, that Zane didn't mean anything to me. Not a word had left my lips by the time he walked out of the office, closing the door quietly. I hunched over and sobbed.

Chapter 24

By the time Zane, Maurice, Vitaly, and Calista arrived, more or less simultaneously, I had cried myself out and hobbled to the bathroom after using all the tissues in my office. Blowing my nose on a piece of toilet paper, I examined my face in the mirror: red, swollen eyes; red, raw nose; bruises; ratty hair. I sniffed. If I belonged on any reality show, it was *Survivor* since I looked like someone who'd been living in a lean-to on a tropical island for a month, eating ants, injuring myself doing outrageous challenges, and fighting with the other obsessive nuts vying for a million dollars. My expression suggested I'd just been booted off the show. I tried a smile. It looked pitiful. Hearing the outer door open, I hurriedly blew my nose again, splashed cold water on my face, and prepared to tell everyone I looked this way because of the crash.

Maurice had filled everyone in by the time I emerged so I didn't have to go through the story again—thankfully. "Can you dance?" Vitaly said, at the same time Zane said, "You can't dance."

"Of course I can dance," I said. "I finished a competition with a broken toe once when I was sixteen. We were named Rising Stars at the end of it. This is nothing."

Zane eyed me doubtfully. Calista looked up from her texting and said, "You need a hot stone massage."

"A massage is a good idea," Maurice seconded. "Wait until after I'm done with Thelma and I will drive you to my therapist. She has magic fingers."

"Don't forget our 'out and about' jaunt with Kristen and the cameras this afternoon," Zane said. "Nigel asked me to remind you. We're all going this time."

Too weary to argue any further, I let them talk me into going downstairs to rest until Maurice finished with his student. I could faintly hear the music and footsteps coming through the floor and I felt guilty about not practicing with Zane, but not guilty enough to drag myself back up there. I guess I fell asleep, because the next thing I knew Maurice was knocking on the door.

After an hour on the massage table, and several more painkillers, I felt almost human. I thanked Maurice profusely when he dropped me back at my house. Turning to go inside, I heard a car door clunk shut and saw a man approaching me. Detective Lissy. Rather than open the door, I took a step toward him, hoping that I wouldn't have to invite him in. The breeze toyed with a wisp of his comb-over, but otherwise he was as precise as ever. The sun reflecting up off his polished shoes made my eyes hurt. He stopped three feet away and studied me.

"I heard about the accident, Ms. Graysin. How are you feeling?"

"Not too bad."

He nodded. "I'm glad to hear it."

He seemed sincere and I relented, unlocking the door to let us in. It was too hot to stand on the sidewalk in the baking sun. "What can I do for you?" I asked. I settled on my new chair by the parlor window and nudged the ottoman toward Lissy with one foot since it was the only other seating surface in the room. He remained standing.

"The report said your brakes were tampered with. When did you last drive your car? Who had the opportunity to cut the brake line?"

For answer, I pushed myself out of the chair and led him through the kitchen and out the back door to my carport. I pointed toward the rental car. "That's where I keep my car," I said. "I don't have a garage or anything, so anyone could have gotten to it. I keep the car locked, but . . ." That wouldn't stop someone from crawling underneath it and sabotaging it. I tried to think when I'd last driven it. "I think I last drove it on Monday, when I came to see you."

Lissy looked dissatisfied. "This is Wednesday, so the saboteur had a wide window of opportunity: Monday afternoon, Monday night, and all day yesterday. My money's on Monday night."

"I didn't hear anything."

"Cutting a brake line is not a difficult or noisy task." He strolled past the carport and looked up and down the alley. I knew there wasn't much to see: garbage cans, the openings to my neighbors' carports or garages, a few scraggly plants, and a big Dumpster being used for the trash from the last house on the left's renovation. "We'll canvass the neighbors," Lissy said, not sounding like he thought it would do much good. "Got to cover all the bases."

"Thanks."

He eyed me consideringly. "I never know if telling you to lay off is going to have an impact, or make you try harder, Ms. Graysin, but I'll say it anyway: lay off this case. You've poked a hornet's nest and gotten stung. I don't need your help. We're making progress and I'm confident we'll make an arrest before long."

"Really?" That was good news, if true. "Who?"

"All in due time, Ms. Graysin. All in due time."

I watched his back as he made his way around the side of the house and back to his car. I wanted to believe he had a viable suspect for Tessa's murder, but his "all in due time" hadn't carried the ring of conviction, no pun intended.

I returned to the house, downed a glass of water, and mounted the interior stairs to the studio. My muscles barely twinged as I climbed and I felt encouraged. Nigel pounced on me as soon as I reached the top.

"There you are, luv," he said. "Good God, your face! They told me you'd had an accident, but I had no idea. What a pity the camera wasn't there. Ariel!"

The young redhead appeared and scanned my face with a professional eye. "Nothing a little foundation and powder won't cover." She led me into the bathroom and worked for ten minutes to cover the bruise on my temple and the top of the one across my chest. "Wear something a little higher cut and that won't show at all," she said, giving me a final dusting with loose powder.

I peeked down toward my cleavage. "I don't own any-thing higher cut." If I'd been thinking, I'd have borrowed something from Danielle.

Ariel laughed. "I'm sure we can dig up a shrug some-where. You're going to the church this afternoon, right?"

"Beats me."

She nodded, curls bobbing. "Some church where George Washington used to attend services. So it's appropriate for you to be covered up anyway."

Even though Christ Church was only a few blocks away, on N. Washington, we loaded into the vans again. Kristen Lee was already on board, her light blond hair French braided, big glasses covering her eyes. She stared pointedly out the window as Ariel, Larry, and I clambered up, and the tote bag on the seat beside her made it clear she didn't want to chat. I sat behind her, next to Larry, and Ariel sat across the aisle. Nigel drove himself, and the other cast members were meeting us there, coming from their apartments or studios or homes.

"I'm glad you weren't hurt too bad," Larry said as the van lurched off. His voice had a soft burr that suggested he was from the Midwest.

"Thanks." He was an ordinary-looking guy; you wouldn't notice him if you passed him in a grocery store or stood in line behind him at the bank. Soft brown hair matched the overgrown beard that partially disguised a long jaw. I felt a little embarrassed about not having had an actual conversation with him, despite the fact that I'd seen him almost every day for more than three weeks. "How long have you been a cameraman?"

"Ever since I figured out that I enjoyed being behind the camera better than in front of it." His beard mostly hid a smile. "I was in all the high school plays back in Illinois, and I went off to school intending to study acting, but then my folks gave me a videocam for Christmas my freshman year, and I was hooked. Said good-bye to acting, and went to film school. I linked up with Nigel shortly after graduation and I've been working on his projects pretty steadily ever since."

The van jolted to a stop at a light and I grabbed for the back of the seat in front of me. "Any plans for directing some day, or producing your own show?"

"Maybe." Larry grimaced. "You've got to be a wheeler-dealer, be able to get in good with the money types to produce, and that's not really my thing. I'm happy with this gig. Nigel might be a little high-strung, but he's loyal to his crew."

"What about Tessa?"

Larry's face closed down and he shifted on the bench seat. "She had a lot of talent. Knew how to get reactions from people. Nigel—he gets a combustible mix of folks together and lets nature take its course, like a chemistry experiment. Tessa—she was better at coaxing a particular reaction from someone, getting them to say things they didn't want to say on camera. She'd plant a seed early on and then three days, a week, later it would bloom. Sometimes like a damned 'Jack and the Beanstalk' beanstalk. I saw her go to work on Hazzard's wife for *Pastors of Hypocrisy*." He clicked his tongue in a little *tch* of admiration. "She had a gift.

"What about you? How'd you get into ballroom dancing?"

I answered Larry's question with half my mind, while the other half wondered if Mickey Hazzard, and potentially many others, might not have described Tessa's gift as a trick or a curse.

The van stopped at Christ Church and we piled out. All the dancers, the pros and the b-listers, gaggled on the sidewalk, staring at the brick building with its white trim and tiered-wedding-cake-looking steeple. Mickey Hazzard was rounding everyone up like he was in charge. My surprise must have shown because Nigel said, "It *is* a

church, and he's a padre. Who better to guide our viewers through the church than a man of God?" He flashed
his sharky grin and moved away to clap Mickey on the
shoulder.

Larry went into camera-guy mode and we all moved
into the church. The interior was simple, without the
kind of ornate decorations or stained glass windows I'd
seen in the cathedrals I'd visited in England when I was
at Blackpool for the Dance Festival; it was a peaceful,
light-filled space. The pews were painted white and
looked like narrow stalls; they actually had little doors
on either end. Red carpets added the only colorful note
since the many-paned windows were clear glass, not
stained. George Washington's family pew was near the
front, on the left-hand side. As I listened to Mickey talk
about the church's history, I let my gaze rest on each of
the people gathered round. It came to me with a start
that I didn't want any of these people, anyone associated
with *Blisters*, to be guilty of killing Tessa. I didn't like
Nigel, but I sort of admired his single-minded dedication
to the show. And Kristen, even though she was snippy
and standoffish, was a woman over forty fighting to survive in an industry that worshipped at the altar of youth.
(I couldn't help the church metaphors; the surroundings
were affecting me.) As for Mickey . . . well, the way he
talked about the church and the Founding Fathers' be-
liefs made me think he was sincere in his faith, even if
he'd screwed up big time. Maybe he was just a good actor, I told myself. Zane, Phoebe, Calista, Nanette, the
others . . . no one came across as a killer and I *liked* most
of them.

I'd liked the woman who killed Corinne Blakely, too,
and I thought for a moment about how that had turned

out. No real justice, only sadness. It gave me pause. Maybe poking into this case wasn't a good idea, and not only because I'd clearly worried someone enough that he or she was warning me off, or because it was creating a rift between me and Tav. It might not be a good idea because I might not like what I uncovered. I worried that around in my mind for a few minutes, missing much of what Mickey was saying as we traipsed up the main aisle and examined the pews. But the alternative was worse: letting a killer get away wasn't right, either. I didn't need to take on the responsibility, however. I could let the police handle it, as Detective Lissy was always on me to do.

I had an in that the police didn't, though. I spent hours every day with these people, overheard their conversations, talked to them, danced with them. I couldn't get away from the fact that I was in a much better position to pick up on an inconsistency or a lie than Lissy and his team were. Did the fact that it wasn't, strictly speaking, my job absolve me from responsibility? And the reward money would be hugely helpful to the studio. I sucked on my lower lip, then realized I was ruining Ariel's makeup job and stopped. I glanced around and saw that the cameras weren't pointed my way. Sidling closer to Solange, who stood a few feet away looking like she'd rather be at the dentist, I said, "I didn't know I was signing up for this when I agreed to be on the show."

She stifled a laugh and said, without her usual rancor, "Me, either. He goes on like this all the time, you know. I'm trying to get him to stiffen his knees for the Latin dances and he's trying to convert me. 'Have you accepted Jesus as your personal savior?' 'When was the last time you went to church?' I finally told him I was a Wiccan to get him to leave off."

"Are you?"

She gave me a scornful look. "Of course not. It didn't work anyway; he redoubled his efforts. Doesn't want me to go to hell, he says."

I snorted a laugh and Nigel turned to glare at us. Solange and I bent our heads to hide our expressions, like two schoolgirls caught passing notes in class, and I found myself not quite hating her for a moment, which was ridiculous after what she'd done to me. Must be the church.

"I guess Zane is helping you get over Rafe?" she said with a knowing look.

I went back to hating her. "I don't know what you mean."

"Right. I saw that photo in the newspaper."

I didn't bother telling her what had really happened.

"I guess you don't mind sharing."

I frowned. "What's that supposed to mean?" Could Solange know that Zane and Danielle had gone out a couple of times?

"Oh, please. Like you don't know that he and Tessa were an item."

"A long time ago. It's been over for years."

"It didn't look over on the dance floor the night she disappeared. They were going at each other like teenagers at the prom. Pretty convenient for you that Tessa's out of the picture." With a sidelong look to see if her dart had struck home, she sauntered up the aisle to join the rest of the group, which was clustered around a commemorative plaque.

I stood alone, feeling chilled despite the lightweight

sweater the stylist had found for me, and hugged my arms around myself. I was pretty sure she'd more or less accused me of killing Tessa, but I wasn't going to think about it. I might not ever think again. Closing the distance between myself and the other cast members, I pasted a smile on my face for the camera.

Chapter 25

When we finally left the church, Nigel grabbed my elbow and steered me toward his rented sports car. "Ride with me, Stace. I've got a proposition for you."

Not giving me a chance to decline, he all but stuffed me into the passenger seat, trotted around to the driver's side, and zoomed away before the van was half-loaded. He drove fast but well, and I relaxed into the leather embrace of the bucket seat.

"You've got potential," he said, keeping his eyes on the road. "The camera loves you. The viewers love you. Our focus groups show you're especially popular with the eighteen- to forty-four-year-old male demographic, but the females like you, too. Say you'd be fun to meet over coffee."

"I'm flattered," I said, not knowing what else to say or where this was going.

Nigel shot me an approving look. "That's right, luv. I think you've got something this show needs. Not just for this season, but long term."

I crinkled my brow. "What—?"

"We've been talking to Hannah Malik's people, but that's not going to work out. Donny and Marie have other commitments. My team and I were saying just yesterday that having a host who actually knew the ins and outs of ballroom dancing, as it were, might give the show a new zing. How do you feel about giving an audition a whirl?"

He was asking me to host *Ballroom with the B-Listers*? He wanted me in addition to Kristen Lee . . . or instead of her? Before I could ask, his phone played Bono and he picked it up. I hated when people did that.

"Whiteman." There was a pause while he listened, and then he said, "You did? Where?" Another pause. "I'm on my way." He clicked off, tossed the phone into the console, and flipped a U-ey.

I grabbed the door to steady myself and had a flashback to the crash that made cold sweat pop out. After a moment, when we were cruising safely up the George Washington Parkway, I said, "Where are we going?"

"The airport. That was the car agency. They've found Tessa's rental in the parking lot."

"Why'd they call you?"

"The cars are all rented by the production company. It's my name on the paperwork."

"Shouldn't the police know?"

"The rental company already called them. I'm hoping we can beat them there."

"Why?"

"Tessa's computer and papers are production company property. I don't want them impounded or read by Old Bill."

The car sped up until we were zipping past the other traffic. We swung onto the curving exit that led to Reagan Airport and Nigel barely slowed. When the parking structure came in view, he was forced to hit the brakes and stop to take a ticket. We wound through the dark garage, making our way ever higher, and the cool felt good after the sun's glare. On a floor about midway up, Nigel slowed at the sight of a young man in a jacket with a name tag standing by a Mercedes SLK, identical in all but color to the one I sat in. It was parked nose in to the outer wall. Nigel pulled up behind it, not caring that he would block other cars attempting to reach higher floors.

He bounded out, and approached the nervous young man, giving him a two-handed handshake and a hearty clap on the shoulder. I got out with a grimace of pain. How had Tessa's car ended up in the airport garage when Tessa ended up in the river? There could be only one answer: whoever had killed her had driven the car here, either hoping Tessa's body wouldn't surface and the police would think Tessa had flown somewhere, or to hide it. That was cold.

I approached the green two-seater Mercedes. Nigel was pointing to a broken headlight, which might have happened when the car was parked since the bumper was touching the wall. Addressing the rental agency clerk, he said, "We are not responsible for that damage. This car was stolen. I don't want to see charges for that showing up on my account."

The clerk, who seemed intimidated by Nigel, bobbed his head and made a note. Making a visor of his hand, Nigel peered through the driver's side window and then tried the door. I was about to tell him it would probably be better not to touch anything because the murderer might have left fingerprints, when he held out his hand to the clerk. "The key."

Hesitating, the clerk said in a reedy voice, "The police said—"

"Whose name is on that contract? Bugger the police."

After a moment, the clerk handed over the key fob, caving to Nigel's sheer force of personality. Nigel beeped the remote and swung the door open. I'd been holding my breath, but when nothing and no one tumbled out of the car, I let it go in a long sigh. Despite my misgivings, I inched closer. The car looked empty and emitted a faint scent of pine from the tree-shaped air freshener swinging from the rearview mirror.

Nigel leaned in. "Nothing but a blasted pop can," he said. He thumbed the glove box open and shuffled some papers. "Car contract. Damn." He twisted to inspect the backseat. "Where the hell could her laptop be?"

"Maybe whoever killed her took it. Or threw it in the river," I said.

Nigel backed out of the car and stood, frowning. I didn't get the feeling he was mad at me; it felt like he was lost in his thoughts. I couldn't help wondering what was on the laptop that was so important.

"The trunk?" the clerk suggested in a nervous voice.

"Righto." Nigel beeped the trunk open with the remote. The lid sprang up. "Aah." Nigel's pleased sound told me he'd found the laptop. He lifted it from the trunk and carted it to his car as another vehicle nosed around the corner and slowed. It wasn't a patrol car, but it looked like a police vehicle and I could see lights embedded in the grille as it drew closer.

"Shut the boot!" Nigel barked.

The flustered clerk scurried to the trunk and slammed it closed. The noise reverberated against the concrete floors and walls but was drowned by the roar of a jet taking off. Nigel draped his jacket over the laptop on his backseat. "Mum's the word," he ordered the rental clerk.

Detective Lissy stepped out of his car and approached us, his gaze going from the rental clerk, to me, and lingering on Nigel who now stood, hands in his pockets, near Tessa's car. "This is the car Tessa King was renting?" Detective Lissy directed the question at the clerk who bobbed his head.

"Yes, sir. That is, it's in the name of White King Productions and Mr. Whiteman here, but it was assigned to Ms. King."

"You have the key?"

The clerk sent an anguished glance to Nigel. Nigel dangled the key fob. "Just about to check things out, Detective."

"Good thing you didn't," Lissy grunted, taking the remote from him and beeping it. The locks clunked down and Lissy shot Nigel a look. The clerk gulped.

"I already unlocked it," Nigel said, not one bit perturbed by Lissy's suspicious stare.

Lissy drew on latex gloves and eased the door wider. "An evidence team will be along shortly, but in the meantime . . ." Careful not to touch anything, he examined the interior of the car. "Not much to see," he said, withdrawing. He scanned the empty space behind the seats and then clicked the trunk button. The trunk yawned open, displaying a whole lot of nothing.

I shifted from foot to foot, the knowledge of the laptop weighing heavily on me.

Lissy turned to face us. "I was rather hoping to find her laptop in the car," he said, narrowing his eyes. "Several people mentioned that she had one, but it wasn't recovered in her room."

"Maybe the murderer stole it," Nigel said, "or tossed it in the river."

I almost gasped at hearing him repeat my words.

"Why would he do that?" Lissy asked.

"Why does a murderer do anything?"

The silence stretched between them. I blurted, "It was in the trunk. It's in Nigel's car." I pointed to the backseat.

All three men stared at me—Lissy with surprise, Nigel with fury, and the clerk with the kind of look centurions must have given Christians being ushered into the arena to make nice with lions: recognition of impending doom tinged with admiration. I met Nigel's gaze defiantly. I didn't owe him anything. If he decided to kick me off the show, or make things tough for me and Zane, so be it. My betrayal ensured I wasn't going to get that audition, but I didn't care. I was a dancer. I couldn't see giving up ballroom dancing to read from a telcprompter, model gorgeous gowns (okay, I'd like that part of the job), and interview disappointed or frustrated contestants. I wasn't going to participate in Nigel's theft of the laptop, not when it might give the police a better chance at finding Tessa's murderer.

"Interesting," Lissy said. "How did it come to be there?"

"It's my property," Nigel said, attempting to conceal his chagrin under his usual sangfroid. "It belongs to White King Productions. I have a perfect right to take it."

"It's evidence in a murder case," Lissy responded, banging his palm onto the roof of Nigel's car. "I could arrest you for obstruction."

After a moment where I could practically hear him grinding his teeth, Nigel said, "Fine. Take the blasted computer." He yanked open the door and reached in.

"Don't touch it," Lissy said. He moved Nigel out of the way and picked up the laptop in his gloved hands. "What else did you touch?" he asked, his tone telling Nigel he'd be happy to throw him in jail if he lied.

"The car door. The glove box. That's all."

Lissy raised an eyebrow at me and I gave a small nod to confirm Nigel's account, feeling like the class tattle-tale.

"He made me give him the key," the clerk piped up.

A van and two more cars pulled up and the evidence team members climbed out. After a brief moment's consultation with Detective Lissy, they hauled out their gear and got to work. Telling Nigel that he might have more questions after examining the computer, and thanking me for my help, Lissy left. Nigel vented his spleen by chewing out the car agency clerk in a savage undertone, then slid into his Mercedes, and peeled out. The clerk slunk away to the elevators, and I realized I didn't have a ride home. I wondered if Nigel had left me behind by accident, or if he'd deliberately stranded me. I suspected the latter. If worse came to worst, I could hop on the Metro and catch a cab from the King Street Station. For now, I was fascinated by the evidence collection team.

I'd never been much of one for cop shows or *CSI*, even though my dad watched all of them. If a show didn't have dancing or singing, like *Glee* or *Smash*, I wasn't much interested. Still, it was interesting to watch this team do their thing. The two men and one woman all wore identical coveralls and latex gloves. The woman twirled a brush coated with fingerprint powder, I assumed, around the locks and door handles of both doors and then got to work on the steering wheel, the dash, the glove box, the gear shift—any surface someone might presumably have touched. One of the men used a small vacuum to suck up debris from within the car.

"What are you looking for?" I asked, moving closer. I spoke loudly to be heard over the vacuum's whirring.

He looked up quickly but then refocused on his task. "Hair, fibers, cigarette ash . . . anything the perp might have left behind. We all shed, you know, like cats and dogs. Most perps don't get that. They think if they wear gloves, or wipe away fingerprints, that they're cool. They're shocked when the evidence I collected and analyzed gets them a nickel at Lorton. Stand back, please, so you don't contaminate the scene."

I scooted back a couple of steps, tickled by his pride in his work. "Sorry."

Turning off the vacuum, he eased out of the car and smiled at me, his smile growing bigger as he took in the details of my appearance. Being blond, slim, and stacked has its advantages. "Where do you know Lissy from?" he asked.

I guessed he'd overheard Lissy thanking me. "Oh, here and there," I said, not wanting to admit Lissy had considered me a suspect on more than one occasion. "I've helped out on a couple of his cases." Even if Lissy didn't want to admit it.

"Lissy's one of the best," he said, "even if he's totally anal about evidence and procedure. You know, if you were interested, I could give you a tour of the crime lab sometime, maybe take you to lunch after?"

The photographer's flash went off practically in our faces before I could answer.

Having photographed the car from a distance, the photographer was now crouched beside the front bumper, taking close-ups of the headlight damage. As I

watched, a thought pricked me. There was no glass on
the ground; the headlight had been broken somewhere
else. As I came to that conclusion, the photographer motioned toward the technician I was talking to.

"Hey, Brad . . . this look familiar?"

With a word of apology, Brad left me to inspect the
headlight. From where I stood, I could see that a cres-
cent-shaped piece was missing from the headlight. Brad
studied it for a couple of seconds before snapping his
fingers. "Yeah! The hit-and-run. We recovered a piece of
glass shaped just like that. Came from a Merc, too. I'd say
we found ourselves the guilty car." The men high-fived
each other.

I told them I had to be getting back, gave Brad an
evasive answer about touring the crime lab—it sounded
fascinating, but I didn't want Brad to think I was interested in him—and headed for the elevator and the airport Metro station. My mind buzzed. Tessa had been
involved in a hit-and-run the night she got killed. I
vaguely remembered hearing about the incident on the
news, and recalled Lissy mentioning it. Where had it happened? I wasn't sure. Getting into an elevator smelling
of stale pizza, I tried to imagine a sequence of events.

Tessa and her companion, whoever he was, hit someone. Tessa got out to check on the victim—maybe in a
spot with no road shoulder?—and got hit by a passing
car. Somehow, she fell into the river. Or—I backed up
my thinking—the accident knocked the hit-and-run victim into the river and Tessa jumped in to save him. She
landed on something that broke her legs, or got hit by
something. Would there have been boats on the river at
that hour? I had no idea what kind of commercial traffic
traveled the Anacostia River. I gave up on trying to fig-

ure out how Tessa ended up in the river to concentrate on how her car ended up at Reagan National. Her companion searches for her, can't find her, and drives her car to the airport. I frowned. Ludicrous. Why on earth would someone do that? As the door dinged open, a thought came to me. Maybe her companion was someone who couldn't afford to have his name associated with Tessa's. A married man seemed most likely—hadn't Phoebe mentioned Tessa was seeing someone?—although it could also be a source, someone involved with one of her projects. I couldn't even begin to speculate who that might be.

I tried to puzzle through the case on the Metro, crowded with rush hour commuters, but the car's swaying lulled me into a semi-sleeping state and I woke up in time to get off at the King Street Station. I caught the trolley back toward my end of town and walked into my house shortly after. My muscles had stiffened up again on the Metro ride and I was ridiculously tired, considering it was only a bit after six o'clock. Deciding not to fight it, I ate a light dinner, soaked in the tub (trying not to think about the brick that came through my window last time), and crawled into bed a bit after seven.

Chapter 26

Thursday morning brought a slight improvement in my flexibility after more pain meds and twenty minutes of stretching on my bedroom floor. A hot shower helped, as did a breakfast of scrambled egg whites, low-fat mozzarella, and avocado. Feeling almost human again, I pulled on lavender capri leggings and a flowered tank top, grabbed my dance heels, and was about to trot upstairs to the studio, when my doorbell rang. Who could it be at this hour?

Peering through one of the narrow panes on either side of the door, I saw Danielle. She was facing away from me, but she turned when I opened the door. Her face was tear-streaked and she wore no makeup, even though she was dressed for the office in a blah greige suit and boring pumps. She'd put her hair up in a loose bun, but strands were falling out of it to dangle beside her face and down her back.

"Danielle!" I pulled her into a big hug. She was shaking. "What's wrong?"

She sobbed against my shoulder and mumbled something.

"What? I can't hear you, sweetie." A terrible thought knifed through me. "Mom? Did she fall?" Mom had had a couple of serious riding accidents in the past and I worried about her more as she got older.

Danielle drew back far enough to say, "Not Mom. Coop." She snuffled into a tissue as I pulled her inside and closed the door.

"What's happened to Coop?"

"He broke up with me." She started bawling again. I tried to urge her toward the kitchen, but she sank onto the bottom-most stair and crumpled in on herself.

"Oh, Dani, I'm so sorry." I scrunched in beside her and wrapped my arms around her, rocking gently. I wanted to punch Coop's nose in the worst way. She cried for at least ten minutes, leaning heavily into me, and I stroked her without saying anything. Finally, her tears dwindled.

Sniffing, she said in a raw voice, "He said Tricia understands him better, that they're completely *simpatico*, whatever that means. How can he just dump me, like our five years together don't count for anything?"

"Wait here." I hurried to the kitchen and returned with tissues and the pint of Triple Caramel Chunk ice cream I'd bought in a moment of dieting weakness but eaten only two spoonfuls of. I handed her the cold container and a spoon. "Eat."

"It's breakfast time."

"I know. That's why I brought ice cream instead of booze. Both have medicinal qualities."

She blew her nose, and then stabbed the spoon into the ice cream. After she'd managed a couple of bites, she said, "We had history. What do he and Tricia have except chess?"

I couldn't answer that. "He'll be sorry he left you for Heifer Girl. You're beautiful and kind and smart and funny and she ... plays chess."

Dani managed a watery chuckle. The ice cream was half gone. "I have to go to work, but I needed to tell you. I shouldn't be so surprised since we'd agreed to see other people, but I didn't see it coming. I think it's the shock that's getting to me as much as the actual breakup."

I didn't believe her, but I pretended like I did. "Of course. Look, why don't you call in sick today? Take a mental health day? We'll go do something." Nigel would blow a gasket if I skipped out on today's rehearsals, but too bad.

"Can't. We're organizing for a possible strike and I've got to be there." She pushed to her feet, leaving the ice cream container on the step.

"At least fix your hair."

I returned the ice cream to the freezer while she ducked into the powder room. She emerged with her hair neatly pinned up and her face free of tear stains, although her eyes were puffy and her nose red. She tried a brave smile. "I love Coop, you know—"

I nodded.

"—but I'm not sure I appreciated him enough. I should have gone to some of his chess tournaments with him, even though they bored me to tears, just because I loved him. I should have worn the red lace bra and pant-ies he got me last Valentine's Day more often. They made me look like a hooker, but Coop said I was the most beautiful woman he'd ever seen. I never said any-thing like that to him."

I could tell she was headed for tears again, so I joked, "Maybe you would've if he'd worn lacy lingerie."

It worked. She gave a burp of laugher and said, "You know what I mean. I was so quick to criticize Coop, to moan about him forgetting to take the trash out on trash day, or getting the wrong size sweater for my birthday present, or forgetting the anniversary of the day we met."

"He's the one who cheated on you," I said, hating to see her blame herself. "I wish you'd never met the bastard."

Dani shook her head. "Oh, no. Even though this hurts more than . . . more than having my hair yanked out by handfuls, I couldn't ever wish that. I wouldn't trade my time with Coop for anything, not a winning Lotto ticket, or a wish-granting genie, or even for Mom and Dad to still be together." Her melancholy smile told me she was reliving happy Coop memories. "I wouldn't be the me I am now if I hadn't been with Coop." Giving me a long, convulsive hug, she left.

"I'll text you later," I called after her. "We can do dinner, if you feel up to it. My treat. I'll bring more ice cream. And booze. We can pour Bailey's on the ice cream."

I sighed as I closed the door, knowing no amount of ice cream or alcohol was going to make Danielle feel better for more than a few seconds. I thought about what she'd said, and Tav's face materialized in my head. I'd been taking Tav's presence in my life for granted, I realized, and I was in danger of pushing him out of my life because I was afraid I'd get hurt again, like Dani was hurting, like I'd hurt after Rafe cheated on me . . . and when he'd died. But Tav wasn't Coop or Rafe. He'd shown up after Rafe's death and helped me get through that time. He'd stuck by me even when the police suspected me of murder, and helped me get the studio onto solid financial ground. Now, he was leaving. I suddenly knew with total certainty that I couldn't let that happen.

Rushing impulsively out the back door, I climbed into the rental car and headed for Rafe's—now Tav's—condo. It was still early. I hoped he'd be there. I considered calling him, but didn't know what I'd say. I was hoping the right words would come if I was face-to-face with him. I slid the car into a spot at the curb, uncaring that the rear hung out into traffic. Dodging cars, I scurried across the street and into the building, taking the stairs when the sluggish elevator didn't appear immediately. I didn't want to chicken out.

I was panting slightly when I emerged on the fourth floor. I stopped in front of his door. Maybe this wasn't such a—

The door opened.

"Stacy!"

Tav stood there, dressed for work in a light gray suit, darker gray shirt, and yellow and turquoise tie that made his tanned skin appear darker. His black hair was brushed back from his forehead and still damp. He smelled like soap and the light cedar-scented cologne he used. Before he could say anything, I rushed into speech.

"I'm sorry. About the investigation, about Zane, about all of it. I don't want you to leave. I want you to stay. It scares me that I want you to stay so much, but I do. I didn't want to not tell you, in case, well, in case it makes a difference. I'm not sure what happened with Zane, or why, but it's you I l—like. I don't know what will happen with the show now that I've pissed Nigel off, or whether the studio will be able to turn a profit, or—"

He kissed me. His hands cupped my face and his mouth found mine. My lips opened under the pressure of his and the kiss deepened until I felt dizzy. My hands went to his shoulders so I wouldn't fall and his arms slid around me, pulling me tightly against his hard body. I seemed to hear the sensuous rhythms of the rumba in my head as I shaped myself to Tav. He was so like Rafe ... but so not like him, too. The similarities had confused me at first, but not—

A door down the hall opened and Tav and I sprang apart. A businessman emerged, dressed like Tav, but older. He gave us a knowing look as he picked up his newspaper, tucked it under his arm, and headed for the elevator. "Take it inside, lucky man," he murmured as he passed us.

I blushed furiously, and Tav tugged at my hand. "Perhaps we should talk inside."

I let him pull me inside, feeling hideously self-conscious. What had I done now? I was used to my impulsiveness getting me into hot water, but this—! "I shouldn't have come," I said.

"Let me get you some coffee," Tav said, not trying to resume our previous activity. I was partly relieved and partly miffed. He clinked around in the kitchen and I perched on the edge of the sofa, noticing that Tav had replaced Rafe's navy blue one with a warmer-seeming couch upholstered in an umber chenille piled with pillows in terracotta, cream, and teal. I ran my hand over the soft nap. "Nice," I said, as he handed me the coffee. I took a swallow, mostly to have something to do, and burned my mouth. "Ooch!"

Tav sat in the recliner, not beside me on the sofa, and I cupped my hands around the mug, suddenly needing its warmth.

"Why, Stacy? Why are you here?" He'd withdrawn.

Emptiness swelled inside me, crushing my organs and making it hard to breathe. Was I too late? But the way he'd kissed me . . . "I'm sorry," I said.

"For what?"

"For being a big chicken, for being so worried about how a relationship between us might end that I wasn't brave enough to give it a go. Ironic, huh, since I'm usually the impulsive one."

"One of your many adorable, and sometimes exasperating, traits."

His words, and the light in his eyes, encouraged me. Shyly at first, and then with more confidence, I told him about Danielle and Coop breaking up, and about my realization that I didn't want him to go. "I don't know where I want us to go, if there is an 'us,' but—"

"Oh, there is an us," Tav said. "At least, there is if I have anything to say about it."

Relief and happiness coursed through me.

"Savage?"

"Our relationship, if you can even call it that, was a matter of proximity. We were competing together—still are—and investigating Tessa's murder, and all that tension turned into . . . something. But not much," I hastened to add. "He's gone out with my sister more than with me. He was easy," I said, "because he's leaving, and I didn't have to think about being with him longer than a few weeks. It's not easy with you because you're Rafe's brother, and we're business partners, and you're not going anywhere, I hope." His smile sent heat curling through my body. "I didn't think I could stand it if you stayed mad at me, if you sold your share of the studio or gave it to me, and returned to Argentina."

"I thought you wanted to own the studio outright." He reached for my hand and held it in a firm clasp.

"I do, but—" I stared at him with exasperation. "Why do men have to make things so hard?"

"Men?" He arched his brows. "Women arc the ones—"

"Men." I continued on before he could argue further. I didn't want to upset him, now that we seemed to be on the same page, finally—and a very nice page it was—but I needed to say something. "About the investigation . . ."

Tav interrupted me. "I was wrong to give you an ultimatum. You are an adult and I was treating you like a little girl. If finding out who killed Tessa is important to you, then you need to do it."

"Really?"

He nodded. "However, I would prefer you not get killed."

"I'm in favor of that."

His thumb traced lazy circles on the back of my hand and I shivered. "Why not tell people you have given up, that the police have warned you off the case—whatever it takes to make them believe you are backing off? Also, you need someone to stay in the house with you. It is not good for you to be there alone, vulnerable."

I expected him to offer to stay at the house and I was wondering how I could turn him down without hurting his feelings—I wasn't ready to take our relationship to *that* level, yet, and I knew we'd end up in bed if he stayed overnight—when he said, "Perhaps your sister could come stay?"

"That's not a bad idea," I said slowly. Danielle might welcome a change of scenery for a few days. "I'll ask her."

Tav nodded. "And do not be alone with anyone associated with the show. Anyone."

I twisted my face doubtfully. "That could be a little tougher. Zane and I have to practice."

"Make sure Maurice or Vitaly is always on hand, then," Tav said. "They adore you—they will do what is necessary to help keep you safe." He glanced at his watch and sprang up. "I am late for a meeting with the man who will, I hope, cut us some slack on the tax bill. I am sorry, but I must go, Stacy."

"It's okay," I said, walking with him to the door.

Before he opened it, he kissed me again and caressed my face. "So beautiful."

We parted on the sidewalk, with him calling after me, "Stay safe!"

I planned to do my best.

Zane noticed the change in me almost immediately.

I was half an hour late for our rehearsal and Zane, Nigel, and Larry were all on their cell phones when I came in. I could hear Vitaly and Calista practicing in the small studio, and Maurice emerged from the office to smile at me. No fear of being alone with the killer today.

"Finally!" Nigel said, snapping his phone closed.

"I'm so, so, so sorry," I said, slipping on my dance shoes. "Something came up."

Zane led me a little aside as we entered the ballroom. Hair flopped over his forehead in that boyish way that was so ridiculously endearing it had half the teenage girl population of the country pinning his poster to their walls fifteen years earlier. "Is everything okay?"

I met his eyes briefly. "Fine. I had something I had to take care of." I wasn't sure I owed him any explanation after a couple of not-quite-dates and a kiss or two, and I certainly didn't want to get into it now, with the camera peering over our shoulders. "Are you warmed up?" I pulled him to the center of the dance floor and began leading him through the moves we'd practiced yesterday.

We stopped an hour in for a water break, and Vitaly bounced into the ballroom, towing Calista, to consult with me on a tricky bit of choreography. While we worked it out, Nigel came forward, beckoning Larry closer. "So, Stace," he said, his grin tighter than usual and I knew he was still royally pissed, "why don't you tell the viewers about finding Tessa's car yesterday? That's a big break in your case, right, luv?"

I felt everyone's heads whip toward me and I wanted to slap Nigel, although he'd given me the opportunity I was looking for.

"You know, Nige, I didn't find the car. The rental car company called *you* when they found it at the airport because it was rented in your name. And it's not my case. The detective told me to steer clear and I plan to do that. The police know what they're doing, and I'm sure they're going to make an arrest soon." I smiled sweetly into the camera.

"Cut," Nigel said irritably. When Larry lowered the camera, he said, "What the hell?"

"I'm done investigating. Through. Finished. Finito. I'm here to dance and that's where I plan to put my efforts." I nodded my head emphatically so my ponytail swished.

"What game are you playing now?" Nigel narrowed his eyes.

"For God's sake, Nigel, leave her alone." Calista

paused in her texting to glare at Nigel. "She's shaken up from the car crash. Anyone would be. Give her a break."

"She's right," Zane said. I didn't know if he meant me or Calista. "We have no business mucking about in a police investigation. We should stick to dancing."

"We are dancers, not Remington Steeles," Vitaly added.

Nigel gave the four of us a disgusted look and stomped out of the room. Larry followed him.

"Did you mean it?" Zane asked when they were gone. The four of us clustered in a little conspiratorial circle.

"Yes." I met each of their gazes in turn. "Detective Lissy really tore into me yesterday. Threatened obstruction of justice." Okay, he'd threatened Nigel with obstruction, but I was sure he'd be happy to sling the same charge at me, although maybe I'd earned a few brownie points by telling him about Tessa's computer. "I'm ready to concentrate on winning the Crystal Slipper."

"Let's do it," Zane said, striking a *Saturday Night Fever* pose.

Chapter 27

Maurice greeted me in my office when we were through for the morning and the others had left to get lunch. "I overheard your conversation," he said. "Did you mean any of it?"

I hesitated just long enough to make him sigh. "I didn't think so."

"Tav and I thought it would be smart to make the killer think I was off the case so I don't have any more 'accidents.' Tav also suggested I get someone to stay with me, so I'm going to ask Danielle if she'll camp out at my place for a couple nights."

"Tav, eh?" Maurice gave me a knowing look and, to my fury, I blushed. He didn't say anything more. "What's your next step?"

Reading his question as acceptance, if not approval, I said, "I thought I'd go to the hospital."

"Are you feeling worse?"

"No, no. I want to talk to the hit-and-run victim. I know his name and the hospital he's in." His name had been in the paper and I'd overheard Lissy's partner mention the hospital. "He might be able to tell us something. According to the evidence technicians who were at the airport yesterday, Tessa's car hit him. I want to see what he remembers. Detective Lissy said something about him being hit by a Dodge, but Tessa's car is a Mercedes."

A line appeared between Maurice's brows. "Puzzling. Look, Anastasia, why don't you stop investigating for real?" He forestalled my protest by raising a hand. "Not because it's distasteful, but because it's gotten too dangerous."

"We're supposed to be filming this show for six more weeks," I said. "I can't spend the next forty-two days watching my back, wondering if the killer's still out there. We can use the reward money, too. And," I grinned ruefully, "you know I'm not good at letting go of something once I've sunk my teeth into it."

"Don't I just." Maurice smiled.

Mindful of Tav's instruction not to go anywhere alone, I asked, "Want to go to the hospital with me?"

Maurice shook his head. "Can't. I've got students coming in this afternoon, now that you TV stars are out of the way for the day."

On the words, the outside door opened and a woman trilled, "Maurrrice, I'm here."

Maurice left to work with his student, and I twirled the ends of my ponytail around my finger. I wanted to go to the hospital now, but it looked like I was going to have to wait. Maybe Danielle would go with me later. The thought reminded me that I needed to see if she would stay at my place for a couple of nights. I called her at work. When I explained what I wanted, she agreed immediately.

"I'd just as soon not be home tonight, anyway," she

said. "Coop's supposed to come over and pick up his stuff."

"You could toss it out the window."

"That wouldn't be fair. He didn't really do anything wrong, except fall out of love with me." She sniffled.

I was tempted to say, "Who cares about fair?" but let it drop. "We'll have fun this evening," I promised, "after we go to the hospital." I hung up without explaining.

Finding Figueroa's room number was as simple as asking at the information desk. He'd been moved out of intensive care a couple of days earlier, a helpful geriatric volunteer said, and could be found on the fourth floor. "Take those elevators and follow the yellow arrows," he said.

"Why are we here again?" Danielle asked as we whisked down wide halls with their helpful color-coded arrows painted on the linoleum.

"If Tessa's car was involved in a hit-and-run the night she was killed, it's got to have something to do with her death, don't you think? This man might be able to help us figure it out."

Danielle wore a dubious expression but helped me look for room numbers on the doors. When we came to the right one, I took a deep breath and knocked lightly on the half-open door. An orderly pushed a dinner cart past us, trailing the odors of steamed peas and gravy. Ick. Danielle and I planned to stop off for Chinese takeout on our way home. My tummy rumbled at the thought.

"Mr. Figueroa?" I called.

"Sí?"

We entered the room. It was small, but private. I'd read that more and more hospitals were going to private rooms to cut down on the risk of infection. A bed with metal rails was parked in the back left corner by a window that looked down onto an open space between wings. It let in light, but no one could say it had a healing view. Metal rails surrounded the bed where a small man sat in a half-raised position, watching the television bracketed into the corner.

He was awake, alert, and seemed pleased to see me and Danielle, I noted with relief. An arm and a leg were in casts, but he wasn't hooked up to any tubes or monitors. Then I realized he was watching a Spanish language station and my heart sank. He looked at us with bright brown eyes from a seamed face the color of Tav's new sofa.

"Buenas tardes."

"Hola." My schoolgirl Spanish had never been good and I hadn't used it since passing Spanish 2 as a high school sophomore. But I gave it a go. Too bad I hadn't brought Tav instead of Danielle. *"Nosotros"*—I pointed to Danielle and myself—*"estan . . . er, estamos* Stacy *y* Danielle."

The man looked slightly puzzled, but said, *"Soy Esteban. Mucho gusta."*

I thought he'd said something like "Please to meet you," so I responded with *"Gracias."*

"El pelo rojo—muy hermoso." Esteban stared at Danielle's hair admiringly. She smiled at him.

"Quiero"—I want—*"decir a tí about la accidente."* I had no idea what the word for accident was, so I made one up and mimed driving a car and crashing it into Danielle. She giggled. I was about to frown her down when I realized how silly I must seem. To Esteban, I must sound as incoherent as Vitaly sometimes sounded to me. Worse, even.

"No lo recuerdo."

"Por el río?" I hoped he translated that as something like "Were you by the river?"

"No recuerdo. Solamente Dakota."

"Only Dakota?" I looked at Danielle. "Isn't that a Dodge truck?" The police were right, after all. But that didn't explain the missing glass from Tessa's Mercedes matching the glass found at the hit-and-run site. Maybe the crime scene technicians were confused?

"Yeah, it's a truck," Danielle said. "Coop's brother has one."

Esteban looked from me to Danielle and nodded. *"Sí, Dakota. Dakota vino."* He flung himself back against the pillows, as if to reenact the accident, then winced when his cast nicked the swing-arm tray.

For a moment, I thought he was talking about wine, but then the verb *"venir"* surfaced from some long-unused part of my brain and I realized he was saying a Dakota came. "It hit you?"

Esteban nodded rapidly. *"Sí, sí. Dakota."*

A scrubs-clad nurse came in, pushing a mobile blood pressure machine. "I need to take Mr. Figueroa's vitals," he said, "and then the patient needs to eat. You can come back after dinner, if you want."

"Thanks. We'll get out of your way." Danielle and I headed for the door as the nurse wrapped the cuff around Esteban's upper arm.

"Are you with the police?" The nurse eyed my lavender leggings doubtfully. Danielle looked more like a cop in her greige suit and his gaze lingered on her, as if expecting her to produce a badge. "I thought you'd already talked with Mr. Figueroa. Did you find out who hit him?"

"We're not cops—just friends. *Amigos*," I said. "*Adíos*,

Esteban." I waved to the man who waved back with his uninjured arm.

Danielle and I scurried into the hall before the nurse could ask any more uncomfortable questions. I didn't see how the hospital could object to us visiting Esteban if the patient himself didn't mind, but I didn't need the nurse mentioning our visit to Detective Lissy. I could envision his reaction to the news that I'd been interviewing his hit-and-run victim.

"Well, that only muddied the water," Danielle pointed out as we crossed the parking lot to my rental car. "He says he was hit by a truck, but the CSI crew says he was hit by Tessa's car. He clearly doesn't remember the accident, so maybe he's confused about the car. Maybe he saw a Dakota earlier that day, or he used to own one, and it's gotten mixed up with his memory of the accident. He must have banged his head when the car hit him—maybe it jarred a few connections loose and reattached them incorrectly."

My sister, the brain surgeon. "Could be," I said, pointing the car toward my favorite Chinese restaurant. "What if," I said slowly, "he's saying Dakota like the name? I have a student named Dakota in my ballroom aerobics class. I also have a Montana."

"Esteban knew the person who ran into him?" Danielle sounded doubtful. "That doesn't sound likely. How do you work Tessa into that scenario? Someone named Dakota runs him down, and Tessa stops to help but accidentally hits him again so the crime scene dudes think her car was involved? Or, Tessa hits him and Dakota stops to help; in which case, why wouldn't he have called nine one one?"

"You're right," I said. "Assuming Esteban's confused

and the evidence experts are right, it still doesn't clear anything up. Tessa hits Esteban and then—what?"

"Gets out to help him," Danielle said. "Or, she panics and drives away."

I considered that. "Okay," I said slowly, thinking hard. "She panics. She's smart enough to know that her car will show damage, have Esteban's blood on it—whatever— and so she decides to dump it at the airport. Hm." This was a new way of thinking about the case. "Tessa hides the car at the airport and then catches the Metro or takes a cab back to her apartment."

"Didn't you say she was with someone?"

"The drug dealer said that. Suppose she and her companion split up. He's someone she met at the club and he's not interested in being mixed up in a hit-and-run case. He goes his way, she goes hers. The murderer abducts her while she's waiting for a cab."

"Or she calls a friend for a lift and he or she kills her for some reason," Danielle said. "That makes more sense than a stranger abduction since the attacks on you prove it's someone involved with *Blisters*."

I smacked the steering wheel. "I hate this."

"Murder. What's not to hate?"

Chapter 28

Saturday finally arrived. Tonight was the second round of competition. At the top of the show, Zane and I would find out if we'd survived the first round. Even if the viewers had eliminated us by not voting for us, the judges had a chance to save us. They could vote unanimously to retain a couple the viewers had voted off, but they could do that only once per season. I was surprised by how anxious I was about the whole thing. In fact, everyone seemed tenser than usual at Graysin Motion that morning.

"People really dressed like this in the eighties?" Calista asked, emerging from the studio, which the wardrobe people had commandeered again. She wore a gold lamé, disco-inspired jumpsuit. It had cutouts in strategic spots and skintight pants that belled out from the knee. A stylist had crimped her hair and pulled it back with a glittery headband so it frizzed past her shoulders, framing her face. "No wonder people say 'Disco is dead.'"

"I look just as goofy," I told her, gesturing the length of my turquoise halter dress and its handkerchief hem, with rhinestones sparkling on the bodice.

Vitaly emerged from the temporary dressing room, wearing a costume that matched Calista's. His gold shirt was open to the waist and displayed a lot of white, hairless chest. Nigel winced and bellowed, "Ariel! Spray tan!"

"Nyet." Vitaly shook his head. "I am allergics."

"Oh, for God's sake." Nigel scrubbed both hands over his bristly head.

Ariel appeared, twisting an elastic around her hair, and said, "I've got a self-tanner for sensitive skin," she said, appraising Vitaly.

Tav walked in on the chaos and cast a comprehensive glance around. He wore jeans and a blue Oxford shirt, sleeves rolled up, a casual weekend look that was even more handsome on him than his weekday suits. Ariel gave him a flirtatious smile, but he missed it because his eyes were on me, the warmth in them making me curl my toes inside my dance shoes. I felt Zane stiffen beside me. "All ready for the big night?" Tav asked.

"Calista and I are moving up the leader boards tonight," Vitaly announced, doing some pliés to keep his muscles warm. "They"—he pointed to me and Zane— "are going down with flames."

"*In* flames," I said. "And you're full of it. Zane and I are taking home the Crystal Slipper. You and Calista may come in second," I graciously allowed.

"Good, good," Nigel murmured as we sparred good-naturedly. He twirled a finger so Larry would keep the camera rolling. His appraising gaze fell on Tav. "You, Acosta. Tonight . . . what do you say to a small argument with Savage over Stacy here? No real violence—we can't risk marks on Savage's pretty face. I'm thinking some pushing and shoving, a little display of testosterone. Before the show . . . no, backstage, after they do their number. It can look like you were riled up by their closeness on the dance floor, like you've come backstage to reclaim your woman." He sped up as he talked, clearly enthused by the idea.

Tav arched his brows and shot me an "Is this guy for real?" look. "I do not think so, Whiteman. Stacy is her own woman."

I smiled at him.

Zane gave a disgusted head shake. "Hell, Nigel, can't the show just be about the dancing?"

Shooting him an incredulous look, Nigel stalked into the ballroom, pulling out his cell phone and murmuring something about "Kim will do it."

I wondered uneasily what Kim would do, but put it out of my mind and let the wardrobe mistress help me out of my costume. When I came out, ready to dance, only Zane was left. Nigel had hustled Vitaly away for a prearranged, one-on-one interview with Kristen somewhere, and Ariel and the wardrobe people had packed up and headed for Club Nitro. I didn't know where Tav had gone; he might be in the office. Before I could check, Zane popped out of the bathroom, wiping his nose, and said, "Ready for some last-minute practice?"

"Absolutely." We moved into the ballroom and spent an hour putting the finishing touches on our routine. The hardest part of the choreography was the overhead lift and Zane finally got it, setting me down lightly so we were pressed together from chest to thigh.

He looked down at me, his hazel eyes searching mine. "I'm not blind, you know."

I eased myself away, so I could answer him honestly. "I'm sorry."

"I thought we had something going."

I cocked my head so my ponytail fell over my shoulder and gave him a look. "Zane, we've never even been on a date. You took me dancing so other women wouldn't hit on you and so you could ask questions about your old girlfriend's death. We've hung out at the Laundromat and strolled the scene of a murder. We've spent a lot of time cooped up in this ballroom, dancing, but that's not real life. You're beyond hot and I'll admit you can get me going, but Tav and I . . ." I didn't need to share my complicated feelings about Tav with Zane. I wasn't sure I could explain them to myself.

Shifting his jaw from side to side, he said, "So that's it? You're really into this Tav guy?"

I nodded. "I am."

He forced a smile and moved away to root out his water bottle from his gym bag. He found it, took a long swallow, recapped it, and said in a deliberately jaunty way, "Well, that's that, then. You win some, you lose some." He slid me a sly smile. "What's Danielle up to after the show tonight?"

I was taken aback for a moment, but then I laughed with him. "As a matter of fact . . ." I told him about Danielle and Coop breaking up. "She could use a little cheering up."

"I am well known for my cheering up abilities," Zane said.

As we resumed dancing with only a little awkwardness between us, I pondered whether or not to warn Danielle not to take Zane too seriously, but finally decided there was little danger of that. She was a big girl. She wasn't going to leap into a rebound relationship with a former child star trying to reestablish his acting career.

She knew Zane was headed back to Hollywood the moment *Blisters* wrapped, or we got kicked off, whichever happened first. I let myself enjoy the rest of our practice and went downstairs to shower before noon, crossing my fingers that we would survive the kickoff and get the chance to perform our dance on live television.

One o'clock brought the return of Kristen Lee and Larry to film our interview. It was supposed to be a "day in the life of" format, and Kristen listed the activities that supposedly made up my daily life, ticking them off on her slim figures. "We'll get a few shots of you at the gym, lifting weights," she said, "and then we'll talk while you pick out wine at the cutest little wine store that's advertising on *Blisters* for the first time this season. It's on Fayette Street. We'll finish up near the waterfront—Nigel likes the visuals—with you getting your nails done at a darling little salon—"

"Let me guess: that's advertising on the show."

"You catch on quick," Kristen said with a curt nod. She seemed frostier than the last time we'd met and I wondered why. "It's a lot to fit into one afternoon, so let's get going. We need to be at Club Nitro no later than four for makeup." She led the way to the van and I followed.

At the gym, Kristen wanted to film me on the thigh machine, but I refused to be seen forcing my legs wide and squeezing them shut on national television. We compromised with me doing bent over rows in a racerback bra top, which gave Larry the chance to film a lot of cleavage, but was better than the alternative. Kristen asked a flow of mostly innocuous questions about what a dancer's life was like, what I liked best about it—using my body to create art—and what I liked least—the business side of running a studio. She asked about my family and my routine. I gave her brief answers, knowing from watching Solange's segment on last week's show, that the whole afternoon's work would be edited to little more than three minutes for the broadcast.

The wine store was a pleasant space decorated with barrels and swags of grape clusters, and lined with racks of wine. It smelled vaguely musty, bringing to mind images of wine cellars beneath ancient Loire Valley châteaux. Not that I'd ever been in one, but I'd seen a Travel Channel special. Kristen lobbed a question at me as I dutifully examined the bottle of Cabernet the wine shop owner had put in my hands. "Is it true," she asked in her brittle voice, "that your mother abandoned your family when you were a teenager? How did you react to that?"

I almost dropped the bottle, and satisfaction slid across her eyes before she blinked them to give me—and the camera—her usual innocent gaze. "My mom's a champion equestrienne. She competes internationally so she has to travel frequently. It was tough on us kids, I'll admit, but my dad picked up the slack." It was toughest on Danielle, I knew, and a recent vacation together on Jekyll Island—me, Danielle, and Mom—had only partly healed the wounds.

"So you didn't mind that she abandoned you in favor of horses?"

I wished she'd quit using the "A" word. I said through gritted teeth, "I can understand her choices, especially since dance is my life, like horses are hers."

"That's very enlightened of you," Kristen said in a voice that implied I was either lying or an idiot. "But what about—"

I thrust the Cabernet at her and she took it reflexively. "Would this go good with steak?" I asked. "Or would this be better?" I grabbed the nearest bottle from a rack and put it in her hands. "This Pinot Noir looks tasty." I added a third bottle and she clasped them to her enhanced bosom, looking frustrated, before saying, "Cut."

As soon as Larry lowered the camera, I leaned in and whispered. "We are through talking about my mother and my family."

Letting the anxious shop owner take the bottles from her, Kristen flipped back her straight hair and turned away. "We're done here, Larry. Let's move on to the salon so we can wrap this up and get downtown."

Fine by me. I followed her out to the van, let the makeup guy—not Ariel—powder my nose again, and alighted a few blocks away in front of a salon that had tubs of pansies, petunias, marigolds, and geraniums sitting on either side of the door. They let out a spicy scent that was immediately canceled out by the stink of nail polish remover when we walked in. The place was small—six stations—and almost deserted, ready for us to take over and film. Fluorescent lights glared from overhead and a countertop fountain splashed near the cash register.

"Chelsea Irving!" the shop's sole customer exclaimed as Kristen walked in. The middle-aged woman dropped her credit card and fumbled to retrieve it, having a tough time of it since she wouldn't take her eyes off Kristen.

Kristen barely glanced at the fan, conferring with Larry until the salon owner hustled her out and turned over the Closed sign.

"What about you, Kristen?" I asked as Larry tested the light, wanting to make amends for my harshness. "Where did you grow up? What was your family like?"

The smiling salon owner gestured for me to seat myself at a narrow table and choose a polish. I pointed at one at random.

"Battery problem," Larry announced, and exited, probably to search for a replacement battery in the van.

"Me?" Kristen gave me a suspicious look. "My people are from Dallas. My daddy was in oil. My brothers both played football for UT, but I went to SMU. I majored in theater and entered a beauty pageant my junior year on a bet with my Gamma Phi sisters. I didn't win, but I got a commercial out of it. One thing led to another and I ended up in Hollywood. *Irving Crescent* was my big break."

"You played Chelsea for ten years," I said. "I met a man the other night who remembered—" I cut myself off, realizing in the nick of time that Kristen wouldn't be pleased to hear that a drug dealer remembered her performance on the nighttime soap.

Her long eyes narrowed. Waving the manicurist away, she leaned in and I could smell her late afternoon breath. "I know who you talked to," she said softly. "Ever since Tessa died, you've been nosing around in other people's business. I know Nigel talked to you about replacing me."

Ah, so that explained her new hostility. She gave a satisfied nod with her pointy chin at my surprised look. "I've got sources and I know more than most people realize. If you think I'm going to let some small-time *dancer*—"

She made it sound like I used a pole in a strip club.

"—steal my place on this show, you can damn well think again. I like this gig and I'm going to hold on to it, age be damned. If Vanna White can be a spokesmodel coming up on sixty, I can stick with *Blisters* until it folds. Tessa tried to get rid of me, too, and look what happened to her."

Larry and the manicurist returned simultaneously and Kristen drew back, sending home her point with a long look at me. Almost immediately, she pasted on the faux smile and launched into more fluffy questions— Who was my favorite singer? What movies had I watched recently?—and ended the interview abruptly when only three of my nails were painted.

"We've got enough," she said. "Let's pack it in, Larry." She marched out of the salon, her back straight as a knife in her red sheath dress.

I took the remover-soaked cotton ball the manicurist handed me and wiped the three orange nails clean. "Thanks," I told her.

She smiled conspiratorially. "That Chelsea's a bit uptight, isn't she? What can you expect from a girl who would steal her stepfather away from her own mother?"

"She's not really—" It wasn't worth trying to explain that Kristen Lee hadn't really done the things her character had done. An amazing number of people, it seemed, had trouble separating TV fiction from real life. "Vote for me and Zane tonight," I said instead.

As I gathered my purse and traipsed out to the van, a thought punched me so hard I stopped, causing a woman pushing a stroller to run the wheels over my feet. When we had exchanged apologies and I had climbed into the van, I sat across from Kristen with Larry and the makeup guy a couple of rows back, both texting. I was tense, almost bursting with the significance of my idea, but I waited until the van slid into traffic to ask in what I hoped was a nonchalant voice, "Kristen, did you ever play a character named Dakota?"

Chapter 29

Saturday night. Showtime.

The celebs and pros and crew were all gathered in Club Nitro, which was closed to the public for the night. It looked like chaos to me, but the crew seemed used to it. Technicians tested lights and sound systems. The band, wedged into a small space beside the bar, played phrases from the night's songs, trumpets and saxes clashing with each other. A vocalist warmed up with "mi-mi-mis." Invited guests filed in, their IDs checked at the door by members of Nigel's staff, and crowded into the booths and makeshift seating that ringed the dance floor. Kim Savage, Tav, and Danielle were seated side by side, with Mickey Hazzard's ex-wife to Danielle's right. Why in the world was she here? I recognized her from the news stories; she was much prettier in person, although a bit older looking. Mickey almost tripped when he caught sight of her, so he hadn't known she was coming. I suspected Nigel had something planned and had arranged for ex-Mrs. Mickey to be here.

Since arriving at Club Nitro, I'd been shuttled from

wardrobe to makeup to preshow rehearsal, and hadn't had two seconds alone to think about my new idea. What if Esteban was naming someone he'd seen at the accident site—Dakota—only he was using a character's name, and not the actor's name? Kristen had denied ever playing a character named Dakota, and hadn't even asked why I wanted to know. I gazed around the room, wishing I'd spent more time watching TV and movies so I might know if Kim Savage, who used to act, had ever been a Dakota, or if Calista or Zane had, or even Phoebe who stood beside me, fidgeting with the fringe of her brown jumpsuit.

"I almost hope me and Nikolai get kicked off," she whispered, "so I won't have to dance in this lame outfit tonight."

The stage manager hushed her as the band started playing the theme music and the audience applauded on cue. Kristen glided into the center of the dance floor, stunning in a periwinkle lace gown slit almost to her crotch, and read from the teleprompter. She was very smooth and connected well with the audience; I didn't know why Nigel and Tessa wanted to replace her. She introduced the b-listers and their partners and Zane and I smiled and struck a pose on cue. "After the break, we'll reveal which couple will be going home tonight, never to dance again on *Dancing with the B-Listers*," she said in thrilling accents.

We were hustled to our spots during the commercial, the places we stood to hear our fate announced. Zane was jittery beside me, doing shoulder rolls, tapping his foot, and looking around. "Why so nervous?" I asked in a low voice.

"The viewers, the voters, have to think I care," he

whispered. His gaze landed on his mother, who nodded at him and glared at me. Beside her, Danielle gave me two thumbs up and Tav smiled. I wanted to stay in the competition, wanted to win the prize money, but my world wouldn't come crashing down if we got eliminated tonight.

The band played a bridge, the lights came down, and Kristen went into the long, teasing drill of "Will this couple dance for us tonight?" or "Will they be packing their bags?" The first "retained" couple she announced was Vitaly and Calista. Calista smiled smugly, but Vitaly went wild with joy, pumping his fist and lifting Calista off her feet. The audience cheered. I clapped as hard as I could, beaming at Vitaly.

Next, Kristen announced that Mickey and Solange were "in danger" and then told Nanette Fleaston, the pet psychic, and Marco Ingelido that they would dance again tonight. Nanette said, "I knew it. Jezebel shook herself after her bath today and I thought how much it looked like she was doing the salsa, and I knew right then that Marco and I would be performing our salsa for all of America tonight." She kissed both hands and flung them out to the audience. I concentrated on not rolling my eyes.

The spotlight landed on Zane and me and I fixed a smile on my face, determined not to look worried or show disappointment if the audience had voted us off. An overhead screen showed snippets of our performance last week and a few of the judges' comments, and then Kristen announced, "Zane Savage and Stacy are . . ." She drew it out. "Still in danger!"

Zane let his shoulders slump as if devastated at the thought of going home, and I gave his hand an encouraging conspiratorial squeeze as we moved to stand next to Mickey and Solange. Kristen quickly announced that Phoebe and the reality show runner-up guy and their partners would dance for everyone tonight. As Kristen wound up for the big reveal, I caught sight of Nigel behind one of the cameras, and wondered at the intense look on his face. Since he must already know which of us was hanging up our dance shoes, I didn't know why he looked so interested.

Thinking about Nigel, I missed part of Kristen's lead-in, but tuned back in in time to hear her announce, ". . . will dance for us tonight!" Damn, I hadn't heard her say who.

When Zane picked me up and whirled me around, I realized she'd said our names. Zane set me down, grinning broadly, and I saw Solange sag with disappointment as Mickey Hazzard dropped to his knees. For a moment I thought he had collapsed, but then I realized he was praying. Against the backdrop of the clapping audience, Angela Hazzard suddenly stood up and lunged across the dance floor, sinking gracefully to kneel beside Mickey. Her demure dress of cream silk puddled around her.

"My husband has suffered enough," she declared in dramatic accents. "He has been punished and he has repented. Mickey," she said, cupping his bewildered face in her hands, "I want to reconcile with you. We can be married again, live out our lives together." She threw her arms around him. Mechanically, he put his arms around her, his jaw dropping slightly. His eyes scanned the audience. It crossed my mind that Mickey was not over the moon about his ex-wife wanting to get back together. Perhaps he'd already moved on to a young girlfriend or two who would not be pleased with tonight's developments. I wondered cynically what Nigel had paid Angela to stage this affecting scene.

Mickey finally got into the spirit of it, kissing Angela's lips, and saying, "My prayers have been answered."

"What?" A young brunette, no more than eighteen, stood up in the back row. "You said you loved *me*, Mickey, that we were meant to be together for all eternity." All eyes were riveted on the slender girl in a peach, one-shoulder dress she'd probably worn to her prom last month as she wiggled through the crowd to the dance floor. Nigel looked delighted at this turn of events; he was practically dancing a jig.

"Ivy, honey," Mickey started, struggling to stand.

Angela, eyes turning to slits, said, "I should've known." Still on her knees, she thrust her shoulder against Mickey's legs as he was rising, and sent him sprawling.

"Don't you hurt my Mickey," Ivy shouted, balling her hands into fists.

"Fight, fight, fight," the crowd started to chant.

Kristen looked to Nigel for guidance and sputtered, "We'll be right back after a word from—" The show went to commercial and crew members hustled Mickey, Angela, and Ivy offstage before blood could be drawn. Nigel, rubbing his hands together with glee, approached Kristen and whispered in her ear for twenty seconds. The band played a lively tune to distract the crowd and drown out the sounds of Mickey and his harem arguing behind the panel that separated backstage from the dance floor.

"How much of that do you think was scripted?" Zane asked as we followed the remaining pairs to the room set aside for us to wait in.

"Freakin' all of it," Phoebe said from two paces in front of us. "That Nigel." She shook her head and I couldn't tell if she was admiring or deploring him.

"I don't think he knew about Ivy," I said. "I was watching him and he seemed surprised."

"She must have looked like so much ratings manna from heaven," Zane said.

"I'm not sure how much heaven has to do with any of it," I said dryly.

Entering the room, we found the other couples already seated and drinking water or energy drinks. The room was intended as a private party room for the nightclub, and boasted comfy seating for ten, a low table, and mirror-tiled walls that were giving me a headache with the way they reflected everyone to make the room seem like it held dozens more people than it did. Nanette Fleaston was bent over, patting the small pig. Jezebel snorted contented little snorts and then nudged Nanette's leg when the psychic stopped stroking her and straightened.

"She's cute," I said. Hoover would probably see her as a tasty hors d'oeuvre, but she *was* cute. Apparently sensing my appreciation, Jezebel trotted to me and wrinkled her nose. I patted her head gingerly, surprised by how rough her coat was.

Nanette clapped her hands delightedly. "Oh, she likes you. Jezebel is very discerning. She wouldn't go near Solange, for instance."

At the mention of the name, we all looked around the room, as if expecting to see the kicked-off pair of Mickey and Solange. I was sorry Solange wasn't there to hear that Jezebel preferred me to her. On second thought, maybe it was just as well since my rating higher on a pig's preference list probably would only make Solange say something about pigs liking muck or swill.

"Nanette, Marco, on deck." A crew member poked her head in to summon the pair.

"Stacy, make sure Jezebel doesn't follow me, okay?" Nanette said as she flitted out the door. The pig made a move to follow her mistress, but I grabbed her by the collar. She let out a squeal that made Vitaly jump, but then settled down by my feet.

"You should adopt a pig next, Vitaly," I told him. "She'd be good company for Lulu."

Vitaly eyed the pig and curled his lip. "Lulu is not liking pig."

I thought Vitaly was not liking pig, but I didn't say anything, only exchanged an amused glance with Phoebe. With everyone gathered together, it seemed like a good time to test my "Dakota" theory. I wished I had access to my cell phone and could look it up, but the stage manager confiscated everyone's phones before the show went live to ensure someone's ringtone didn't interrupt the broadcast.

"Hey," I said casually, "did any of you ever play a character named Dakota?"

"What a funny question," Calista said. "I played a Cheyenne once, does that count?" She didn't look up from the Tweet she was composing.

"Don't think so," Zane said, clearly not interested.

"Uh-uh. I knew a Dakota in high school," Phoebe said.

The television in the corner played the opening bars of Nanette and Marco's music, and someone hissed, "Ssh." We watched as they danced a clean performance. Nanette had very precise footwork, but Marco had apparently overemphasized the fun, "party" feel of the salsa because she kept throwing her head back and smiling like she'd had three too many appletinis. The judges scored them a point higher than last week. Marco and Nanette bounced back into the room, sweaty and smiling. Jezebel ran to greet Nanette.

"They looked good," Zane murmured.

"We look better."

A stagehand appeared at the door and beckoned to us. Zane pulled me to my feet. "Did I mention I like that outfit?" he said, peering down my cleavage. I bumped his hip with mine, and said, "Keep your mind on the hustle."

"I thought that's what I was doing."

"Good luck," the others called. Vitaly and Phoebe might actually mean it.

The show was still in commercial as Zane and I positioned ourselves on the dance floor. Ariel blotted the sheen off Zane's forehead and whisked a little more sparkly powder across my collarbone. "You guys look great," she said. "Show 'em how it's done."

We did our best. I counted "*And* one, two, three," under my breath as the music started. With the band doing an enthusiastic version of "Funkytown," we hustled our hearts out. We had incorporated some popular disco moves from the 1970s, along with some harder elements, and I was thrilled when Zane managed to swing me around the world in a layback position without stumbling. Bracing my hands on his hips, I arced back, feeling the strength in his arms where they were locked across my back. My feet left the ground as we spun.

"Great," I murmured. The mirror ball spun shards of colored light across the floor and the harsh TV lights kept me from seeing anything beyond the dance floor. The music rose to a climax.

Zane smiled fiercely and readied himself for the lift. We finished with me sinking into the splits at his feet. The crowd gave us a standing ovation and the judges, famous for their poker faces, even smiled. Zane gave me a hand up and we glided over to where Kristen waited for us. Tav and Danielle applauded wildly while Kim Savage looked strangely disgruntled. The judges liked our energy and athleticism and thought Zane got into the character of the hustle. They scored us a full three points higher than last week and we practically bounced into the wings. Zane pumped his fist jubilantly for the camera that preceded us down the narrow, makeshift passageway.

"I am going out to celebrate tonight," Zane said. "Champagne for everyone. You'll drive me home, right? Oh, I forgot. Maybe Danielle will be my designated driver." He grinned and leaned over to kiss me on the cheek.

Designated driver . . . The words opened up new possibilities in my mind, but before I could think through the scenario that presented itself, a hand on my upper arm wrenched me around. "Keep your mind on dancing and your hands off my son." Kim Savage, dressed in a black and white outfit she might have stolen from Cruella DeVil's closet, stood glaring at me. The camera guy moved in closer and I realized that this is what Nigel had meant when he said Kim would do it. Kim would cause a scene. Kim would act up.

"Fine," I said lightly. "You got it." I wasn't going to follow Nigel's script and get into it with Kim.

"Mom!" Zane said, hovering between embarrassment and anger.

My reaction slowed Kim down, but she recovered.

"You can give me that 'butter wouldn't melt in your mouth' look, but I know what's going on." She put her hands on her hips. "I won't have it. Zane has a future in Hollywood and I'm not letting you get in the way of that."

"Believe me—" I started, but Zane interrupted.

"That's enough." He ripped the mike pack off and flung it down the hallway. It skittered to a stop against the wall. He glared at the cameraman until he reluctantly lowered the camera. Zane approached to within inches of his mother and leaned down until he was nose to nose with her. "I have. Had. Enough. This is my life, my career, and my love life. If I want to be with Stacy, I will be." He grabbed my hand and yanked me into his arms. In front of his horrified mother, he kissed me. There was more anger than lust in the kiss and he mashed my lips against my teeth. It hurt. I struggled against him, furious at being used, but he kept the kiss going for a good thirty seconds while his mother bleated, "Stop! Zane, don't be a fool," and the cameraman resumed filming.

I finally stamped my heel onto the top of his foot and he loosed me with an, "Ow." Standing on one leg, he bent to massage the injured foot. All the things I wanted to say sounded stagey and melodramatic—"Don't you dare do that again!" "Touch me again and I'll make you sorry!"—so I clamped my lips shut and stalked off. Kim threw her arms around Zane, presumably to stop him from following me, and knocked him off balance. They tumbled to the floor in an ungainly heap. I hoped Kim had ripped her multithousand-dollar ensemble and that Zane had broken his nose or chipped a tooth. I had had it with both of them.

I vaguely heard Zane call my name as I marched

straight out the side door we'd used more than a week ago. Ignoring him, I let the door snap shut behind me, and took a deep breath through my nose. I needed four more such breaths before I felt my heart rate begin to return to normal. The valet parking lot held the big rigs that had hauled the show's sets and lights and I could barely see through the trailers to the park across the street. Lights glimmered in one of the truck cabs and honky-tonk music filtered through a cracked door. A faint "Raise you five" made me think the drivers might be playing poker.

A shadowy figure large enough to be Li'l Boni moved into the small slice of park I could see and I impulsively struck out in his direction, weaving through the semis to reach the street. The odor of diesel exhaust hovered in the parking lot. Hardly stopping to think, I trotted across the street, wincing as I realized that I was ruining the soles of my dance shoes. "Li'l Boni!"

The huge figure stilled at the sound of my voice and the silhouette he was talking to, distinctly feminine, darted away. Li'l Boni moved closer and I could see his downturned mouth in the faint wash of moonlight. He was not a happy camper. Maybe it was stupid of me to come over here alone and interrupt a drug dealer at work. Strike that "maybe." His expression lightened somewhat as he took in my attire. "Lookin' good, dancer chick. You wan' to join Li'l Boni's stable?"

It took me a split second to realize what he had in mind. I hadn't realized he had diversified business interests; I'd thought he just dealt drugs. I glanced down at the plunging neckline of my turquoise dress in dismay. "No! No, I mean, thank you for the offer, but I just have a quick question."

He half turned away. "I don' got time for no mo' questions."

"Wait! Please. The other night . . . did Tessa get in on the driver's side of the car, or did the other person?" I shifted from foot to foot, and glanced over my shoulder at the lights of Club Nitro. They formed a pool of safety.

"Other dude," Li'l Boni said.

A low-slung sports car pulled to the curb fifty yards away and I made my escape while Li'l Boni was distracted by his customers. I scurried back across the street, handkerchief hem whipping around my calves, and wondered what to do now. I was sadly afraid that I knew what had happened the night Tessa died. Zane's casual words about a designated driver had rearranged my thinking. What if Tessa hadn't been driving her Mercedes on the way home from the club? Her blood alcohol level, according to the autopsy report, was well over the limit. What if she'd arranged for a designated driver? Who was that likely to be, other than the person she drove to the club with? Li'l Boni said he'd seen a man waiting for Tessa at the car, but Phoebe was tall, strongly built. In the dark, at a distance, she could easily be mistaken for a man. And who was more likely to be waiting at the car than the woman Tessa had come with?

My steps slowed as I crossed the valet parking lot. As soon as I could retrieve my phone, I'd call Detective Lissy and tell him what I'd figured out. In fact, I'd use the nearest phone I could find; there had to be one in the club's office or behind the bar. I pulled on the door. It stuck. I yanked harder and the door jerked open. I barely had time to register the figure standing there before a hand grabbed my shoulder and twisted me, and an arm like an iron band pressed against my neck.

Chapter 30

"Quiet," Phoebe Jackson commanded.

Her voice was a whisper, but I sensed the resolve behind the soft words. I panicked and kicked back, hoping to connect with her shins. Her arm tightened against my throat until my vision got fuzzy. I quit kicking. The hall was dimly lit and momentarily deserted. The band's rendition of a Spice Girls song drowned out any other sounds. Calista and Vitaly would be dancing.

I made a gargling noise against the pressure on my throat. I couldn't scream. I wanted to pry that arm away, but she'd somehow pinned both my wrists at the small of my back.

"In here." Phoebe nudged me with a knee to the back of my thighs and I stumbled forward a few steps. My shoulder banged against a door and then it was closing behind us. It was dark. Pitch dark. Cave dark. From the smell, I figured we were in the room Club Nitro used to store its booze. I tried to remember what it looked like. Stacked boxes, sliding doors into a refrigerator area . . . that was all I could come up with. My knee banged something that yielded like cardboard and glass clinked. Phoebe did not turn on a light.

She eased her forearm away from my throat slightly. "Don't yell," she said, "or I'll put you out."

I had no doubt she could do it. "Okay," I whispered.

"Damn, girl." Phoebe sounded sad and very weary. "Why'd you have to keep pushing?"

"You killed Tessa."

I felt her nod behind me, her chin brushing my hair. Not being able to see a blasted thing was disorienting. It made no difference whether my eyes were open or shut. My heart was racing so fast the blood drummed in my ears, making it hard to hear, as well. Phoebe was behind me and to my right, still pinning my hands in the small of my back. My wrists ached from the pressure. I could feel her exhales on my cheek. The floor beneath the thin soles of my dance shoes was hard and chilled my feet. Cement, maybe. I took a couple deep breaths. Was I imagining it, or did the air taste like beer?

Phoebe shifted with a rustle of fabric, and I continued, "She went to talk to Li'l Boni about being in her documentary, and met you back at the car, just like you'd arranged. It was you, not a man, that Li'l Boni saw. You're big enough that it's an understandable mistake. She'd had a few too many drinks and you were the designated driver. You started back to the apartments and then I think you must have hit Esteban Figueroa, right? What happened then?" Her closeness, feeling the heat of her pressed so close to my back, her strong fingers clenched around my wrists, was both strangely intimate and unpleasant.

"Oh, God, girlfriend," Phoebe said. "It was a nightmare. I got turned around getting off the bridge and ended up on some little road down by the river. I never saw him. It wasn't until the impact that I even knew he was there. That thud—that sound will stay with me forever." She breathed heavily, the moist warmth unpleasant on my ear. "We got out, me and Tessa. The man was lying there, bleeding, his leg at a weird angle. I thought he was dead. Then he opened his eyes and looked straight at me. 'Dakota,' he said."

"You lied to me about not playing a character named Dakota."

"It was a small role on a detective show. It only lasted eleven episodes. But that man said 'Dakota' again before he died, and I knew he recognized me."

"What did Tessa do?"

Phoebe laughed bitterly. "What does Tessa always do? She went for a camera, started talking about what good TV this would make."

"Neither of you thought to call nine-one-one?"

"There was so much blood. He kind of choked after he said 'Dakota' and I thought it was over for him."

I leaned forward, trying to put more distance between us. She slowly released my hands. "Don't even think about trying to get past me. I'll put you down so hard you'll never know what hit you—and you won't dance for months."

I believed her. At least she hadn't said anything about killing me. Some of my fear ebbed and waves of regret washed over me. Feeling my way cautiously forward one step in the pitch dark, I touched a box at head height. Letting my fingertips trail along the edges, I found the end of the stack and sat down on a box facing Phoebe. Even though I couldn't see her, I knew she was a mere foot in front of me. I felt like crying. Not because I was scared of what Phoebe might do, although I was, but because I liked Phoebe and this all felt so wrong. I swallowed hard.

"I told Tessa to put the damned camera away, told her I couldn't get arrested for drunk driving, for hitting the man. I was already a two-time loser—I couldn't face a third strike. Even if they'd have tried me in D.C. or Maryland—I don't even know where we were, exactly—I couldn't do prison again. Nuh-uh. No way."

Fear tightened her voice.

"What did Tessa say?"

"She kind of laughed, said it wouldn't come to that, but if it did, we could make another documentary, bring my story full circle. She wasn't thinking about a thing except her damned filmmaking, another Emmy or an Oscar."

I had trouble blaming Phoebe for being bitter about Tessa's reaction.

"I got back in the car," she continued. "I was going to drive away. I don't know to where, but I figured if the cops didn't catch me at the scene, it would be Tessa's word against mine, and the car was Tessa's after all. I was only planning to drive away. . . ." She trailed off.

"What happened?" I kept my voice low, non-accusatory. My hands worked to pry up the sealed edge of the box next to me, hoping to extract a bottle I could use as a weapon. The rough corrugations bit into my fingers. My thumbnail snagged on a heavy-duty staple and ripped off well below the quick. I sucked my lips in and bit down to keep back the yelp.

For the first time I sensed hesitation in her. "I must have left the car in reverse somehow. When I pressed on the gas pedal, it shot backwards. The car knocked into Tessa. I heard her cry out."

"Did you get out to help her?"

"It was an accident! I figured she couldn't be hurt too bad, not at that speed. Someone would come along. She had her phone. I just needed to get away. How was I to know she'd been knocked into the river, that she would drown?"

Even through the whisper, I heard the lie. Terrified of returning to prison, Phoebe couldn't afford to leave any witnesses. I didn't know if she'd deliberately run into Tessa or not, and I didn't want to visualize her getting out of the car and dragging the injured woman toward the river, but I couldn't stop the images from forming in my mind. I guessed Esteban was lucky that she'd thought he was dead. I didn't ask about the camera; it was at the bottom of the Potomac. "So you drove her car to the airport."

"You figured it all out, girl. I left the car in long-term parking and walked back. Couldn't risk being identified by a cab driver if the police found the car. It must have been eight or ten miles. I barely made it home and got cleaned up before it was time to meet Vitaly for practice. My ass was dragging."

I imagined her jogging along the roadside in the wee hours, covering five or six miles an hour. Even as fit as she was, it must have been scary. She'd have been running on adrenaline and guilt, replaying the scene in her mind, ducking out of sight when a car passed. I didn't want to empathize with her. "You tried to kill me."

"No way, girlfriend! I tried to warn you off. When the brick through the window didn't work, I cut your brake lines, figuring you'd have a fender bender, maybe get banged up enough to give up investigating. I'm not a killer."

Good to know. My nervous system wasn't reassured, however; goose pimples had sprung up on my arms and I shivered. "What are you going to do with me?"

She shuffled her feet. "I just need time to get away."

"I'll give you an hour before I tell anyone," I lied.

She chuckled in a sad way. "Liar. I need you out of the way for a few hours. I meant to catch you in the parking lot and pop you into the trunk, but Nigel came into the Green Room right after you left and I couldn't get away. You came back too quickly. Now . . ."

She trailed off, apparently considering her options. "As soon as you started on about characters named Dakota, I knew I'd have to run for it. I'd heard on the news that the man survived, but when the police didn't come for me, I figured he hadn't been able to tell them what happened, or that he didn't remember. But when you showed up tonight, asking about Dakotas, I knew. You talked to him, didn't you?"

I nodded, then realized she couldn't see me. "Yes. He said 'Dakota came.' I didn't know who he meant, but then someone called Kristen 'Chelsea' this afternoon, and it got me thinking about how the public confuses actors with their characters sometimes."

"Why'd you have to keep at it and at it?" Phoebe asked angrily. "It was just a game to you, a challenge, trying to figure it all out. You had to win, just like on the dance floor. Nothing else mattered. You didn't stop to consider that you were ruining my life."

A lump lodged in my throat and I swallowed hard. Was she right? Had my competitive nature taken over so completely that . . . no. "*You* ruined things by killing Tessa," I said. I slid my fingers under the box flap and pulled. The ripping sound alerted Phoebe.

"What're you doin'?" Her hand landed on my shoulder.

I was out of time. I didn't know what she had planned for me, and I didn't want to wait around and find out. I yanked a bottle from the box, my palm slick on the smooth neck. I struck out, the weight of the bottle and the force of my swing pulling me off the box. The bottle glanced off Phoebe, maybe her arm, and she grunted. Her hand landed on my shoulder and her fingers bit in. I didn't have the angle to hit her again. Frantic, I drew my arm back and flung the bottle as hard as I could. Glass shattered explosively, showering pebbles and shards over us, so many I knew the bottle had hit the sliding glass door of the refrigeration unit. Cold bathed us and the sweetish smell of rum saturated the air. Phoebe sprang away from me as footsteps sounded in the hall.

She jerked the door open and a figure stumbled in, hand still wrapped around the doorknob. Shoving him or her toward me, Phoebe dashed into the hall. I could see her silhouetted against the dim light as I crawled out from under the bewildered Club Nitro bartender and scrambled to my feet. I blinked. My outfit was damp with rum along the left side, and one of the halter straps was flapping, but I took off after Phoebe. "Call the police," I shot at the bartender. Gabriel.

On the threshold, I looked toward the outer door. It was ajar, and I thought for a moment she'd gone out. Then the odor of cigarette smoke and the sound of voices told me a couple of employees were taking a smoke break. Phoebe couldn't have escaped that way. I ran the other way, toward the dance floor, yelling, "Stop Phoebe!"

The door to the temporary Green Room opened as I neared it and Nanette, Vitaly, Zane, and Marco peered out. "Phoebe!" I yelled to their startled faces.

"Phoebe is not being here," Vitaly said as I passed.

My foot caught on something and I almost went sprawling; as it was, I fell against the wall. Grunting and an outraged oink told me Jezebel had tripped me. The small pig galloped down the hall.

"Jezebel!" Nanette cried.

I followed the pig, knowing Phoebe must have gone this way. I saw her duck into the passageway that dancers used coming off the stage following their numbers. She glanced over her shoulder and I caught the whites of her wide eyes. She saw me, and plunged forward. She was headed for the front door and freedom. Chances were she'd make it since the audience would be too startled to react as she ploughed through them.

I was close on her heels as we burst onto the dance floor. The reality guy and his partner were performing their East Coast swing as Phoebe skidded on the slick parquet. She recovered her balance and leaped onto the judges' table to avoid colliding with the couple whose spins were already a bit out of control. The audience gasped. The judges, as one, looked toward Nigel, clearly wondering if this was something he'd staged. Audience members began to stand, trying to get a better view.

"Stop Phoebe," I gasped. "Killed Tessa." I'm not sure anyone heard me.

Taking advantage of everyone's indecision, Phoebe jumped lightly down from the table, landing in a fighting crouch. She looked tall, determined, and lethal. Before I could stop my forward momentum, she spun and planted a foot firmly in my diaphragm. I went down hard, pain jolting from my tailbone clear to the top of my head as I skidded backwards. I gasped for air. Jezebel, concerned, nosed my armpit and oinked. Vitaly, Zane, Nanette, and Marco erupted onto the dance floor. Someone bumped into the dancers doggedly trying to finish their number, and the reality guy joined me on the floor.

I saw Tav start toward me as I struggled to my feet. I waved him away with pushing motions. "Get Phoebe," I yelled. My voice was hoarse, but he got the message and nodded. With an agility I imagined he'd developed on the soccer field, he wove through the excited crowd, hot on Phoebe's tail. Avoiding Vitaly's questions, Zane's concerns, and Nanette's upset over Jezebel, I climbed on a chair to see over the crowd's heads.

A uniformed police officer appeared in the doorway—summoned by the bartender?—and Phoebe veered my way. Seizing my chance, I leaped onto her back, wrapping my arms around her head and my legs around her waist. She bucked and snapped her head back, cracking her skull into my chin. She'd have had me off in a second, but Tav was right there. She made as if to snap a kick at him, but he dodged it and tackled her at the knees, bringing us both down.

Phoebe landed at the bottom of the pile and let out an "Oof!" as my weight slammed into her. I lay dazed for a second, draped over Phoebe. I felt her lurch beneath me, then still as three pairs of cops' shoes surrounded us at eye level. Phoebe went limp and I felt her shudder. "Why couldn't you just let me go?" she said in a low voice.

I didn't have an answer. She'd killed someone, and even though I liked her and had some sympathy with her motives, they didn't justify the act. "I'm sorry," I said. I was. Very, very sorry.

The police manhandled Phoebe to her feet and cuffed her. Tav helped me up, his hands gentle, and I turned my face into his shoulder. He stroked my hair for a moment, not saying anything, and I felt his strength flowing into me. "Thanks," I murmured, pulling back slightly. He ran his index finger under my eye; I hadn't realized until then that I was crying.

"It will be okay," he said.

I wasn't convinced.

Vitaly came up behind us and I stepped away from Tav. "I cannot believe Phoebe killed Tessa. Why she is doing this?" His brow crinkled with confusion and betrayal as he watched the police lead his former dance partner to the door where Detective Lissy stood waiting. After exchanging words with the officers, he made his way through the crowd to us. I stiffened, waiting for him to chew me out for interfering in his investigation.

"Ms. Graysin, Mr. Acosta, Mr. Voloshin," he greeted us, nodding at us each in turn.

"Detective Lissy," we chorused.

"I understand you tangled with the suspect," he said, looking me over. His gaze made me wonder just how beat up I looked. "Are you all right?"

I rotated my shoulders, feeling some twinges, and suddenly became aware of new aches, especially in my abs and tailbone. "I'll live."

"Thank you for your help in apprehending Ms. Jackson," he said, surprising me. "I understand she confessed to you?"

I nodded.

"When you're done here"—he gestured toward the

chaos that surrounded us — "I need you to come down to the station and give me a statement."

"Will do."

As Detective Lissy turned away, Nigel Whiteman bounded toward us with a blazing smile. Larry trailed him, camera strapped to his chest, and I wondered how much of the chase, fight, and apprehension they had captured on film. Probably all of it.

"This is brilliant, Stacy, brilliant! I couldn't have staged it better myself. I can't believe that Phoebe Jackson did in Tessa. I rather thought it was Savage, myself. Just goes to show, doesn't it?" The way he said their names made it sound as if he were talking about movie characters, rather than people he knew and cared about.

I couldn't help wishing it had been Nigel, and that he was the one in handcuffs being hauled off to jail.

"Anyway, we've got it all on film, and I want to do a two-hour special, to air after the *Blisters* finale, that features you talking about what led you to Phoebe and how you cornered her. You can talk about your investigative techniques, the evidence you uncovered, what made you suspect that Phoebe was a vicious killer. We'll intersperse it with clips of Phoebe's movies and bits from Tessa's documentaries, as a tribute to her. What do you say? You'll be famous!"

The punch I launched at Nigel dislodged my halter top, which was dangling from a single strap, so he got what he'd wanted from the first: a wardrobe malfunction. He also got a bloody nose.

While he clutched his nose with both hands and howled for a doctor, Vitaly, Tav, and I headed for the door. Contract or no contract, we were done with *Ballroom with the B-Listers*.

Chapter 31

Two months later, Tav and I sat snuggled together on the chair and a half in my sitting room. It was a tight fit, but I wasn't complaining. We were watching an entertainment news show on my new TV because the promos promised an update on Phoebe Jackson and the pending trial. Tav tightened his arm around me as the pert anchor reported that Phoebe Jackson was free on bond, awaiting trial, and had sold the movie rights to her story to a producer—not Nigel Whiteman—to pay her legal team.

"Are you worried about the trial?" Tav asked.

I gave a small nod. I was dreading it.

"Maybe she will make a deal and you won't have to testify," he said.

I hoped so. It felt like only last week that I'd been struggling with Phoebe, had seen the police haul her away in handcuffs. Yet, so much had happened in the interim. Nigel was forced to cancel the *Blisters* season after Graysin Motion resigned from the show and Zane got a part in the up-and-coming director's new movie and pulled out of the competition. Nanette Fleaston also withdrew, saying that Jezebel told her something bad would happen if she continued on with the dance competition. Personally, I couldn't imagine what the pig thought would be worse than murder, unless it had something to do with pork chops. Kevin McDill's article, largely based on interviews with yours truly, made it unlikely that *Blisters* would ever have another season. Zane's new movie was filming in North Carolina and he and Danielle saw each other on the weekends sometimes. She'd driven down there twice, even though I suggested she might want to take things slowly. Little sisters always have to learn things the hard way. Lately, there'd been hints in the gossip columns about Zane and his lovely costar, so we'll see. Regardless, I won't say "I told you so," and I've stocked up on pints of Ben & Jerry's, just in case.

"Any regrets?" Tav asked, sensing my pensiveness. His breath moved the hairs along my temple and I shivered.

"I wish I could've spent some of the reward money on something *fun*," I admitted.

Nigel's production company ended up paying a third of the reward to me and a third each to Li'l Boni and Esteban Figueroa when I told the police how their information helped me figure out Phoebe killed Tessa. Figueroa used his windfall on medical bills, and I didn't know what Li'l Boni used his share for. Once the government took its cut and Graysin Motion made a down payment on the property taxes owed to the city, my share was gone—poof! On top of that, I was having to pay legal fees: Club Nitro sued me for damages resulting from my chasing Phoebe through the club. "No good deed goes unpunished," as my lawyer, Phineas Drake, likes to say. He was confident I wouldn't have to pay the club anything, but his fees are so exorbitant that I won't have enough money left in the bank to buy a new lipstick.

"We can have fun without any money at all," Tav suggested, nibbling my ear.

"You think?" I turned my head so our lips met.

Tav and I are taking things slowly—unlike Danielle—but sometimes I have to pinch myself I feel so happy. I may not have come away with a Crystal Slipper, but I'm still the luckiest woman inside the Beltway: I'm dating the world's sexiest, nicest man; I get to ballroom dance for a living; and my studio's doing really well now since there hasn't been a death in the ballroom community in over a month. We'll be turning a profit by Christmas as long as there's not another murder. And, really, how likely is that?

Reaching blindly for the remote, I clicked off the television and gave myself over to the swirl of sensation stirred by Tav's kisses and wandering hands. Fade to black . . .

ALSO AVAILABLE FROM

Ella Barrick

Dead Man Waltzing
A Ballroom Dance Mystery

After quickstepping through her first murder
investigation, champion dancer Stacy Graysin is looking
forward to slowing down the tempo a bit and focusing on
her dance classes at Graysin Motion. But when Corinne
Blakely, the grande dame of American ballroom dancing is
poisoned at a luncheon, Stacy is spun into
another investigation...

"Perfect for all your dance show fans."
—Library Journal

Available wherever books are sold or at
penguin.com

facebook.com/TheCrimeSceneBooks